Kings of Mayhem
Kings of Mayhem MC Series Book 1

Penny Dee

This book is a work of fiction. Any references to real events, real people, and real places are used fictitiously. Other names, characters, places and incidents are products of the Author's imagination and any resemblance to persons, living or dead, actual events, organisations or places is entirely coincidental.

All rights are reserved. This book is intended for the purchaser of this book ONLY. No part of this book may be reproduced or transmitted in any form or by any means, graphic, electronic, or mechanical, including photocopying, recording, taping, or by any information storage retrieval system, without the express written permission of the Author. All songs, song titles and lyrics contained in this book are the property of the respective songwriters and copyright holders.

Disclaimer: The material in this book contains graphic language and sexual content and is intended for mature audiences, ages 18 and older.

ISBN: 978-1795662857

Editing by Elaine at Allusion Graphics
Proofreading by Stephanie Burdett
Formatting by Swish Design & Editing
Cover design by Marisa at Cover Me Darling
Cover image Copyright 2019

First Edition
Copyright © 2019 Penny Dee
All Rights Reserved

DEDICATION

To Rachael, Stephanie & Laurie,
my beta beauties. xx

PATH OF FAMILY

The Calley Family
Hutch Calley (deceased) married Sybil Stone
Griffin Calley
Garrett Calley (deceased)

Griffin Calley married Peggy Russell
Isaac Calley
Abby Calley

Garrett Calley married Veronica Western
Chance Calley
Cade Calley
Caleb Calley
Chastity Calley

The Parrish Family
Jude Parrish married Connie Walker
Jackson Parrish
Samuel Parrish (deceased)

Jackie Parrish married Lady Winter
Bolt Parrish
Indigo Parrish

The Western Family
Michael 'Bull' Western
Veronica 'Ronnie' Western

ORIGINAL CHAPTER

Kings of Mayhem MC

Bull (President)
Jackie (VP)
Cade
Caleb
Isaac
Grunt (SIA)
Davey
Tex
Vader
Joker
Cool Hand
Elias
Griffin
Jacob
Matlock
Maverick
Tully
Irish

Nitro
Hawke
Freebird
Ari
Picasso
Caveman
Chance (on tour)
Reuben (honorary member)

Employees of the Kings
Red (Chef, clubhouse housekeeper)
Mrs Stephens (Bookkeeper, administration)

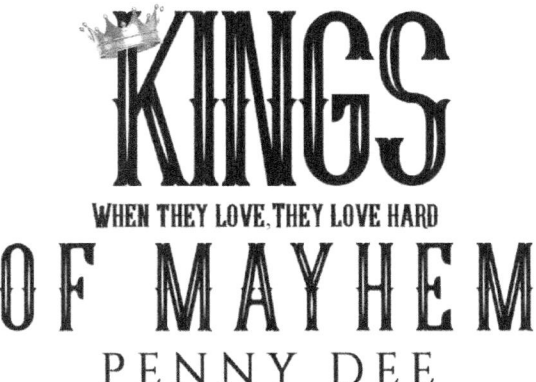

PROLOGUE

West Destiny High School

We hid under the desks. The entire room was quiet except for the occasional sob from Leslie Winters a few desks away.

"Ssssh," Brody Meyers, the school star quarterback hissed. "Or you'll get us all killed."

He was crouched awkwardly beneath a science table, his body shaking as he clutched onto one of the table legs.

Across the aisle, Leslie sobbed again but this time it was silent and she dropped her head to her chest as another round of terror wracked her body.

I watched them, wishing they'd both shut the fuck up before they got us killed.

My eyes shifted to Indy crouching beside me. She was biting her bottom lip and her eyes were filled with fear. I'd known her my entire life and I had never seen fear in those beautiful eyes of hers. Indigo Parrish wasn't someone who scared easily. But right now her big brown eyes were gleaming with it and I knew I had to do something about it.

I leaned forward and mashed my lips to hers. Her eyes widened when I pulled away and began backing out from under the safety of the desk.

"Cade, no ...!" She pleaded. But it was just a whisper, because somewhere out in that hallway, Travis Hawthorne was on the hunt for blood, and if he heard us he would come and kill us all. We knew he was strapping some serious firepower with the sole intention of taking out as many of us as possible.

I gave my girl the cocky, lopsided grin I knew she loved. The one she spent hours kissing because she was so damn in love with me. It was my way of silently comforting her. Of letting her know that I would always protect her. I had loved her my whole life. Ever since we were little and she used to climb into my bedroom window and slip into my bed because her parents were fighting again and she needed to escape. We were neighbors. Our parents were friends. We were club kids. She was the love of my life.

"I'll be back," I whispered with a wink.

I snuck across the room and paused at the door, my heart thundering in my chest.

"Cade, get down!" Our chem teacher, Mr Lemon, hissed. "Get the hell down now before you get shot!"

I ignored him and said a silent prayer as I opened the classroom door. I swallowed deep. The hallway wasn't empty. Travis Hawthorne was only a few feet away, stalking the corridor like a hunter stalking his prey. His back was to me but he swung around when he heard the quiet click of the door behind me. His face was dark and sinister. His eyes bright and crazy. He was clearly surprised to see me, and for a moment we just stared at one another and all I could hear was the pounding of my heartbeat in my ears.

Travis was brandishing a 12-gauge shotgun, which he aimed right at my chest.

Standing there I figured this could go one of two ways: Travis Hawthorne could shoot and kill me—which would set off a world of trouble for the Hawthorne family. Or, I could use my greatest weapon—my ability to talk myself out of most situations—and we would both live to tell the story.

I held my hands up in surrender.

"Dude, you don't want to shoot me," I said. Not the smartest of one-liners, but it was the first thing that came to mind.

Clearly, I hadn't thought this through.

"What are you doing?" Travis's eyes narrowed as he came toward me, walking with the determination of an approaching soldier. A yard away from me he stopped and yelled, "What the fuck are you doing, Cade?"

It was a good question. All I knew is that I had my girl to protect.

"I hate to say it, Travis, but you know who my family is—this isn't the first time I've had a loaded 12-gauge pointed at me."

Up this close, I could see the crazy in his eyes. Yep. Chances were this wasn't going to end well.

"You are a cocky son of a bitch," he snarled.

"Probably."

I nodded and he aimed his gun higher, taking it from my chest to my face.

"What makes you so fucking sure that I won't shoot you?"

I thought for a moment, my mind racing, but I was calm as I asked, "Do you love your mom?"

Not expecting the question, he looked confused. Then he frowned. "What?"

"I said, do you love your mom?" I tried to keep my voice steady, but my heart was going like a racecar in my chest. "Your sister? What's her name? Eve? The pretty little thing with the long blonde hair…"

His eyes narrowed. "What the fuck are you talking about, Cade? Don't you talk about my mom!" He jabbed the business end of the 12-gauge shotgun closer to my face as he yelled. "And don't you talk about my sister like that! What are you doing?"

"You kill me, Travis, and you know my family will go after yours." My eyes held his steady. And I talked fast, because at any second this psychopath could blast me across the corridor and into the chem lab with a gaping 12-gauge shotgun wound to my chest. This was a fucking stupid idea. I should never have left the classroom. But there was no turning back now. I had to keep my voice steady and my confident façade in place. "If you shoot me, they will go after everyone, Travis. Your mom. Your dad. Your sweet, sweet sister. Hell, Travis, they'll even go after your cousins. Second and third cousins, too. And they won't stop until every last one of the Hawthorne's are wiped from the face of the Earth."

Going by the look on his face, he hadn't expected me to say that. He hadn't considered it. His eyes narrowed and he went to say something, but I stopped him. He was probably going to shoot me now anyway, so I might as well get as much in as possible before I went down in a hail of shotgun lead. I was too far in to back out now.

"And I promise you this, Travis—what my family will do won't be as pretty as the shotgun blast you take me out with. What they'll do to them... it will require getting up close and personal. Especially with your mom. Especially with your sweet, sweet sister Eve."

What I was implying wasn't true.

My family wouldn't hurt the women. They wouldn't touch them. Or rape them. My family might be mean sonsofbitches when they needed to be, but they didn't vent vengeance on women. And they certainly didn't rape. My granddaddy would roll over in his grave, cursing the day he ever started the MC if they started doing that shit. Sure, they didn't exactly treat all women well—especially the young, eager ones who hung around the club waiting for MC cock—but they did look after their old ladies. Most of the time.

But my daddy could be unpredictable. And boy, he could be mean. *Vicious*. You didn't fuck with Garrett Calley and get to walk away. But he didn't hurt women. And he wouldn't let anyone in the club get away with that shit either.

But Travis didn't know that. He dropped his aim a little. He knew the Kings of Mayhem were bad motherfuckers. Which was good, because I wanted him to think the worst. And judging by the flicker of unease in his eyes, it was working.

But he suddenly frowned and raised his aim again.

"Don't you say that!" he yelled, shaking the barrel of the gun and jabbing me in the chest.

I shrugged, like it was no big deal. But my heart was doing its best to beat itself out of my body.

"It's the truth, Travis. You pull that trigger and your entire family is gone." I was desperate to swallow the big damn lump in my throat. But more determined to show him that I wasn't afraid of him. Which wasn't true. Because I was fucking terrified. But I had Indy to think about. And my younger brother, Caleb, and my cousins, Isaac and Abby, who were somewhere nearby. I also had an entire high school of friends cowering under desks, terrified they were going to be blown away by this psycho.

Ha. And I was the one they called crazy.

The tip of the shotgun pressed deeper into my chest.

Then again, maybe they were right. After all, I was standing in front of this nutball with a loaded shotgun pointed at my chest—so clearly my peers had a point.

"Think about your mom, Travis. Think about Eve."

At the mention of his sister's name Travis Hawthorne's eyes unfocused and he looked distant.

It took a split second for me to grab the barrel of the shotgun and rip it out of his grasp. Panicking, he reached for the Glock he had holstered to his hip, but he lost his grip when I hit him in the jaw with the butt of the shotgun.

I took aim, but he grabbed me and we both crashed to the floor. The Glock and 12-gauge spun across the linoleum and we both struggled to reach them with our outstretched arms.

With one well-placed knee I got him straight in the balls, and he growled with pain and curled up like a Roly poly. I launched for the closest weapon, and the instant my fingers curled around the handle of the Glock, I leapt to my feet and took aim.

Then I shot him.

For as long as I could remember, Indy and I had always talked about going away to college. When she got into med school, I applied to a college nearby and was accepted. Excited, we spent the summer planning our home together. Life was looking good. We would be far away from the club life that Indy hated so much.

Me, I didn't mind club life. I liked growing up in the club. I liked the camaraderie and brotherhood. But I loved Indy more, and if she moved to hell, then I'd follow her. She was my girl and I'd walk through fire for the rest of my life if I had to.

Until the West Destiny High School shootings, our life had been pretty good. But Travis Hawthorne shooting up our high school set off a string of events that changed everything.

When I shot Travis, I only wounded him. A bullet to the right shoulder stopped him from carrying out anymore of his psychopathic plan. He would live, but it would probably have been better for him if he hadn't.

Me, I was labeled a hero. Cade *fucking* Calley—the son of the President of the Kings of Mayhem MC—a fucking hero.

Who would have thought?

For years I was the bad boy of West Destiny High School. The one who would never amount to much. The one who surprised the fuck out of every one of his teachers when he achieved the high SAT scores and got his choice of colleges. All of a sudden, he was the good guy.

At first, my dad was pissed at me for confronting an armed Travis. He said my balls were bigger than my brains and that someday they'd get me shot dead. My mom was furious and called me a stupid asshole. The police were pissed at me, too. They were all right, of course. What I did was stupid. Plain stupid. I was lucky I wasn't lying in the funeral home.

Three nights after the shooting, the MC decided to celebrate my heroism with a party at the clubhouse. MC parties were legendary. They could go on for days and, more often than not, they got very messy and rowdy.

The afternoon of the party I lay with Indy on her bed in her room. Her mom was at the clubhouse with the other old ladies setting up for the party, while her dad—the club's VP—was out with my dad.

We spent the afternoon naked and enjoying every inch of one another's bodies. Looking down at her, I felt so crazy in love with her that I had to make love to her again.

"You're such a hero," she teased.

"I did it all for you," I whispered against her ear. "Because you're my girl."

She had snuggled into me, and the familiar smell of her had made all my insides feel warm and happy. She was the light in all my darkness.

"I feel so safe with you," she whispered.

I cupped her face in my hands. "I'd do everything and anything to keep you safe, baby."

She smiled and dragged her teeth across her bottom lip. "Tomorrow we start our new life together, college boy."

I grinned. "Are you sure you won't come to tonight's thing at the clubhouse?"

She pulled a face and went rigid in my arms. "No. I'll let you enjoy that on your own."

I wish she had come with me to the clubhouse.

Maybe then I wouldn't have drank too much.

Maybe then I wouldn't have fucked up our future together.

CHAPTER 1

CADE
Twelve Years Later
Now

Without a word of a lie, I woke up with some chick's hand on my cock. I was on my bed in my room at the clubhouse, sleeping off an eight-hour ride back from Missouri. Despite a party going on in the clubhouse, I was way too tired to party and wanted nothing more than to be left the fuck alone. Yet, there she was. A brunette with great tits and an even greater ass. Pressing herself all over my body and pushing her hand down my jeans.

"Whoa …" I said, blinking awake.

A surge of pleasure streamed though me—completely involuntary because I wasn't interested. Except according to my cock I was.

"You like that, Cade?" The brunette asked, squeezing a little tighter. My balls contracted and tightened with a surge of pleasure.

"What do you think you're doing?" My voice was husky from being in a deep sleep.

"Waking you up." The brunette looked up at me through thick, false lashes before pulling my jeans and boxer shorts down. She straddled me, her hand firmly gripping the base of my hard-as-fuck cock. She was wearing nothing but a g-string. It was one of those really tiny ones with the thin straps, and I could feel the gentle tickle of her pubic hair through the almost non-existent fabric. And I was wrong—her tits weren't great—they were fucking amazing.

She started to stroke, and dear God, if she kept that up I was going to blow my load.

Using every ounce of mental strength, I pushed her hand away and she pouted. "You don't like that, Cade?"

"Ain't nothing I can't do myself, sweetheart," I said. I wanted her off me. Granted, she was hot. But I wasn't in the mood. Which lasted all of five seconds. Because she grabbed my hand and forced it between her legs, and she was dripping wet. My cock throbbed and begged me to fuck her.

But I'd decided a while ago that I wasn't that guy anymore. After twelve years of trying to fuck *her* out of my head, I realized that *she* wasn't going anywhere, and no matter how many women fell into my bed, I was never going to fuck her out of my heart.

Her.

Indigo.

Her being gone didn't make me want to fuck a hundred women to get over her anymore.

Her being gone didn't make me want to share my bed with faceless women, night after night.

Her being gone made me mad.

Twelve years.

Twelve fucking years and not a fucking word.

I was an asshole. It was my fault she left. I broke her. I broke us. I never denied it. But she ... she was the one who turned and ran.

I clenched my teeth.

She was the one who ended us.

The brunette rubbed herself with my hand and I swear to God there was only so much restraint a man could show when a hot babe was rubbing her pussy all over him. Maybe I'd been a bit hasty in saying I wasn't interested. Maybe I was—

Oh God.

Juicy lips closed over the head of my cock while a wet, talented tongue sucked me into the deep cavern of her throat. Yep, no point in fighting it. No fucking point at all.

I let out a deep groan as her mouth began the slow glide down the length of me, her tongue pulling me deeper into her throat. *Fuck.* She had one hand curled around the base of my cock and it hit her chin as she moved up and down, up and down, slowly gaining more momentum as she expertly sucked me like a goddamn lollipop ...

I gave into the pleasure stirring in my balls and sank back into the pillows. She was good. *Damn good.* And the little moans she made as she licked and sucked me put me on a train straight to Pleasureville.

My orgasm was rapid and it surged through me, cartwheeling across my brain. I thrust my head back into the pillow and shot into the back of her mouth. She whimpered but didn't stop sucking as I continued to pump more and more down her throat. She lapped it up, milking me with her lips and tongue, and moaning as she emptied me of every last drop.

When she was sure I was done, she looked up and greedily licked her lips. "I love how you taste, Cade."

My post-orgasm indifference was already kicking in and I wasn't in the mood for small talk and lies. Pulling on my jeans I raised an eyebrow at her. Ergo, if a girl tells you she loves the taste of your cum, chances are she is lying.

I hoped she didn't plan on hanging around. I wasn't into small talk.

But it wasn't small talk she was after.

She pushed me back down on to the bed and ran her palms across my abs and up my chest. "You're so big," she breathed. "All the girls think you're beautiful." Her fingertips whispered across my chest to my shoulders. "So big and strong." She slid her legs on either side of my hips and began rubbing herself against me. "They all want to fuck you," she moaned, getting off on the zipper bulge of my jeans. For me, nothing was going on behind it. I was done. But I was slightly intrigued by her performance. She leaned down and moaned in my ear. "I can't wait to feel you inside me."

When she tried kissing me, I turned my head.

I didn't kiss. I fucked. And I fucked well.

"I want you to make me come," she whispered in my ear as she ground her pussy against me. "And then I promise I will make you say my name—over and over again."

That wasn't going to happen.

I didn't know her name.

And I didn't want to.

A sudden pounding on the door almost sent her flying off the bed. The door flung open, and Caleb, my younger brother, filled the doorway. He didn't flinch at the sight of a near-naked girl sprawled on my bed.

"You've gotta get out of here, brother," he panted. Going by the alarm in his voice and the commotion out in the clubroom, something was wrong. Something was very wrong.

Over the muffled music I heard shouting in the bar. I flew off the bed and quickly followed Caleb out of the room and down the corridor toward the noise.

It took me all of a nanosecond to work out something had happened to one of my MC brothers. Jackie Parrish—our Vice President—was lying on the floor, his eyes closed, a look of pain etched on his face. His wife, Lady, was kneeling over him, crying, yelling, and swearing.

"What happened?" I asked, dropping to my knees next to Jackie. I turned to no one in particular and yelled, "Turn the goddamn music down!"

Red, our clubhouse cook, crouched next me. "One minute he was just sitting there laughing, the next... he bent over and fell to the floor. He was f-fine and then he w-wasn't ... *cunt! Fucker!*"

Red had Tourette's.

I checked for a pulse. But Jackie's heart had stopped and his pulse was still. I knew CPR and I wasn't about to give up on one of my brothers.

Without hesitation, I started to work on the old man. Doing compressions. Blowing air into his whiskered and beer-drenched mouth.

But he was unresponsive. He didn't move or open his eyes and yell at me for getting up in his face. He didn't sit up and make some lame-ass joke about me trying to kiss him. But I kept going, knowing I was the only thing standing between him and the Reaper. It wasn't until the paramedics turned up and took over that I sat back, utterly exhausted. I didn't know how long I had been going because of the adrenaline thundering through my veins.

Devastated, I watched the paramedics work on him, but as the minutes ticked by with excruciating slowness, it was suddenly real that nothing more could be done for Jackie.

"He's gone," one of the paramedics finally said.

A ripple went through the men in the room. Lady, let out a howl.

I raked a hand down my face. "Fuck... "

Penny Dee

Grief settled across the club. Lady sobbed into our prospect's shoulder.

Jackie was dead.

Our Vice President was gone.

I sighed. "Someone had better call his daughter."

CHAPTER 2

INDY
Now

It was a stare-off.

He was trying to outstare me. *Me.* The Queen of Stubborn.

He had no idea he had met his match.

I folded my arms, arching one eyebrow...you know, to show that I wasn't an amateur. We needed to get one thing straight—I was in charge.

"Be honest, Jeremy. You put it there, didn't you?"

He shook his head.

He being Jeremy Dixon. Five years old and not nearly as terrified of my stern doctor face as he should be.

I held up the plastic bead I had just extracted from his nasal cavity. It was the fourth one this month. Any more and I could make a bracelet.

"So, how did it get in there, if you didn't put it there?" I asked.

He shrugged, his eyes not leaving mine.

"Did it crawl in there by itself?

"Maybe."

"Really? Because I don't see a pair of legs on this sucker."

"They fell off."

"Of course, they did." I dropped the bead into the plastic basin in my hand. "Do you think anymore of them are going to grow legs and take a tour through your nasal cavity, Jeremy? Or are we done with this? See, the way I see it, that's four times now and every single time the same thing happens. You shove it up your nose and your mama has to bring you in here so I can pull it out of your nostril. Be honest …" I picked out a lollipop from my coat pocket. "…is it for the candy?"

His big brown eyes grew round at the sight of the lollipop.

Just then, one of the ER nurses ducked her head into the cubicle. "We have a GSW on its way in. ETA less than five minutes. We're going to need you."

I nodded and turned back to Jeremy, and held up the lollipop.

"I'll make a deal with you, Jeremy. I'll give you this here piece of candy on one condition. No more burying any beads up your nose. Got it?"

He nodded and I smiled. Bribery. It was the perfect deal sealer.

I pulled the lollipop away, just long enough to reaffirm our understanding. "We've got a deal?"

He nodded again, and I grinned at him as I handed him the candy.

Two minutes later I met the ambulance at the front of the hospital. I heard them before I saw them, thanks to the violent vocals of the burly patient on the gurney.

Showtime!

Snapping on my gloves, I absorbed the image unfolding in front of me. The man on the gurney was about six foot seven, covered in tattoos and apparently well educated in the art of swearing. He clutched his belly and cussed at the EMTs as they tried to do their job. Blood soaked into the white sheet beneath him.

Here we go.

"Okay, what have we got?" I asked one of the paramedics who was struggling with the patient.

"Gunshot wound to the belly. No exit wound. We've given him morphine for the pain and managed to slow the bleeding."

I ignored the abuse of the patient who appeared to also be an expert with terms of endearment such as *cunt, motherfucker,* and my personal favorite, *motherfucking cunt.* I ignored his abuse because I was good at shutting shit out. I had years of experience. It was like my superpower.

When I pressed down on his belly, he grabbed my wrist, and with a roar yanked me to him. "I've been fucking shot, you cunt...!"

I neither flinched nor looked concerned, and I didn't care that his face was so close to mine, apart from his retched breath. Because I was the perfect distraction while my colleagues got ready to fill his veins with enough sedative to knock down a horse.

"I hate to break it to you, sunshine, but if you knew where I came from then you wouldn't even bother with this intimidation shit," I said, making sure I held his attention. To my left, one of the paramedics was able to get a line in and anesthetize him with some serious knock-out juice, and less than ten seconds later, Prince Charming was down for the count and being prepped for surgery.

On my way to wash up, Karen, one of the ER nurses, stopped me. "Dr. Parrish, you have a phone call. Line three."

"I'm just heading into surgery."

"They say it's urgent."

I nodded at her and thanked her. Thinking I could make it quick, I made my way toward the administration station where my best friend Trinity caught up with me.

"Hey, are we still on for tonight?" she asked, rushing by, one hand full of patient files, while the other held a half-eaten, iced donut.

"Of course. What do you want to do?" I asked as I headed toward the nearest phone. "Quiet drinks somewhere, or is this going to be an all-night thing?"

Trinity pulled a face. "Honey, I gave up the all-night thing back when Bieber didn't need to shave. Let's just grab a few quiet drinks and see what happens."

I laughed. "Sounds like a plan," and then picking up the phone, said, "Doctor Parrish."

There was a bit of a pause, and for a moment I wondered if the call had dropped out. But then I heard her—the familiar voice of my mom.

And she was crying.

My body stiffened. "Mom, what's wrong?"

"It's your father, Indy," she sobbed. "He goddamn went and died on us."

For a moment, I said nothing. I hadn't been expecting the phone call and I certainly hadn't been expecting the news. Actually, that wasn't exactly true. My father was on the wrong side of fifty, overweight, and he smoked and drank like he was a goddamn immortal. It was only a matter of time before his stupid-ass lifestyle took him out.

I nodded silently and fiddled with the phone cord in my hands.

Damn it, Daddy.

CHAPTER 3

CADE—Aged 5
Then

"Why do I have to play with her? She's a stupid girl!"

I smashed the two toy trucks together because I was so mad.

"Because I am your mama, and you do what your mama says," my mama said, putting her hands on her hips and fixing me with one of her looks.

"But—"

"No *buts*, Cade Calley."

I smashed my toy trucks together again. *Angry*. I didn't want to play with our new neighbor's little girl. But this morning mama told me we were looking after her because her parents had to go to work, or something. Her mama baked cakes for money and her daddy was in the same motorcycle club my daddy was in, The Kings of Mayhem. That meant I didn't get to go with daddy's friend, Freebird, to his family farm out near Walton Grove. He helped out there during the week, looking after the animals and stuff. And on Mondays I got to go with him. I got to play with the goats and baby pigs, and sometimes

Freebird would let me feed the horses, too, and let me ride with him on the quad bike when he had to fix some of the fences down by the creek. Mondays were my favorite because I loved the farm. But now we had to look after the stupid new girl next door and I couldn't go.

Mama knelt down next to me. She's real pretty, but when she gets mad she gets a fire in her eyes and a look on her face that is still pretty, but scary at the same time. Our daddy was a big, powerful man, but our mama, she could stop a train with one look.

"Now, Cade, you need to be nice to little Indigo Blue," she said. "She is new to town. She doesn't know anyone. And she'll be starting school with you next week, so it will be nice for her to have a friend when she does."

Mama said our neighbors had moved here from Humphrey, which is the next town over. It's bigger than Destiny.

"You could be her best friend," she explained. Mama's eyes were real blue. Like bright blue stones. "Everyone needs a best friend."

"What's a best friend?"

My mama thought for a moment.

"It's that one friend you can always rely on to be there for you. The bestest of all your friends."

"Like Batman and Robin?"

Batman was a superhero. Robin was his friend who helped him.

Mama pointed to my Batman bedspread and winked. "Just like Batman."

When my young brother Caleb started wailing in his crib, Mama gave me another wink before she walked out of the room.

I frowned and glanced out my bedroom window. It looked out onto our new neighbor's house and my bedroom window looked straight into the little girl's room, but I had only caught a glimpse of her since she moved in last week. My frown pulled back in surprise when I saw the window lift up and a small leg swing out, followed quickly by the other one. I straightened my back. The little girl from next door was climbing out her window.

I watched as she settled on the window ledge with her legs dangling over the side.

"Indigo Blue, where are you?" I heard her mama call out to her from inside the house.

The little girl glanced over her shoulder, her face scrunched up into a frown. "I ain't no baby, and I don't need no babysitter," she hollered.

She eyed the patch of grass below her window.

"Indigo? Where in the blue blazes are you, child?" Her mama called out again.

"I told you. I ain't going," she yelled back through the window. "And you can't make me!"

Next thing I knew, the little girl jumped out of the window and tumbled onto the grass below. I stood up. She had landed badly and I would bet all my baseball cards she had twisted her ankle. I watched her face fold and her chin begin to wiggle as she fought the need to cry.

She was hurt. And even though I was mad at her, I knew I had to help her. I quickly climbed out of my window, and jumped onto the grassy patch below, landing solidly on my two feet.

I knew how to do it properly because I had done it a thousand, trillion times before.

The little girl looked up and her pretty face went from sad to surprised.

I stopped.

Pretty?

Uh. Uh.

She wasn't pretty. She was ugly! An ugly, stupid girl who made me miss going to Freebird's family farm and I hated her.

"You can't just jump," I said, annoyed.

She scowled as she looked up at me. "You blind? I just did."

"And you hurt yourself. You gotta line up your jump. Make sure you land on two feet. Not one, dummy."

"I ain't a dummy," she huffed, rubbing her ankle.

I felt bad. Mama said name-calling was for people who didn't have many words. They weren't smart enough to get their point across. So they used mean names, instead.

I reached down and offered her my hand. But she ignored it and kept rubbing her ankle.

Feeling bad, I knelt down beside her. "It don't look broke," I said softly.

She looked at me again and her face softened. Up close, she *was* pretty. *Real pretty*. She had big brown eyes and shiny, pink lips. Her blonde hair was pulled into two pigtails and held there with elastic bands with big, colored-plastic bubbles on them. She was wearing denim overalls and a blue and white striped t-shirt underneath. When she looked up at me again, I noticed her lashes were long and dark.

"I just need a minute." Her voice was softer than before, but her brows were pulled back as she continued to rub at her ankle. "It will be okay with a bit of rest."

Still feeling bad for calling her a dummy, I shoved my hands into my jeans.

"I can show you how to climb out your window without hurting your ankle," I said, and then shrugged. "I mean, if you want."

Again, she looked up at me. But this time she smiled and my tummy started to hurt, just like it did when I was hungry. She looked at me, her nose crinkled up and her head tilted to the side.

"You have blue eyes," she said. "Like blue diamonds."

Again, my tummy rumbled and my cheeks went hot.

"They're real pretty," she added, squinting as she stared at me.

"Boys aren't pretty, they're tough," I said.

She shrugged. "They can be pretty."

"No, they can't."

"Yes, they can."

I rolled my eyes. "You want me to show you or not?"

She climbed to her feet and dusted off her knees. But as soon as she tried to walk, her ankle gave way and she almost fell. I had to move quickly to grab her and stop her from falling to the ground.

"You're hurt," I said, holding her up. She smelled like flowers and soap.

Before she could reply, her mama came around the corner.

"There you are!" She threw her hands up in the air. "I've been looking everywhere for you." When she saw I was holding her daughter up, she put her hands on her hips. "Oh, for crying out loud, Indigo Blue! What have you done to yourself now?"

"I'm fine, Mama."

"Aha. That's why you're using this handsome young man here as a crutch."

I stuck out my hand. "Hello, ma'am. My name is Cade. Cade Calley."

The little girl's mama looked at my hand and smiled. She was real pretty. Her blonde hair was piled up on her head, and when she smiled, her blue eyes sparkled like stars. "Well, now, it's a pleasure to meet you, Mr. Cade Calley. My name is Lady Parrish, and this here is Indigo Blue."

"But don't be calling me that," the little girl interrupted with a frown. "My name is Indy. Only my mama calls me Indigo. If you call me that, I won't answer, you hear me, Cade Calley?"

"I can see you two have already made friends," Lady said. "We were just on our way to meet you, Mr. Calley."

"You can call me Cade," I reassured her.

Again she smiled. "Well, Cade. Shall we go see your mama? I believe she makes a great cup of coffee and I've just baked a beautiful pecan pie."

"Pecan pie is my favorite. We have a pecan tree in the backyard," I declared.

"You do? Well, now. I'll make a deal with you, young man, when you pick the pecans, I'll make the pie. Deal?"

I nodded. I liked Lady Parrish.

"Shall we go?" Mrs. Parrish asked.

I tightened my grip around Indy and helped her along the side of our house to our front porch. She tried standing by herself, and because her ankle didn't hurt as bad anymore, she could walk up the steps to the porch. But I walked behind her just in case she slipped. Because that was what a best friend did.

And we were going to be best friends.

Just like Batman and Robin.

CHAPTER 4

CADE
Now

I woke up to blinding sunlight. I was lying across my bed with one arm over my eyes. My throat was dry and my mouth felt like a wad of cotton balls had been shoved into every available space. I hadn't gotten to bed until dawn thanks to a solid drinking effort in Jackie's honor, and I'd forgotten to draw the blinds before falling in a drunk heap on my bed, and now I was paying for it.

I sat up and the bedsprings wheezed and groaned beneath me as I rubbed my eyes. I looked around. I wasn't in my room at the clubhouse, I was in my bedroom at my mom's.

I sighed, trying to shake the fog that filled my head from lack of sleep and too much damn bourbon. The smell of bacon hit me and I groaned. No matter what happened, today was going to suck.

I pulled on jeans, a white tee, and a flannel shirt, then clipped my wallet chain to my jeans and shoved my wallet into my back pocket. On my way to the kitchen, I stopped quickly to brush the taste of hangover out of my mouth and wash the sleep out of my eyes, then headed downstairs to face the day.

Not surprisingly, my mom's house was already full of people. Mom and Red were busy fixing breakfast, while at the twelve-seater dining table, Lady—Jackie's widow—was being comforted by my younger brother Caleb and his girlfriend, Brandi.

Lady's head was in her hands. I gave her a comforting rub on her shoulders as I walked by, and she looked up at me with eyes that were raw from crying. At the end of the table, my cousin Isaac's son, Braxton, let out a loud giggle. At four years old he was the spitting image of his father with his blonde hair, blue eyes, and dimpled chin. He was playing with his cereal while his mom, Cherry, tried unsuccessfully to convince him to eat it and not play with it.

I sank down in the chair next to him. I love kids. I wanted a whole tribe of them. But I was nearing thirty, and so far kids hadn't even come close to my radar. There'd been no one serious to have a family with. Besides Indy, there'd only been one other girl I'd considered getting serious with. Krista. Dark and beautiful. We had dated for almost a year but it just didn't work out. Why? Because no matter how hard I tried—no matter how hot or beautiful the chick was—my heart still belonged with the girl I gave it to when I was five years old.

Braxton looked at me with his big, adorable eyes and when I winked at him, he winked back. So, with a jerk of my chin, I gave him the biker's nod, and he gave me a tough biker's nod back. I snarled my top lip and growled, and he snarled his right back. I couldn't help but grin and he burst out laughing, Christ, the kid was so damn cute. Grinning, I ruffled his hair.

"What are you up to today, big guy?" I asked him.

"I have swimming lessons."

"You do?" As I replied, my mom sat a cup of black coffee in front of me. I smiled up at her but kept my attention on Brax. "You're doing pretty well with those lessons, huh, buddy?"

He nodded proudly. "I'm the best in my class. I can almost swim the whole pool."

I looked at him, impressed. *Damn.* The little dude was a freakin' fish.

But when I looked at his mom, Cherry, she shook her head with a grin and mouthed, "No, he can't."

I couldn't help but laugh as I turned back to my cousin's son. "Sounds like you're kicking some butt."

Red put a plate of bacon and eggs down in front of me. "Small man got some ribbon at school for runnin', too, didn't you, Brax?"

I gave Brax a big grin. "You did? Dude, you must be amphibian."

Brax looked at me like I'd spoken alien.

"That means you can easily get around on land *and* in water," I explained to him.

Apparently, I was still speaking alien because Brax just stared at me with those wide, blue eyes.

Red walked back over with a frypan full of hash browns. "You want hash, Cade?" He scooped a couple up but as he let them slide onto my plate he let out a loud, "Mother. Fucker."

To which Braxton quickly copied. "Mudder. Fucker."

I fake-frowned at him, "Oi!" But I had to force myself not to laugh. I shook my head and took a sip of my coffee. "Amphibian, he can't say. But mother fucker he has no problem with."

"That's my boy," Isaac said, sitting down between Cherry and his son.

I dug into my bacon, eggs, and hash browns. Being six foot and pretty much hard-as-fuck with muscle meant I could eat whatever the hell I wanted. But the biker lifestyle was hell on the body. Booze. Drugs. Cigarettes. Partying. No sleep. Women. *Lots of women*. It was a combination just waiting to take you out with a heart attack before you hit fifty. I didn't plan on being a statistic, so I countered my booze and hard partying ways with daily, hard-core weight sessions at the gym.

A lot of my brothers did. Including Isaac.

"How you doing this morning, Lady?" he asked as my mom placed his breakfast in front of him.

Lady looked up from the coffee in her hand gave him a small smile. "I'll get there, babe."

Isaac winked at her. "Indy will be here soon."

And just like that, the activity around the table stopped and all sets of eyes fell on me. Even Lady gave me a concerned look. It was because everyone seated at that table knew that the infallible Cade Calley had one huge motherfucking Achilles' heel and her name was Indigo Parrish. I had lost my shit over her once and everybody wanted to know if I was going to turn psycho again when she returned.

"I'm looking forward to meeting her," Brandi said. "What is she like?"

Caleb's girlfriend was new to the club and I didn't think she'd be around long. She was nice looking, had a decent set of tits and some serious come-fuck me eyes, but Caleb wasn't known for his commitment to the opposite sex. He had a limited attention span and would grow tired with the same body in his bed night after night. Plus, Brandi had a serious case of the *I can't shut the fuck up* in every situation.

"You'll meet her soon, babe," Caleb replied.

"She's a bit of a legend amongst the ladies," she continued, missing the prompt from Caleb to stop. "I've already heard stories about her. Boy, she sounded wild." She glanced at Lady. "And very beautiful. I've seen photos of her in the showcase at the club."

Kings of Mayhem

Again, a strange vibe hung in the air. Yep. These motherfuckers were all walking on eggshells.

"You're right," I said, and as soon as I opened my mouth, again, everyone looked at me. "She is very beautiful." I looked at Lady. "When are you expecting her?"

"She's on a plane from Seattle now. She's going to pick up a car at the airport and drive herself into town."

A familiar sensation tightened in the pit of my stomach at the thought of seeing Indy again, and I forked more hash browns into my mouth to ignore it. Just like I had drunk it away the night before with too much bourbon.

I tried not to acknowledge that it was a two-hour drive from the airport to Destiny. That in a couple of hours we would be standing in the same room as each other for the first time since she ran.

I frowned and jabbed a forkful of eggs and bacon into my mouth.

"You ready for hurricane Indy?" Isaac asked, grinning.

I glared at him. The motherfucker loved drama.

"As ready as I'm ever going to be."

He looked at me and his smile faded. "Can we talk?"

"Sure." I looked at him over my bacon. Grease dripped over my fingers. It was pure heart attack material, but damn it was doing my hangover some good. "You need to talk now?"

He nodded and something about the way he looked at me concerned me.

Outside, he lit a cigarette and squinted in the early morning sunlight. "You're going to be voted in VP."

"How do you know that?"

"Because I suggested it." He looked at me through a furrowed brow. "Not one person has disagreed. Bull thinks it's a good idea."

I shook my head. Holding any kind of rank within the club was a responsibility I wasn't sure I wanted. It came with a shit load of obligation and little room to fuck up.

"We need to leave this until after we bury Jackie," I said.

He nodded. "Yeah. But think about it."

I put my hand on his shoulder. "I will. Thanks, brother."

Isaac was my best friend. While I was close to my brothers, Chance and Caleb, Isaac and I were the same age, born two days apart, so we'd grown up close. We were like brothers. I could read him like a book so I knew something was gnawing at him. It didn't surprise me when he changed the subject.

"Hey, I gotta talk to you about somethin' else," he took a deep drag on his cigarette and looked worried. Something was obviously troubling him.

"Is everything okay?"

His brow creased again. "I did this deal."

Already, I didn't like where this was going.

"Deal? What do you mean?" I studied his face. This wasn't good. If he was setting up deals without taking it to Chapel first, then it was the last thing the Kings needed. The club had had a run of bad luck lately. A lot of good, solid deals had fallen through. The last thing we needed was for one of our members to do rogue deals.

The opening of the sliding door interrupted us, and my mom stepped out onto the porch. "There you are." She took the cigarette from between Isaac's lips, sucked down a toke before handing it back to her nephew. "We need to get going. They're expecting us at the funeral home in half an hour."

I looked at my cousin. "You okay to finish this later?"

He hesitated, but quickly relaxed and nodded. I watched him drop his cigarette to the ground and grind it out with his boot.

"Yeah. This can wait." He smiled broadly and patted my back. "Come on. Let's go make sure Jackie gets sent off right."

CHAPTER 5

INDY
Now

I hadn't been back to Destiny since the day I had walked away from the club and my family twelve years earlier. Now I was in a rental car with the air conditioning cranked up to high and the familiar landscape of small town Mississippi scrolling past the window. Lynyrd Skynyrd's *"Free Bird"* filled the car and despite the air conditioning, I had the window wound down as I sped toward the town I had desperately run away from as an eighteen-year-old girl.

The past was already coming back to claim me, filling me with familiar sounds, smells, and memories I hadn't thought about in years. I sucked in a deep breath of the warm spring air to settle the butterflies taking flight in my stomach.

I was sad about Daddy. I was sad that he was dead and that I'd never had the chance to say goodbye. I was sad that we hadn't spoken in several years. I was sad he was such a monster and that I wouldn't miss him. He had been a mean sonofabitch and we'd both let go of each other a lot sooner than the day I left town.

Despite my hesitations about returning to Destiny, my head was surprisingly clear and it actually felt good to breathe in the familiar smells of the place I had once called home.

Since finding out about my daddy, my head had been filled with a million thoughts of the past. Thoughts about my childhood. Of my family. Of growing up in Destiny as an MC kid.

Of Cade.

I sighed. I wanted to see Cade about as much as I wanted a hole in the head. From what I'd heard, he was neck deep into the club now. According to my mom—on the rare occasions that we talked—he was a popular member of the MC and there was an expectation that he would rise through the ranks to be president one day.

Not that I was worried about seeing him again. I wouldn't be hanging around long enough for it to matter.

Get in and get out. No distractions. That was the plan.

I'd be there for my mom, bury my daddy and then get the hell out of dodge.

The truth was, I didn't need Cade Calley getting into my head. It had taken a lot of time and a lot of tequila to get over him.

A lot of tequila.

As I passed the timber-carved sign welcoming me to Destiny, Steppenwolf's *"Born To Be Wild"* filled the rental car, and I experienced a fractured moment where the years peeled back and I was an eighteen-year-old MC kid again.

My eyes shot to the black script on my inner forearm.

Yeah, darlin', go and make it happen.

I'd gotten the tattoo the day before the party at the MC clubhouse in honor of Cade's heroism during the school massacre. The day before everything had fallen apart.

I tugged the sleeve of my shirt down to hide the tattoo and changed the radio station. I wasn't that girl anymore. I didn't need to travel down memory lane and rehash all the gory details of some guy doing wrong by me and breaking my sorry teenage heart.

Okay, so Cade was never just *some guy.* At one point in time the asshole had been everything to me. My cocky, beautiful MC man with the confident, manly swagger and piercing blue eyes that defied Mother Nature.

And I had another tattoo to prove it.

My eyes shifted to the elaborate daisy on my ring finger. It hid the fine black script underneath that simply read: *Cade.*

Yep. Like a prized fool I'd gotten his stupid-ass name permanently inked on my ring finger. Not hard to do when you are eighteen and raised in a motorcycle club full of tattoo artists. It was the one time my mom got pissed at me about my ink. But at the time I had truly believed Cade and I would be together forever, and that I'd never have a reason to *not* have his name on my finger. It was ironic, really, that four days later we broke up and I walked away from him for good.

Sometimes it was funny how things worked out.

My cell phone rang, and with one tap I put it on speaker.

"Hey, beautiful, are you in Mississippi yet?" It was Anson.

"Yes. I'm in the car heading toward Destiny now. I got in about half an hour ago."

"Any hiccups?"

I turned down the radio. "Damn airline lost my luggage. Otherwise, things are great."

"I wish you'd let me come with you."

"There was no need. I don't plan on staying long enough to show you the sights."

"They have sights in Destiny?"

I laughed. "City snob."

He laughed back. "Hick."

I smiled. Anson always had a way of pulling me out of my funk. Maybe bringing him with me would have been a good idea. You know, be the safe buffer between me and my old life.

Between me and Cade.

I shook my head as if I could rattle the thoughts of Cade out of my brain.

"Don't you worry about me, I will be fine," I said.

"You're lying. Your voice just went up an octave."

I grinned. Anson knew me so well. "Oh, shut up…I'll call you in a couple of days."

"Okay. Love you."

I smiled. "I love you, too."

CHAPTER 6

CADE
Now

When my granddaddy formed the Kings of Mayhem MC, he wanted a legit club. The rules were simple. No drugs and no guns. And women were to be worshiped, not enslaved. My granddaddy had seen enough shit in Vietnam to hold onto these values with determined grit.

My granddaddy hated drugs. And he hated guns. He had been a dust-off pilot during the Vietnam War and had risked his life flying an unarmed chopper into the jungles of battle to save the lives of the wounded. More often than not, he'd flown his Huey chopper into heavy gunfire to save soldiers who'd been shot or blown up, or trapped by enemy forces. And in the three tours he did, he had the scars of two near-fatal gunshot wounds and a chopper crash to remember it by.

He never spoke much about the war, and he died when I was thirteen years old, so I never really had the chance to talk to him about it. But his aversion to guns and drugs were legendary in the club. He always said they were the reason so many of his buddies never made it out of Vietnam. Illegal guns had found their way into enemy hands and had been used against his Army buddies. And the heroin that was so prevalent in the area at the time had claimed the lives of so many of his friends and military brothers. To my granddaddy, heroin was a dirty word. He had watched it destroy not only the lives of soldiers, but doctors and medics, too.

When granddaddy had come home from the war, he had been rocked by the lack of empathy and pride for what he had done over there. The fact that he'd risked his life to save American and allies' lives meant little to the society that had been permeated with a deep, anti-war movement.

The lives he'd saved meant nothing.

The missions he'd flown into enemy territory to save the lives of wounded soldiers meant nothing.

In the end, he'd slowly withdrawn from society. He'd climbed on board his Harley and hit the road.

He had ridden out to California to catch up with Hank Parrish, his crew chief on the Huey, who was experiencing the same lack of empathy and difficulty in re-joining society. Hank joined him on the road, and the Kings of Mayhem MC was born.

The name had been a natural selection. Mayhem had been their call sign in Vietnam.

Nowadays, to make a legitimate income, the Kings had several sources of income: prostitution, pornography, custom choppers, and tattoos.

We owned a brothel called The Den. A few miles outside of Destiny, The Den was pure high-class shit. A place where both the average Joe and the executive could enjoy the finer comforts of a pleasurable establishment in the company of clean, beautiful, and accommodating women.

The Den was managed by Megan, a tall, dark-haired beauty with a knockout body and killer Egyptian eyes. Seriously smokin' hot, she had a way about her that grabbed your attention and kept you mesmerized. Her voice was husky but as smooth as bourbon, and she had a way of slow blinking that you felt all the way to your goddamn balls. Megan and I had a weird relationship. A strange kind of mutual respect for one another. She got me. And I fucking admired her head for business—as well as the way she gave it. Yeah, we'd gone there numerous times. But we both knew the deal. There was nothing serious. A head job here and there, and the occasional night spent in her big bed. But nothing more. It suited both of us just fine.

The brothel aside, the *Kings* also ran an adult entertainment production company that included adult movies, as well as sexual documentaries. You know, sex for dummies, that kind of thing. It made the club a fuck load of money and staved off the need for us to look for other lucrative, yet illegal, means of income—like drugs and guns. Which suited me just fine, because just like my grandaddy, I hated that shit.

Our movies were made in our studios just off Highway 54. A place aptly named Head Quarters. It was an old converted warehouse, fully equipped with all the amenities of a well-appointed production studio, and guarded by security guards with guns twenty-four hours a day. Guards who went by the names Bubba, Tank, and Gigantor.

Other interests included a strip club in town called *Spank Daddy's*—which was definitely not high-class shit like *The Den*, and a security detail service that was completely off the books.

Before I got so involved in club business, I used to work at *Sinister Ink*, the tattoo shop that bordered our clubhouse. Next door to that was our custom chopper shop, *Shadow Choppers*, run by a creative mastermind called Picasso. His custom paint jobs were legendary throughout the South, all the way up through the Bible belt and across the northern borders.

After visiting Jackie at the funeral home and helping Mom and Lady with some of the funeral arrangements, I headed out to Head Quarters to check out how things were going. It was Tuesday, and every Tuesday and Friday I checked in with the production manager, Tito, to make sure everything was running smoothly. Tito was a creepy looking pervert. Four-foot nothing with ill-fitting suits and a combover, he liked things a little weird. I had busted him jerkin' his gherkin once. Not so unusual, until you factor in the detail that he was wrapped in Saran wrap and Vaseline, and rocking backward and forward on a big black dildo stuck up his ass. I'd shown up just in time to see him squirt the money shot all over his hands.

Like I said, he was a little odd. But damn he knew the porn business, and damn he was good at managing our interests.

So what if the oddball liked it a little weird?

As long as he didn't get up in my face with his creepiness and kept things going well at Head Quarters, then I didn't give a fuck.

Today he was in a fluster about God knows what. While I had been at the funeral home, he had rung my cell, hollering about *not putting up with this craziness* and if I didn't *come and sort out this insanity* then he was going to *go where his genius was appreciated*.

Pulling into the parking lot of Head Quarters, I saw a cherry-red Mustang convertible parked by the front door, and Tito's meltdown started to make sense.

That cherry-red Mustang was a warning to batten down the hatches.

"Jesus Christ," I muttered as I parked my bike next to it, and shoved my aviators into the front of my cut. "This is going to be fun."

CHAPTER 7

INDY
Now

After hanging up from Anson, something in the distance caught my eye. It was at least a mile up and it looked like a plume of dust or smoke rising up off the side of the road.

"What the hell?"

As I got nearer, I noticed a woman kneeling in the dirt on the side of the road and the air around her was thick with a settling cloud of dust. I quickly pulled over and hurried out of the car, my skin tingling with the same electrical charge I had right before an emergency came into the ER.

I knew I'd just stumbled upon something—what, I had no idea. I did a quick scan of our nearby surroundings, but couldn't see anything out of place.

I quickly raced over to the young woman on her knees in the dirt. She was bruised and dirty and moaning as if in labor, and the moment I got to her I knew her shoulder was dislocated. My first thought was that she had been thrown from a car.

I crouched in front of her.

"It's okay, honey, I'm a doctor."

At the sound of my voice, she looked at me. Her face was grazed and bruised, and drool was dripping from her mouth as she continued to moan in agony. I knew I wasn't going to get any coherent details from her until I stopped that excruciating shoulder pain.

When I reached for her arm, she flinched.

"Your shoulder is dislocated. I can fix that, okay. I can make it stop hurting. But first, I need you to tell me if you're hurt anywhere else."

She looked at me with large, mascara-smudged eyes, and finally shook her head. As another spasm of pain washed over her, she moaned again.

"What's your name, sweetheart?" I asked, guiding her upward so she wasn't so bent over. I needed her to try and relax a little.

She flinched and gritted her teeth. "Michelle. My… name… is Michelle."

I nodded. "Michelle. That's nice. I have a cousin called Michelle." I didn't. But I was trying to build trust. I spoke quickly because time was ticking by and I had a feeling she wasn't going to be the only surprise I found on the side of the road. How she got here and who was involved was probably nearby. But I had to get her fixed before I worried about anything else. "Now, I'm about to get real up close and personal with your shoulder, okay, Michelle, and I need you to be real brave for me… can you do that?"

She winced and started to cry again.

"Look at me," I said as I put her arm in the neutral position and slowly began to rotate it outwards until I felt resistance. She winced again as I moved her upper arm exteriorly. "I promise you, it's only going to take a few moments and you'll feel—"

Kings of Mayhem

The relocation of her shoulder back into its joint was swift and the pain that had rendered her almost incapable of talking seconds earlier eased almost immediately. She looked at me with startled eyes and her panting slowly turned into deep, relieved breaths.

That was when her panic turned up and she started screaming.

And holy hell! This woman did it well.

"Caveman! You have to help, Caveman!" She stumbled to her feet and pointed to the embankment a few yards away. Tire marks ground up the dirt and disappeared over the edge.

That second surprise I mentioned earlier? Yeah. It was at the base of that embankment lying beside the twisted remains of a Harley. A man. A very bloody and broken man.

Oh hell.

I turned to Michelle. "There's a travel first aid kit in the glove compartment of my rental. I need you to run and get it." I thought about my handbag and the bottle of vodka I'd brought for my mom. "And my handbag. I'll need that, too." When she didn't move, I yelled at her in some attempt to get her moving. "Hurry!" I needed that first aid kit. Not that I had any confidence in it having anything too useful to aid a broken biker who was quite possibly already dead.

Michelle took off while I was already calling 911 on my phone. As I scooted down the embankment, I hurried out words to the operator, then dropped my phone to the ground when I reached the body. Straight away I noticed the cut he was wearing and the familiar MC insignia on the front. *Kings of Mayhem.* But I didn't recognize him.

Dropping to my knees, I checked his vitals. He was alive. But he was in a bad way. Clearly both his legs were broken and he was covered in grazes and cuts, but it was the damage to his face and mouth that concerned me the most. It looked like someone had taken to him with a baseball bat. His head and face were covered in blood, and I could tell by the extreme trauma to his mouth that he would be missing teeth.

Just as Michelle slid down the embankment to me, the broken biker began to convulse. He couldn't breathe. Either he had vomited and was choking on it, or his facial trauma had filled his trachea with teeth and other tissue matter, stopping his airflow.

I swung back to Michelle.

"Give me that first aid kit." She handed it to me and I quickly checked the contents. Inside were the usual suspects you would expect to see in a small travel kit. Bandages. Tweezers. Saline solution. Band-Aids. Medical tape. Small scalpel. Gloves.

"In my bag is a bottle of vodka," I said, snapping on the latex gloves. "And a ballpoint pen. I'm going to need both of those."

I opened the unconscious biker's mouth and my suspicions were right. Most of his teeth were missing and were blocking his airway.

Michelle pulled out the vodka and handed it to me, then rummaged through my bag for the ballpoint pen "Caveman… is he… is he going to be okay?" she asked, handing me the pen with shaky hands.

"He won't be if I don't get that airway clear," I said, unscrewing the pen. I glanced at my phone on the ground and gestured to it with a nod of my head. I didn't need Michelle watching what I was about to do. "I need you to get back on the phone with emergency services and see how far away the EMT is. Tell them there is a doctor on the scene but she has to do an emergency crike."

She looked at me with wide eyes. "A what?"

"Tell them there is a doctor on the scene and she is giving the patient an emergency crike," I said calmly.

While she busied herself with the call, I tipped vodka over Caveman's throat in a crude attempt to sterilize the area, then using the very small, but very sharp, scalpel, I slit into his throat.

That was when Michelle decided to pull a gun on me.

"Wha… what are you doing to Caveman?" she cried.

I glanced over my shoulder to reassure her that I was doing the only thing that could be done to save her friend's life, and came face to face with the business end of a handgun.

"Are you fucking kidding me?" I had just put a hole in her friend's throat, and now she decided to confront me? "I don't have time for this, Michelle."

"You're hurting him…!" she cried, her very shaky hands swaying the handgun closer to my face.

I wasn't alarmed about having a gun waved at me—I was pissed. And the adrenaline pumping through my veins had me wanting to *unrelocate* that shoulder of hers just so she would stop being such a pain in the ass while I tried to save this guy's life. He was cyanosed and would die within minutes. I didn't have time to explain it to her, but the fact that she had a Glock up in my face gave me little choice.

"Listen, if I don't get this airway clear, your friend is going to die."

"Boyfriend… he's… my… boyfriend," she corrected me.

Because clearly now was the time to establish that.

"Listen, do whatever it is you're going to do, but right now I have to get this pen into that hole in his throat if I want him to have any chance at survival. Do you understand? He will die if I don't do this."

Time was running out. Caveman was in peri arrest. So I turned away and prayed she didn't shoot me as I continued slicing into the skin of his throat. I pushed two fingers into the cut and felt for the cricothyroid membrane. Blood was bright red as it rose to the surface of the wound and rolled down his throat. I glanced over my shoulder at Michelle, who half had me at gunpoint and half stared at what I was doing to her boyfriend in disbelief.

"How far off is that EMT?" I asked in an attempt to shake her out of her craziness. Shock was settling in and I couldn't afford for her to lose it again while I was trying to save this guy's life.

I turned back to Caveman and inserted the base of the scalpel into the incision, rotating it to hold the hole open wide. With a steady hand, I pushed the pen through the hole, passed the cricothyroid membrane and into his trachea. Not wasting anymore time, I leaned down and gave two quick breaths into the pen and felt a little win when I saw Caveman's chest rise and fall. I counted to five in my head and then gave him another breath of air.

At the sound of arriving sirens, Michelle fell to the ground with a sob and discarded the gun to the side as if it was all too much for her. Shock and distress took over and she stared straight ahead at some invisible entity in front of her.

I nodded toward the gun. "You might want to get rid of that."

She looked dazed at the sound of my voice, but then quickly grabbed the gun and pushed it into her handbag. I checked Caveman's pulse but it was very weak and I didn't hold out much help for him if the EMTs didn't arrive soon.

At the sound of tires on gravel, both Michelle and I looked up the embankment, and within seconds, Sheriff Buckman appeared at the ledge.

"Oh shit!" The fifty-something sheriff exclaimed when he saw us. He quickly scrambled down the uneven ridge. "What the hell happened here?"

"I don't know exactly, other than this is Caveman and that is Michelle," I gestured toward the very confused looking blonde slumped on the ground. "And that's the bike they came off."

Kings of Mayhem

I pointed to the smoldering motorcycle a few yards away.

Sheriff Buckman already had his mobile radio in his hand. "Delores, where the hell is that damned EMT?"

The radio fizzed. "They're two minutes away, chief," replied a crackly female voice.

"Well, get on the line to them, will you? Tell them to make it one minute!"

Sheriff Buckman knelt next to me. "Anything I can do?" he asked, and then as if a light bulb went off in his head, he recognized me. "Wait a minute … Indy? Indigo Parrish?"

I gave him a close-lipped smile.

"Jesus Christ! What's it been…? Seven? Eight years?"

"Twelve."

He looked stunned. "Well, I'll be goddamned."

The voice behind us startled me.

"When you two are quite finished with your *fucking* reunion…"

We both looked around, and there was Michelle pointing her goddamn gun again.

Sheriff Buckman leapt to his knees with one arm out to calm her down. "Now hold on there, Missy…"

"Don't worry about her, Sheriff. She's just concerned about her boyfriend." Turning to look at Michelle, I said reassuringly, "He's going to be okay, sweetheart. The best thing you can do for him now is to put that gun away."

Her wide eyes bounced between Sheriff B and me, and it was like some fucked-up standoff. Thankfully, the sound of approaching sirens and the screeching of the tires on gravel gave us all a sense of relief. Michelle dropped the gun to her side and Sheriff B went to her, putting his arm around her as he disarmed her.

Within minutes, two EMTs had Caveman strapped to a gurney, and with the Sheriff's help we got the six-foot-something biker up the embankment and loaded into the ambulance.

"Nice work," said a very hot looking EMT called Rory.

"Thanks," I replied.

"Would you mind accompanying us to the hospital?" He looked apologetic. "Paperwork. Plus, if he starts crashing again I have a feeling you'll come in handy."

I looked at Sheriff B and he nodded. "You go. I will arrange for someone to drop your car to your mom's." He gave me a questioning look. "You were going to your mom's, weren't you?"

"Yeah, thanks, Sheriff." I gestured to Michelle. "What about her? You know… about the whole pulling a gun on us thing?"

He gave me a blank look. "What gun?"

Sheriff Buckman had been a strong ally of the Kings of Mayhem for as long as I could remember. He wasn't a pushover but he was known to turn a blind eye to a lot of things. It was no secret he wasn't a big fan of paperwork.

I nodded. "I guess I'll see you at the funeral."

He gave me a casual, two-finger salute and walked over to his squad car to call a tow-truck while I climbed into the back of the ambulance. Five minutes later, I watched the town of Destiny come into view as we rode toward the hospital.

I was back in town.

CHAPTER 8

CADE
Now

I heard her as soon as I entered the building.

"It's a classic, sonny boy, and you don't fuck with the classics. Do you hear me? Or has that combover blocked your ears?"

I couldn't help but grin. The voice belonged to Sybil Calley, my formidable, charismatic grandmother. Seventy-something-years old, she was a force to be reckoned with and very rarely backed down in an argument. Any poor soul who took her on was in for a fierce fight, and by the sounds of it, Tito was about to feel the full force of hurricane Sybil.

"It's blasphemy! That's what it is. Blasphemy! Why, I bet Deborah Kerr is rolling in her grave, God rest her beautiful soul. How dare you stain such a beautiful story with your weirdness, you rude little boy!"

As I rounded the corner, Sybil and Tito came into view. Tito was standing with his back to the wall with his arms in the air, while my formidable grandmother yelled at him. He looked terrified.

"Grandma Calley," I interrupted, trying to contain my grin. Seeing me walk in, Tito looked relieved and relaxed his arms.

Sybil wasted no time in getting straight to the point. She held up a DVD so I could see the cover. "Did you know about this?"

I took it from her and couldn't help but grin at the cover. *Pure spank bank bullshit that sells.* But definitely not what you wanted your grandmother looking at in front of you.

"How on Earth did you even know about it?" I asked.

"I might be edging close to buying the farm, Cade, but I'm not quite dead yet. You know I like to keep my finger on the pulse. It's Tuesday, and I know you drop into this pit of despair on Tuesdays, so I came down to speak with you." She gave Tito a withering look. "Ran into this little twerp and found this . . ."

She ripped the DVD out of my hands and held it up. The cover was a rip-off of *An Affair To Remember*, except it was titled, *An Anus to Remember*. Gay porn. It was a bestseller.

"It's a disgrace, Cade. An absolute disgrace." She pushed the DVD into Tito's chest. "You should be ashamed of yourself."

"Ain't nothing wrong with a bit of man-on-man love, Grandma," I said, trying to diffuse the situation. Sybil could be unpredictable at times.

"I know that! Man on man. Woman on woman. I don't give a goddamn! What I do care about is taking a classic and turning it into smut. Now that is not right, Cade. Not right. You don't fuck with the classics."

"Cade, this can't keep happening," Tito moaned.

Sybil turned back to Tito. "I'm seventy-three years old but I ain't dead yet, sonny. I'm the original biker queen and I'm still packing as much attitude as I did back when my old man started the Kings of Mayhem more than fifty years ago. If you ever mess with one of the classics again and put your perverted stamp all over it, I will knock you on your ass, do you hear me?"

Again, I struggled to contain my grin.

Tito, however, looked unraveled. And he had every cause to be because I had no doubt Sybil meant what she said. She was a classy lady who never left the house without taming her bright red hair and putting on a thick coat of red lipstick. But she was a biker queen first. Tough. Fierce. With a mean right hook.

You didn't fuck with Sybil Calley.

Taking pity on Tito, I slunk an arm around Grandma's shoulders and guided her toward the front door.

"Now, Grandma, you can't come in here and get up in Tito's grill about things. Head Quarters is off limits to MC women, remember?"

That rule had come about after Sybil had swept through Head Quarters like a hurricane and upset an entire cast of actresses on the set of a movie we were making called *Some Like It Hard*. Sybil was a die-hard Marilyn fan and managed to put the fear in all the actresses who were on set, leading to a mass walk-out and halting production for three days.

Not that Sybil paid any attention to rules. She was the original rule breaker. She did what she wanted, when she wanted. And if it suited her, she'd blame her *forgetfulness* on her age to get away with it, despite being sharp as a tack.

She waved off the mention of the rules.

"If that little pervert can't handle a seventy-year-old woman, then he needs to take a cup of cement and harden the fuck up." She glanced over her shoulder and narrowed her eyes at Tito as we were walking away, and muttered, "little pussy."

I tried not to laugh because that would only encourage her, so I asked, "Grandma, why are you here?"

She relaxed and smiled. "Now, Cade, you know you're my favorite grandson—"

"You say that to all your grandsons . . ."

". . . and I love you. So I wanted to see how you were feeling about Indy coming home."

"This isn't her home anymore, Grandma. She lives in Seattle now."

"Thank you, Captain Obvious. But you know what I mean." Her face softened as she took my hand. "I know the affect that girl has on you. I just wanted to make sure…"

"What?"

She smacked me hard on the arm. "That you're not going to be an ass about it."

I couldn't help but grin. Good on Grandma Sybil.

"A lot of water has passed under the bridge, Grandma. I'm not an eighteen-year-old psychopath anymore."

Sybil didn't look convinced. "You're a Calley and we're passionate sonsofbitches. When we love, we love big, and if that love dies, then we die a big death along side it. I should know. When your Pappy died, my heart went with him."

I couldn't help but smile at my feisty grandmother.

"I'm sure Jury wouldn't like to hear you say that," I said.

Jury was my grandma's sixty-year-old boyfriend.

"Jury isn't the love of my life. Your grandpappy was. Jury knows I'm just after his body."

I raised an eyebrow at her. "Grandma, there are certain things a grandson should never hear his grandmother say, and that's right up there with them."

She waved me off. "The body may be old and the reflection in the mirror might be slightly different, but the mind is still twenty years old. I might not be able to do it the way I used to but—"

I stuck my fingers in my ears. "Lalalalalalalalala . . ."

She rolled her eyes. "Fine. I'll let you think that I don't do the things I still did when I was twenty."

"Seriously, Grandma . . ." I begged, pained by the mental images.

Sighing dramatically, she changed the subject. "Your mom is making dinner for Lady and Indy. Somehow I was extended an invitation. I assume you'll be there."

To say Sybil and my mom didn't exactly get along would be an understatement. The civil unrest had ended years ago, but in its wake was a frosty cold war of mammoth proportions. Mother-in-law and daughter-in-law didn't exactly see eye to eye.

I nodded. "I'm heading over there now."

"Fine. I'll follow you. Lord knows I've had my fair share of pussy and cock today."

I opened the front door for her and shook my head. "Jesus Christ, Sybil. My ears are bleeding."

CHAPTER 9

CADE & INDY—Aged 6
Then

It was dark but moonlight spilled into my bedroom. The house was quiet, and I was in the middle of deciding who would win between Spiderman and the Flash if they had a fight, when something rattled against my bedroom window. I sat up, straining to hear in the dark. Again, something hit the glass. Pulling my blankets back, I climbed out of bed and went to my window. Peering out into the moonlit night I saw Indy standing by the sycamore tree. She was wearing an oversized t-shirt with a big pineapple on the front.

I pushed up the window and she came toward me.

"What are you doing?" I whispered loudly.

"Can I come in?" she asked.

I glanced over my shoulder. The house was still and no lights had come on in the hallway, so my mama and daddy weren't awake.

"Of course," I said. "But be quiet. My mama will tan my hide if she catches us."

I helped Indy climb in through the window.

"Can I stay here tonight?" she asked, a little puffed. "I promise I won't snore."

"You want to stay here? With me? Why?"

"We can have a sleepover," she said. She was smiling but I could tell it was forced. "We've been friends for a thousand years, Cade Calley, and I've never stayed over. I think it's time we fix that, don't you?"

"Sure," I replied casually, but I was confused. I didn't say anything as I watched her climb into my bed.

"Is everything okay?" I didn't know why I asked the question. There was just something about her tonight that seemed weird.

Indy looked up, surprised. For a moment she looked sad, but then she shrugged.

"I don't like it when my Uncle Calvin stays over," she said quietly. She lay down and pulled the covers over her, leaving half the pillow free for me. She didn't say anymore, so I shrugged and climbed in after her.

For a moment neither of us said anything.

"Why don't you like it when he stays over?" I finally asked, breaking the silence.

Indy shifted closer to me. She was warm but squirmy.

"He makes me feel funny," she said. To my surprise she reached around and pulled my arm around her. "Good night, Cade."

And that was how we went to sleep, with her head on my shoulder and my arm around her waist. When I woke up the next morning, she was gone. But she was back again later that night, this time wearing a big t-shirt with a faded strawberry across the front.

Again, she climbed in through my bedroom window and crawled into bed next to me, wriggling until she was comfortable.

"Indy?"

"Yeah?"

"Is your uncle still at your house?"

I felt her stiffen and nod against me. Then she let out a sigh and wrapped her arm around me. A strange feeling swept through me. A powerful need to hold her tight and keep her safe.

"Indy?"

"Yeah?"

"Why does he make you feel funny?"

I felt her swallow and then breathe in deeply before letting it go heavily. Finally, she said, "He calls me his little princess and makes me sit on his lap. He puts his big hands on my legs and sometimes his fingers rub up and down my back. And he looks at me funny. He always licks his lips and his eyes get all funny looking."

Another strange feeling moved through me. I had no idea what it was because I had never felt it before. But it made me feel angry. I didn't want her uncle doing that to her.

"Does he do anything else?"

She was still for a moment, thinking in the darkness, then said, "The other night, he opened my bedroom door. I could tell he was just standing there in the doorway, watching." She swallowed deeply but she lay rigid next to me. "I could hear him breathing and I got scared. But then he closed the door because he heard a noise down the hall. A few moments later I heard him tell mama he was looking for the bathroom."

I frowned in the darkness. What Indy was telling me didn't sound right. I didn't understand why, but I knew it was wrong. Remembering what I had promised my mama about protecting Indy, I wrapped my arms around her and held her to my chest.

The following night we lay in the exact same spot and the exact same position. I had my arm around her while she curled into my shoulder. She was warm and smelled like soap.

"When is your uncle leaving?" I asked.

I would be pleased when he left because then Indy wouldn't be scared anymore. But at the same time, she would stop coming into my room at night and I would miss putting my arm around her and listening to her breath soften as she fell asleep.

"Tomorrow. Mama said he joined the Army and won't be back for a while." She sighed. "I wish I could tell her . . ."

"Tell her what?"

"That I wish he won't ever come back."

I held her to me, just like I had done every other night that week. But then I did something I had never done before; I turned my head and pressed a kiss into her hair.

"If he comes back, I will protect you."

She tilted her head to look at me. "Promise?"

I nodded and smiled. "I promise."

CHAPTER 10

INDY
Now

"Indy!"

I swung around at the sound of my name and saw my mom hurrying down the hospital corridor toward me.

"Baby!" Catching me off guard, she flung her arms tightly around me. "It's so good to see you, my girl."

"You, too, Mom."

My mom was all of five-foot nothing, even in her six-inch-heeled boots. She held on tight, her arms secured around me as if she was holding on for dear life. It took me a moment to realize I was holding on just as tight. My grief started to rise to the surface in her familiar embrace, and I pulled away before the tears behind my eyes spilled down my cheeks. I didn't realize how much I had missed her.

When Mom stood back, she noticed my bloodied blouse. "You're hurt? Oh my God, Indy, are you hurt?"

"Relax, Mom. I'm fine. It's someone else's blood."

Despite my reassurance, she still looked alarmed. "What happened?"

Not wanting to recap the details of the last half an hour, I said, "I'll fill you in later, okay."

My eyes shifted to Veronica—Cade's mom and the MCs legendary biker queen—who walked up behind my mom. They were best friends.

"Baby girl," she greeted me, her smoky voice low and full of affection.

Veronica, known affectionately as Ronnie, was your quintessential biker goddess. Tall. Leggy. Tight jeans. Tight top showing just enough cleavage to tantalize.

She hugged me, and when our gazes met, her eyes softened and she gave me a gentle half-smile. "Its so good to see you, baby." She brushed hair out of my eyes. "It's been too long."

Ronnie reminded me of Cher, circa 1988, strutting her sexy-stuff on a battleship while surrounded by a platoon of hot Navy guys. Same head of dark curls. Same hooded eyes. Same sassy attitude.

"Hey, how did you know I was here?" I asked.

Sadness swept over my mom's face. "We were downstairs organizing your daddy's funeral."

The town's funeral home was ironically attached to the hospital. It was kind of a creepy, multi-tasking thing.

"Cade called us," Ronnie replied, her voice soothing and smoky compared to my mom's soprano timbre. "He said Caveman had been in some kind of accident and that you were at the hospital with him and Michelle."

"Cade called you?" My stomach twisted.

"He and Isaac are on their way in," Ronnie said.

Anticipation flared in my chest.

"Are you sure you're okay, baby?" Mom asked.

I hadn't seen a mirror since I'd knelt in mud and cut open Caveman's throat. I was pretty sure I was a bloodied, muddied mess.

"Yeah, Mom. I'm fine." I touched her arm. "Are you okay?"

She smiled softly. "I will be, baby girl. I will be."

The elevator pinged and we all looked in its direction. Hell, why did I have a sudden urge to run and brush my hair?

I held my breath, waiting for Cade to walk through the doors, but a mixture of relief and disappointment flooded my body when two men in Kings of Mayhem cuts appeared, and neither one of them were Cade.

"Well, well, well . . . if it isn't little Indigo Parrish," the taller of the two men greeted me. It was Cade's cousin, Isaac. Tall and broad, he looked like a big, blond Viking, strong and commanding. Two sleeves of tattoos colored his arms.

Grinning, he pulled me into a bear hug, slightly lifting me off the ground with his strength.

"Hell, girl! You look like you've been to war," he exclaimed, dropping me to my feet and taking a good look at me.

I looked down at my bloodied white shirt and mud-covered tailored pants. Both were Marc Jacobs. Both were ruined. "Don't worry, I'll be sending your buddy Caveman the dry cleaning bill."

"How is he?" Asked the guy with Isaac. I had been so distracted by the mix of relief and disappointment tearing through me that I had barely recognized Caleb Calley— Cade's younger brother. When I'd left Destiny twelve years earlier, he'd been a weedy fifteen-year-old with pimples and patchy facial hair. Now he was all grown up and handsome. And massive. Just like all the Calley boys. He had the same dark hair and blue eyes as his older brothers, and like his cousin, he had two sleeves of tattoos. I remember my mom mentioning he'd done a stint in prison, but I couldn't remember why.

My smile faded. "He's got two broken legs, some pretty serious maxillofacial trauma and a hole in his neck, but he's going to be okay."

"Maxio-what?" Isaac asked, looking confused.

Sometimes I forgot medical terminology was basically a second language. It was easier to put it in layman's terms to explain it. "His face looks like he's been beaten with a baseball bat."

"Damn," Isaac shook his head.

"Do we know what happened?" Ronnie asked.

"I have no idea." I gestured toward Michelle who was leaving one of the ER cubicles farther down the corridor. She was patched up but still looking shaken and dazed. "You might want to ask her."

Caleb and Isaac both turned to look.

"I'm on it," Isaac said, before walking off toward the bruised and shaken blonde girl.

Ronnie turned to Caleb. "Where's your brother?"

"He had to head over to Head Quarters."

Displeasure bit into Ronnie's face, and she folded her arms across her impressive rack. "What's up at the pussy playground now?"

"Tito."

Ronnie looked even more unimpressed. "What's that little pervert upset about?"

I didn't know what Head Quarters was but I could hazard a guess.

While Caleb spoke to Ronnie, I pulled my handbag over my shoulder and turned to my mom. "Are you heading home?"

I explained how I had to ride in with the ambulance and that Sheriff Buckman was going to arrange for my car to be dropped off at her place.

"I have to head over to Sticky Fingers first."

Sticky Fingers was my mom's cake shop. She was a talented cake designer, well known across three counties for her elaborate wedding and celebration cakes.

"We can drop you on the way," she suggested.

I shook my head. Her cake shop was in the other direction.

"I'll get a cab into town," I said. "The airline lost my bag so I need to pick up a change of clothes."

Isaac jogged up the hallway to rejoin us, his face serious. He looked at Caleb. "Think we need to call a meeting. Looks like we may have a problem," he said.

"What sort of problem?" Ronnie asked.

Isaac's brow furrowed. "Michelle just told me someone deliberately ran them off the road." Caleb and Isaac exchanged a look.

"Payback?" Caleb suggested.

"Don't know," Isaac looked concerned. "But we need to find out. Let's get to the clubhouse and speak to Bull."

Bull was Ronnie's brother, and from what I could make out, the current president of the Kings.

"I'll call Cade." Isaac turned to me and winked. "It was really good to see you."

Caleb agreed. "Welcome home, Indy."

I smiled. "Thanks."

After they left, I turned to my mom. "I'll see you at home?"

My mom hugged me again and we held each other for the longest moment.

"It's good to have you home, baby girl."

Riding the elevator down to the ground floor, I tried to push it all to the back of my mind. Five minutes back in Destiny and there was already drama. I didn't know what the possible payback was about and I couldn't help but wonder what bullshit was going on.

Then I remembered this wasn't my world anymore and I really didn't want to know.

CHAPTER 11

INDY
Now

Because I needed to buy clothes, I took a cab to Main Street. The only clothing shop in town was a department store called McGovern's. It was Destiny's version of Walmart and smelled like a stale old movie theatre. In twelve years it hadn't changed.

I wandered around the drab store feeling out of place and trying not to breathe in the stale air. Lifeless elevator music scratched and crackled through the old speakers in the ceiling, while flustered mothers pushed their carts around trying to shop and drink their extra large Starbucks while their children hollered and whined at their feet. Toward the back of the store, right beside women's underwear, someone had vomited all over the floor.

Thirty minutes later, I had a few pairs of underwear, a change of bras, a pair of black pants, and two blouses.

And probably scabies.

I was about to pay for my items when I heard a voice behind me.

"Indigo? Indigo Parrish?"

I closed my eyes and swore under my breath. I was hoping to avoid anyone while I was here, and I knew that voice.

I sucked in a deep breath and turned around.

"Hi, Mallory," I said brightly.

Mallory Massey. One of my best friends in high school.

"Oh my Lord, it really is you!" she said with a huge grin. Her lips were still painted the bright red she wore in school and her hair still tumbled around her face in thick waves. But she looked older. Frayed around the edges. She was also heavily pregnant.

She pulled me in for a big hug, the bracelets on her arms jangling and her big baby belly pushing into me as she hugged me tight.

"It's so good to see you. I didn't think I'd ever lay my eyes on you again. Aren't you some fancy doctor in the city now?"

"I'm a trauma doctor at SeaTac Medical."

Mallory looked blank.

"In Seattle."

"Wow. That must be exciting." She popped her gum.

I nodded toward her big belly. "Congratulations," I said.

Once upon a time, Mallory and I could talk for hours, but that was a long time ago. Now it was just awkward. Life had definitely taken us down different paths.

"Thanks. This is baby number five." She rubbed the bulge through her dress. "This one's a girl, finally! I have four boys at home, can you imagine?"

I couldn't.

"But me and Brody really wanted a girl this time."

"Brody? As in Brody Meyers?"

She grinned. "Nabbed myself the quarterback."

I nodded. "And five kids, that's . . . awesome."

"Oh, baby number one and three ain't his," she said with a wave of her hand. "Lloyd Peterson got me pregnant just after graduation. You remember, Lloyd?"

I did. He tried kissing me in fourth grade so I had kicked him in the shins and pushed him over.

"Lloyd didn't stick around. He met some fancy girl in college. Then Brody started hanging around and that led to baby number two. But you know, we were young and he left for a bit, so I started dating this guy from outta town and he gave me boy number three." She laughed again. "Then Brody came knocking on my door again, wanting to give things another go. My fourth boy came along nine months later. He's only a year old now, can you believe that? And, well, my man just can't keep his hands off me, and look where we are today." She rubbed her belly again.

I smiled. Mallory seemed happy. Content. It was actually really refreshing.

"Boy, you look like you've been playing in the mud," she said, noticing the mud and blood on my clothes. "Is that blood?"

"I came across an accident on the way into town," I explained.

"Was anybody hurt?"

"Well, yeah . . . that's where the blood came from."

Her eyes went as round as saucers. "What happened?"

I waved it off, not wanting to rehash the story. "A motorcycle accident on the road into town. They're okay."

Mallory looked impressed. "I bet your life is real exciting. Being a doctor in the city and all."

"I do okay."

"You must come for dinner before you leave. We have a real nice double-wide at the park."

"That sounds, you know . . . awesome. But I'm only here really briefly for my father's funeral and then I'll be leaving." I handed my credit card over to the cashier. "But thanks for the offer."

Mallory's face fell, but she gave me a self-conscious smile. "Okay, then. Well, it was real nice seeing you again. Sorry about your daddy."

When she wheeled her cart away, I felt bad for brushing her off. I was keen to get home, get cleaned up, and brace myself for when Cade and I finally came face to face. But Mallory deserved better than a shitty brush off.

"Hey Mallory," I called out. She swung back to look at me. "Is that The Last Stop Holiday Park?"

She looked a little surprised. "Yeah. Van number six."

I nodded. "Would it be okay if I dropped by before I left town?"

She smiled brightly. "I'd really like that."

I smiled too. "Yeah, so would I."

And I really meant it.

CHAPTER 12

INDY
Now

The house looked the same. Even after twelve years, it looked exactly the same. White timber. Dark navy shutters. Slate roof. Little porch.

I paid the cab driver and climbed out, but stood on the curb well after he drove away because being back was a giant mind fuck. I looked around me and clutched the strap of my handbag like it was the only thing standing between me and the horrible memories of my past. Mom's Mercedes was in the driveway. On the next driveway over was Ronnie's Mustang. They were home.

"Baby girl!" I looked up. My mom stood in the open doorway. "Did you find some clothes?"

I held up my McGovern's bag and she pulled a face. "I haven't been there for years. Can't stand the place. Smells like stale popcorn." She smiled across at me. "Well, come on, let's get you inside. Ronnie and I are getting dinner sorted. We thought it would be nice for all of us to have dinner together, but I can fix you something to eat now if you're hungry."

I hadn't eaten since breakfast but shook my head. My stomach was in knots. Dinner *for all of us* more than likely meant dinner with Cade, and I wasn't sure I was ready for that. It had already been a long day.

"Come on, let's at least get you a glass of wine."

I closed the door behind me and followed her into the family room. For a moment I paused, letting the weirdness fill me and the goosebumps prickle along my skin. The smell. The feelings. They were all still here.

I followed Mom into the large kitchen off to the right. It was huge and open planned, with gleaming, granite countertops, and stark white cabinets. I glanced over at the fridge with photos and menus stuck to the front with magnets I had made in craft class when I was twelve. A strange, tingling sensation curled around the base of my spine and began its ascent up my back. Life had changed when I was twelve.

Ronnie pulled a bottle of wine from the rack beside the refrigerator and poured three glasses. She handed me one. "Here, you look like you could use it."

I accepted it gratefully. Wine was a good idea. Lots of it.

"The airline rang," I said to my mom. "They found my bag. It will be here Tuesday."

"In time for the funeral," she said. "If it doesn't get here by then, we can go into Humphrey to get you something."

The knock at the front door made me almost jump out of my skin. We turned all our heads and watched a fiery redhead walk in. Immediately, the energy in the room lit up like a night sky on the Fourth of July.

"Grandma Calley," I whispered in disbelief.

"Yeah, she's still alive," Ronnie muttered beside me.

Sybil Calley shot her daughter-in-law a warning look as she approached. But her face softened when she reached me, and her wise old eyes twinkled as she pressed her palms to either side of my face.

"Beautiful Indigo Blue," she said, using my first and second name. "It is good to see you, my girl."

"It's good to see you, too, Grandma Sybil."

She kissed me on both sides of my cheek. Growing up, I always thought she was the most interesting person in the world.

"I'm sorry about your daddy," she said with a sharp nod.

"Thank you. I appreciate that."

"I don't expect this visit to pass without you and I getting together for a one-on-one catch-up, you hear?"

"Of course."

She patted my cheek. "Such a beautiful girl."

Her eyes shifted to my mom and then back to me. They were wise and knowing, and they glittered as if she was aware of things I couldn't possibly fathom. I smiled uncertainly. Sometimes I had the feeling that Sybil Calley knew about things before they happened.

She took my hand. "Come on, let's get dinner started. I'm famished."

Cade, Isaac, and Caleb were going to be late. Apparently, Caveman being ping-ponged off the road initiated some kind of urgent meeting at the clubhouse. So Ronnie, Sybil, Mom, and I caught up over wine, homemade lasagna, and salad. They told me about Chastity, the youngest of the Calley children, who was away at college in California, and Ronnie showed me a photo of her on her phone.

Being a Calley, she was strikingly beautiful, with raven black hair and bright blue eyes. I didn't doubt she was probably enjoying the freedom of being away from the over-protective eye of the club and her older brothers.

I remembered how smothering it had felt being an MC kid. Always watched. Always protected. Every move scrutinized by someone. Apparently, Chastity was dating someone but refused to bring him home to meet the family because she knew how her older brothers would be, and she wasn't sure if it was serious enough to subject anyone to that.

"Do Cade and Caleb still live at home?" I asked before I could stop myself. I glared at the almost-empty glass of wine in my hand, blaming it for making me ask the question. I didn't need to know anything about Cade and what he did.

"They both split their time between the clubhouse and home," Ronnie replied. She leaned over and refilled my wine glass, then settled back in her chair. "Home is for family. Clubhouse is for *other* interests."

Meaning, Ronnie didn't allow the boys to bring their hook-ups home.

"They've expanded the clubhouse now, so most members have a room there," Mom explained.

I hated the clubhouse. A few weeks before the West Destiny High School shooting, Garrett Calley had asked me to meet him there, under the guise of discussing his graduation present to Cade. Naïvely, I had gone to meet him.

My relationship with Garrett Calley had deteriorated the moment Cade told him he was following me to college. Garrett didn't like it. Not one little bit. He didn't want his son moving away. He wanted him to stay in Destiny and join him in the MC. He'd already lost one son, Chance, to the Navy SEALs, and wasn't about to let his second-born son leave.

When I arrived at the clubhouse I had knocked on the door to his office and walked in, not thinking. Garrett was at his desk, his head dropped back against the leather headrest of his chair, while his hands were tangled in the blonde hair of the MC groupie giving him a blowjob.

Hearing me walk in, Garrett had simply looked at me, grinned, and then come.

Repulsed, I had run out of there, determined more than ever to leave club life behind me.

A week later, I had walked in on his son fucking someone who wasn't me.

Less than a year after that, Garrett Calley was dead.

I stood up and started to clear the table. I hated this fucking place.

As I packed the dishwasher, I heard the rumble of approaching motorcycles and I straightened. Instantly, my stomach knotted into a big ball. Any minute Cade would walk through the door and I would come face to face with my past.

I wasn't ready. I reached for my glass and drained it, accidentally banging it down on the bench. When the front door opened, I jumped and knocked it over.

"Oh, shit!" I said, quickly picking it up. It was broken.

"It's okay," Mom said, taking the broken glass from me and nodding toward the front door. She had a small smile on her face. "I think someone is here to see you."

I swung around and there he was.

After twelve years.

Cade.

My stomach knotted.

He was taller than I remembered. Like, *mountain man* tall. And his hair was shorter than when he was a teenager, but still as dark. Tattoos covered both of his arms, which looked strong and muscular and his broad chest strained against the fabric of his plain black T-shirt. Everything about him screamed big. His lip ring was gone and he no longer had the face of a boy. It was all man. *He* was all man. I could almost smell the testosterone radiating off him.

Blue eyes zeroed in on me as he closed the distance between us, and for the first time in twelve years, put his arms around me.

"Indy." His voice was deep and manly, and his breath was warm and sweet on my throat. I was immediately engulfed in the intoxicating scent of him and accepted his warmth as he held me against him. He was big and strong, and I could feel his power in his embrace, which was all too familiar.

Wanting to put some distance between us, I stepped back. "Hi, Cade."

I forced a smile, unsure of what to do. I had given up on this day ever happening because I'd never intended to return to Destiny. But it had been an unrealistic intention, because my father's partying and hard lifestyle was always going to take him out sooner rather than later. I was always going to have to come back here to bury him.

"I'm so sorry about Jackie," he said gently. "We all loved your old man."

I nodded at him, fully aware of how awkward this was. He gave me a gentle squeeze on my arm before leaving me to greet his mom and grandmother.

Behind him, Isaac and Caleb barreled into the room. They said hi to me, then stopped to greet their mom and grandmother with a kiss, before sitting down at the dinner table and digging into large helpings of lasagna.

"Everything okay?" Ronnie asked, referring to Caveman and why he was run off the road.

"All good," Caleb reassured his mom with a wink, like it was no big deal. "Cade and a couple of the guys are going to meet with the Knights tomorrow."

The Knights—or *The Knights of Hell MC*—had been a rival club since anyone could remember.

I turned away and picked up my overnight bag. I didn't need to get involved.

"I'm going to my room," I said to my mom. "I need to freshen up."

Mom smiled. "It's good having you home, honey."

I placed my hand on her arm but said nothing, simply offering her a warm smile and enjoying being close to her. Glancing across at Cade and seeing his back to me, I smiled at my mom again and then turned and disappeared down the hall.

Walking into my old bedroom was another step back in time. The smell. The same floral comforter on the bed. The same faded curtains hanging in front of the window. My old desk in the corner of the room. I sucked in a deep breath. It was strange how familiar everything was, yet how disconnected I felt from it all.

I sighed and dropped the McGovern's bag on my bed.

Even if my bag hadn't been lost, I wouldn't have bothered unpacking it because I didn't plan on hanging around this place. I would say goodbye to my daddy and be here for my mom. But then I would be gone. I had a life back in Seattle. One that didn't involve a motorcycle club.

Get in and get out. No distractions.

There was a knock at my bedroom door and I swung around.

Cade.

"Let me guess, you're wondering how the fuck you've ended up back here?" he said, casually leaning against the doorframe, those two dimples perfectly in place on either side of his mouth.

I had to look away because those dimples were dragging me back to the past by my hair. Cade was still every inch the handsome guy he'd always been. Only, it seemed the years had given his looks more potency—which seemed a little unfair.

"Am I that predictable?" I asked, trying to shake off the tingling at the base of my spine.

His eyes darkened. "No. You're definitely not predictable."

An uneasiness hung between us.

"I thought I'd come and check on you," he said. "Make sure you're doing okay."

"I'm fine." I looked around the room. "It's just weird, you know. Being back."

We had spent our last day together in this room. We'd talked excitedly about college while making love in my bed a ridiculous amount of times. It was the night of the clubhouse party where everything had fallen apart for us.

"If there's anything you need while you're here . . . let me know. Like I said to your mom, I'm here for you both."

I nodded at him, wishing I knew how to form words because this was so fucking awkward. But apparently, I had lost the ability to speak like a grown-up.

"And thanks for what you did for Caveman and Michelle today," he said. "He's going to make it because of you."

"It was nothing."

"Well, he was lucky you were there."

"I guess."

Twelve years of unspoken words hung between us.

"It's good to see you," he said.

I didn't know what to say to that, because I had been prepared to hate him. Or not be affected by him. Or maybe I had simply planned not to care.

No. I always cared.

"I guess I'll let you get back to it." He nodded to the McGovern's bag sitting on my bed.

I forced a smile. "Thanks."

With little else left to say, he nodded and began to turn away, but stopped. He frowned as he turned back to me.

"You know it was the biggest mistake of my life, right?"

His words took me by surprise and I didn't know what to say. I looked away because it was unfair of him to bring it up when I was so unprepared. What happened had changed everything. What he did broke my heart and stole our future from us. I felt ambushed by the mention of it, and my feisty little heart decided to tell him so.

But when I looked up again, he was gone.

CHAPTER 13

INDY
Now

Much later, Mom took a sleeping pill and I tucked her into the couch in the lounge room because she didn't want to sleep in her bed without Daddy.

But I was too wired to sleep. Instead, I grabbed another bottle of wine and went outside to the tree house in the backyard.

I sat with my legs dangling over the side and took a big mouthful of wine. It was crazy how much life could change in the course of twenty-four hours. Yesterday this place had seemed like a distant, bad memory, and now here I was, staring up at a night sky just like I had done a thousand times as a kid.

I took another big mouthful of wine and appreciated the warmth spreading through my chest. By the third and fourth mouthfuls, my muscles began to loosen up and I started to relax.

As kids, my brother Bolt and I used to play cards for hours on this very spot. Then Cade had taught us poker, and the three of us had spent hours playing the game using a pouch of old poker chips Cade had stolen from his daddy. Bolt had been a terrible player. He wasn't one for being able to hide his emotions, whereas, I had a faultless poker face. I was hard to beat. Even Cade couldn't beat me ... and Cade was good at everything.

I looked around. Carved into one of the floorboards was my brother's name. *Bolt*. On another, *Cade loves Indy*. I ran my finger over the crudely carved letters and felt overcome by nostalgia. A lifetime had passed since any of this had meant something to me.

In my teenage years, the tree house had taken on a whole new meaning. It wasn't the place I came to play with my brother and my best friend. It was the place to escape the grief and arguments that had descended on our family home.

It's where I hid out. Where I smoked my first joint. Where I made love to Cade under a star-scattered sky.

It was also where I decided to escape the club given the first chance I got. I remembered the moment like it was only yesterday.

I was fourteen and life inside the Parrish home had come to completely suck. My mom and dad fought a lot. Daddy had changed. He'd always been gruff, but his tough exterior had always belied a fun and loving guy who loved his kids dearly. But the fun-loving father I knew left us when I was twelve. He became distant. Moody. *Mean.* He spent more time on club rides and immersed in club business. By the time I was fourteen, I had ceased to exist, or so it seemed, and our relationship deteriorated.

Then came the push and shove of the domestic violence kind. When dear old Dad went and hit my mom.

It was during a club cookout in our backyard, to celebrate the Fourth of July. Cade and I were hiding out in the tree house, watching the celebrations in the backyard as we sipped beers he'd stolen from his daddy. It was dark but the yard was lit up by the flames in the 44-gallon drums they used as fire pits.

I don't know how the fight started. Cade and I were drinking and playing poker when we heard the commotion. To this day, I still remember the spread of goosebumps along my skin when I'd heard my daddy's booming voice. He'd raised his hand and struck my mom to the ground. A hush had descended across the people gathered on the lawn, but then, all of a sudden, everyone was busy again, moving about and talking as if nothing had happened.

I leapt off the treehouse to get to my mom. She was on her knees, nursing her mouth, while my monster of a father stood over her, cussing at her and calling her names. Even now, sixteen years on, I could still see the look on his face and the meanness in his eyes. In that moment, I no longer loved him. I hated him. So I stood up to him and told him what an asshole he was. But he'd simply shoved me aside and stomped off.

In a second, my fourteen-year-old self decided to get as far away from him and this fucking MC life as soon as she could. She wasn't ever going to end up like her mom, on her knees nursing a bloodied lip while people barbequed on her lawn and acted like the nothing had happened.

Seeing my daddy shove me, Cade went to say something but I begged him not to. When my daddy drank, he turned into a pit bull and I didn't want any more trouble. Things had a habit of escalating when my daddy was drunk.

I shook off the memory and took another mouthful of wine. My eyes drifted over to Cade's bedroom. The shades were open but it was dark.

I lit the cigarette I'd taken from my mom's packet on the kitchen counter and drew on it, feeling lightheaded because in the real world I had given up cigarettes almost eleven years earlier. But this wasn't the real world. This was my past. And it was fucking weird being back.

When Cade's bedroom light flicked on, my heart knotted. He didn't know I was there. Didn't know I could see him. Didn't know I was watching. He paused and leaned down, resting his hands on the back of the desk chair as he thought about something. Then he straightened, and even from this distance I could make out the broad expanse of his back and the heaviness of his shoulders

I took a second drag on my cigarette and tried to pull my eyes away from him. I wasn't a creeper. But my eyes had a mind of their own. They wanted to watch Cade throw his bike keys onto the dresser and remove his cut. They wanted to drink it in as he placed his wallet and sunglasses next to his keys, and then pulled his black t-shirt over his head to expose a body that was nothing but all man. *All man.* I swallowed deep. This was wrong—all types of wrong, but for whatever reason, I couldn't look away.

His jeans were the next to go, and then his boxers, and finally—finally, I looked away. I crushed the half-smoked cigarette against the wooden floorboard of the treehouse. I drank back more wine. A few hours in Destiny and it was already fucking with my head.

The light went on behind the little window next to his room and I heard the faint sound of a shower.

I lay down and stared up at the starry sky, breathing in the night air tinged with the subtleness of soap. It was weird knowing Cade was only meters from me, naked and showering. Two days ago, he was a memory I didn't visit. Now I was trying not to picture him lathering soap all over his mountain man body.

A few minutes later, the shower switched off and I refused to think about him standing in his bathroom toweling off. I was an all-or-nothing kind of girl. I either held my feelings close to my chest and stayed focused, or I opened the floodgates and let everything tumble out.

And I had no intention of letting anything tumble out while I was in Destiny.

After a while, Cade's bedroom light switched off, and I heard the squeak of the screen door, and then the rumble of a Harley as it bit into the evening.

Feeling empty and strange, I sat up and watched him roar off into the darkness.

CHAPTER 14

CADE—Aged 7
Then

"Who do you think would win a fight between Spiderman and Superman?" I asked Indy.

We were playing jacks on my driveway, sitting on the warm concrete. It was the beginning of summer break, and the days were long and hot.

Indy thought for a moment. She twisted her head toward the sun and bit her bottom lip, frowning a little as she contemplated what I'd asked her.

She shrugged. "I don't know. Spiderman, I guess."

"Spiderman?" I repeated, astonished. "Why Spiderman?"

"Because Superman is from outer space."

"Yeah, so?"

"So . . . Spiderman is from Earth."

I rolled my eyes. "Annnnnnd . . ."

"Earth is his home planet. Superman is on a strange planet. Spiderman has more friends here." She picked up the jacks and threw them up in the air.

I shrugged. "That's crazy. Superman would win. He's the man of steel. Spidey just throws his webs around."

The sound of a motorcycle pulling into her driveway turned both of our heads. It wasn't one of the Kings, and it took me a few minutes to work out who it was because it was a face I hadn't seen in ages.

Uncle Calvin.

I looked at Indy and saw her back straighten. Her eyes narrowed and her dark brows pulled in as she watched him pull up to the garage and climb off his bike. He walked over to where we were sitting and bent down so he was eye level with her. I saw her clench her teeth and her nostrils quiver as she breathed through her nose.

"How's my special girl?" he asked, wiping a lock of her hair away from her eyes. "You got a hug for your uncle?"

She didn't want to hug him. I could tell. And so could he.

"What? I've been away for a year and you ain't got no hug for me?" His voice was lighthearted, but there was a mean gleam in his eyes. I didn't like Uncle Calvin.

Indy rose to her feet and he scooped her up in his arms and held her against him. He was bigger than before. Like he had grown even taller and wider while in the Army.

"That's my girl," he said, planting a kiss on her mouth.

I stood up.

"Hi, Uncle Calvin," I said. I didn't think it was right him kissing Indy like that. "Welcome home."

He let Indy down and smiled at me.

"Hey, little dude." He gave me his hand to shake. He had fat fingers with dirt under his nails. "You keeping my girl here out of trouble?"

My girl?

"We're playing jacks," I said.

Calvin huffed. "Sounds like fun." He stretched and yawned. "Well, I'm going inside for a beer with your mama, Indy. I think you should come in and spend some time with your family."

"Okay. I will be in soon," she said, scuffing her tennis shoe against the concrete.

When he disappeared inside, we resumed our game. But Indy's mood had changed.

"I think Superman would beat Spiderman hands down," I said, throwing the jacks up and letting them scatter on the concrete in front of me.

"I don't care," Indy said. "Superheroes are stupid."

I looked up. "No, they're not."

"Yes, they are. They're always getting into stupid situations. And the baddies are always coming up with dumb ideas."

"Batman is not stupid."

"Batman is the worst!" she said, deliberately trying to make me mad because she knew Batman was my favorite.

"You're wrong!" I stood up. So did she.

"Everybody knows they're stupid," she snapped. "With their stupid capes and their stupid costumes. I think they're the dumbest thing ever!"

Anger made my cheeks hot and my fingers curl into a fist.

"Because you're a stupid girl—"

"And you're a stupid boy—"

She made me so mad.

"I don't know why we're even friends sometimes," I huffed.

"Neither do I."

My eyes widened. "Well, maybe we shouldn't be."

Indy folded her arms across her chest. "What do you mean *maybe*?"

"Fine."

"Fine!"

She turned away and stomped off. So, I picked up my jacks and shoved them into my jeans pocket before trudging off inside my house.

I spent the afternoon angry at her. I didn't know why, but Indy was able to get me more worked up than anyone I knew. Even over dinner I was mad at her, stabbing at my carrots and peas with my fork, and gulping down my milk like I was mad as hell at it.

My mama was going over to Lady's to play chess, but instead of going to play with Indy, I told mama I was tired and wanted to go to bed.

"You and Indy have a disagreement?" she asked, standing in the doorway of the bathroom as I brushed my teeth.

"No," I mumbled through toothpaste foam.

But my mama was no fool. She raised an eyebrow at me and folded her arms as she said, "Cade Calley, I've known you your whole life. And the only time you don't want to visit with Indy is when the two of you are fighting. I've seen you stay up hours after your bedtime just to see her when comes home from visiting her Grandma in Jacksonville." She knelt down in front of me. "Is there something you want to tell me?"

I thought of Indy and our fight. "No. I'm just tired is all."

She let it go. But not before she raised her eyebrow and gave me a knowing look.

While she went next door to play chess with Lady, she had our babysitter come and stay. Her name was Cilla and she was married to someone in the club. We loved it when Cilla came and sat with us because she always brought brownies and ice cream. But tonight, instead of sitting up with her and my brothers, I went to my bedroom and sat in the darkness, hugging my knees to my chest and feeling angry. I watched Indy's window, waiting for the light to come on. When it did, I turned my light on, too, and we both stared angrily at each other.

Finally, Indy stomped toward her window and slammed it down. Well, it was more an attempt at a slam because it got stuck a couple of times and she really had to force it down. To show her I was just as mad, I did the same thing, I slammed it down so hard the glass rattled in the pane. Indy crossed her arms and poked her tongue out at me, so I crossed my arms, too, and pulled a face. She stormed off in a huff, and I saw the main light of her room snap off. So, I turned mine off, too.

But I didn't go to bed. I sat at my window and stared up at the full moon. I thought about climbing out and sitting on one of the branches of the sycamore tree, but I didn't want Indy to think I wasn't mad at her anymore. And, boy, was I mad. I didn't want her coming out to see what I was up to and make me forget about our argument and want to make up. Because then she would think she had won.

I shoved my arms across my chest again and set my mouth.

She would have to apologize first.

A sudden band of light appeared in Indy's room and I realized someone had opened her bedroom door. From where I stood, I could make out a silhouette. It was her Uncle Calvin.

Panic suddenly flared in my stomach.

"Turn and walk away," I whispered, untangling my arms from my chest and pressing my fingers to the window glass. "Turn and walk away. Turn and walk away."

My heartbeat picked up when he didn't. Instead, he stepped into the room and closed the door behind him.

Instantly, I knew Indy was in trouble.

I didn't wait. I climbed out the window and raced across the lawn, and around the side of Indy's house. I knew my mama would be playing chess out on the patio with Lady. When Daddy and Jackie Parrish were away on rides, Mama and Lady spent a lot of time on the Parrish patio playing chess and drinking from fancy glasses.

Feeling my heart pounding I unlatched the gate and ran through to the side garden until I reached the tiled patio. My mama and Lady were laughing but when they saw me, their smiles faded.

"Cade—"

"It's Indy!" I said, panicking. "He's in her room!"

Lady stood up quickly. "Who's in her room?"

"What are you talking about, son?" Mama asked.

I heaved the words out, "Uncle Calvin."

Mama looked at Lady, then a strange look came across Lady's face and she raced inside with me and my mama close behind.

Twenty minutes later, I sat on the front porch watching them load Indy's Uncle Calvin into an ambulance. He was moaning and demanding they give him something for the pain.

Sheriff Elton was talking to his deputy. Like Indy, Deputy Buckman was new to town. He was younger than Sheriff Elton but he had a beard and it was already turning grey.

"Christ, her father made a mess out of him," Buckman said to Elton as they walked toward the police cruiser.

Sheriff Elton stopped walking and looked at him.

"The father didn't do that to him," he said. "The mother did. Lady Parrish."

Buckman baulked. "*She* did that to him?"

From what I could figure out, Uncle Calvin was really messed up. Black eyes. Lots of broken bones, including his nose and his jaw. I overheard the EMT say something about busted ribs. He was probably right. I remember hearing them crack when Lady hit him with the baseball bat.

"You don't fuck with the women of the MC," Elton said.

"Where is the father?" Buckman asked.

"Out of town." He gave Buckman a serious look. "If Jackie Parrish had been home, Calvin Winter would be leaving here in a body bag."

"And that would be a problem?" Buckman asked. "Seems to me, anyone goes around hurting little girls gets what's coming to them."

Elton nodded. "Oh, it's coming to him. Believe me. The MC have a special kind of justice for people who hurt kids. Don't worry, you'll learn to turn a blind eye."

Buckman scoffed. "That's not something I'm going to need to learn, Elton. Not when it comes to dishing out justice to perverts messing with kids."

They disappeared inside the Parrish house and I watched the ambulance quietly pull away.

I sat with my face in my hands feeling helpless. Indy was with her mama and my mama inside, talking to a policewoman. I wanted to go to her and put my arms around her but my mama said I had to wait until the policewoman had finished talking with her.

It seemed like hours before they finished. Finally my mama came and got me and led me down to Indy's bedroom.

"Five minutes and then we need to go home and give Indy and her mama some privacy," Mama said. I nodded and opened Indy's bedroom door. She was curled up in her bed. The lamp on her bedside table was turned on and I could see the tear stains on her cheek as she stared straight into the lamplight.

"Indy?"

She didn't look up, so I walked into the room and sat down on the bed.

"Are you okay? I asked, uncertain of what to say. "Did he hurt you?"

She didn't answer and her eyes remained on the light.

I didn't know what to do. Or say. So, I did the one thing I knew comforted her.

"Do you want me to lie down with you?"

She looked at me, and although she didn't move, her eyes said yes. So, I climbed in beside her and wrapped my arms around her. She snuggled into me and I felt her relax. After a while, she finally spoke.

"He didn't hurt me," she murmured.

"Are you sure? You can tell me if he did."

She shook her head. "He didn't hurt me. But he tried."

I swallowed deeply not wanting to think about him hurting her because it made my stomach hurt and the hair stand up on the back of my neck. "What happened?" I asked.

For a while, she didn't answer me, and I wondered if she had fallen asleep. Finally, she spoke.

"He thought I was sleeping, but I heard him open my bedroom door. I pretended to be asleep and prayed he would go away. But he walked in and closed the door behind him. He came to my bed and put his hands over my mouth and then . . ."

I secured my arms tighter around her. I hoped her Uncle Calvin was hurting bad in the back of the ambulance. I hoped the road to the hospital was bumpy and that he felt every single pothole.

". . . he told me not to say anything. That I would get in trouble if mama heard us. That she would tell my daddy and he would be mad at me. I knew what he was doing was wrong, but at the same time, all I could think about was how his fingers smelled like tobacco smoke and the empty beer bottles your daddy keeps in the garage." Indy's breath left her in a big exhale. "He told me I was his special girl, that special girls got special gifts from their uncles. He kept his hand over my mouth. But his other hand slid up my leg to my panties. That was when I bit him, *hard*, and when he let me go I jumped out of bed and kicked him right in his privates. That was when my mama walked in."

She twisted her head to look at me.

"Thank you for telling my mama, Cade." She hugged my arm tightly.

I felt sick. I didn't know what her uncle would have done to her if her mama hadn't rushed in.

"I'll always be here for you, Indy." I pressed my lips to her hair and settled in behind her. "That's my job."

Indy tangled her fingers in mine and exhaled softly. "I don't want us to ever fight again."

"We won't. We'll stay best friends forever."

"Promise?" she asked.

I nodded and closed my eyes. "We'll be best friends for the rest of our lives."

CHAPTER 15

INDY
Now

The next morning, I rose early and went downstairs for coffee. To my surprise, my mom was up, sitting on the couch looking through old photo albums. I thought about going to her and giving her a hug, but it seemed so alien to me so I poured us a coffee, instead.

"Morning, baby," she said when I joined her.

"How are you feeling?" I asked.

She glanced up, her black-rimmed glasses perched on the edge of her nose, and she smiled. "I'll get there." She accepted the cup of coffee from me and then patted the space next to her. "Come sit with me for a bit."

When I settled next to her, she passed me one of the photo albums.

"I have to find a photo of your father to put on the casket," she said. She sipped her coffee as her eyes passed over the page of the open album on her lap. "If you find a good one, holler."

I hesitated. Reminiscing always made me morose. Teary, even. So, as a rule, I made a point of never looking back. But my mom needed help, so I put my coffee cup down and opened the photo album. Immediately, my eyes met those of my nine-year-old self staring out from an over-exposed photo. I was standing with my brother Bolt who was holding a kitten toward the camera. A sudden jab of sadness hit me in the heart and I quickly turned the page. More photos of Bolt and me followed. Fourth of July firework celebrations. Thanksgiving. Christmas. Us sitting at the base of the ginormous Christmas tree my mom spent almost an entire day putting together and decorating, surrounded by discarded wrapping paper. Bolt and me eating the Christmas cookies my mom always made, our mouths full of the crumbly goodness I hadn't tasted in almost two decades. I bit my lip. I could almost taste the cinnamon sugar.

The last photo was of the four of us. A family photo. Probably the last one taken before things fell apart.

I closed the book and mindlessly reached for another. This one was circa my mid-teens and was full of photos of me and the other MC kids. Abby. Isaac. Cade, and his brothers. His sister Chastity. It was funny, when I recalled my teenage years, I recalled the heartache and the anger toward my father. But in the photographs, I was always smiling. Always laughing or looking happy. Especially when I was with Cade.

I looked at a photo of the two of us. It had been taken at a club barbecue when we were about seventeen. Cade had his arm slung around my shoulder, and my arms were wrapped around his waist. I was smiling up at him with the dreamy look of a teenage girl in love. He was looking down at me, his dimples deep in his cheeks, and his beautiful eyes focused on me like I was the only woman in the whole world. You could see how in love we were. You could see how happy we were together.

Pain trickled into my chest and I turned the page before my mind went there and asked the question I had asked myself a billion times over the past twelve years. *How did we not work out?*

"Here we go," my mom said, removing a photo of my father from the sticky, plastic page. She handed it to me. My father was smiling, which was a rarity in itself, and he actually looked happy. I flipped it over to see if there was a description on the back. *Jack Parrish, 1999. Veterans memorial run. Destiny to Biloxi.* I handed it back to my mom.

"That's a good one," I said. "He looks happy."

My mom smiled, but when her eyes fell to the photograph they turned misty. She absentmindedly played with the crown pendant around her neck. "I know you won't believe me, but your father was a happy guy when I met him. Carefree. Charming. A bit of a good old boy, but a gentleman just the same. We were happy for a real long time, Indy. He was just heartbroken at the end."

Without thinking, I took her hand and gave it a squeeze.

"I like to think he wasn't always like that," I said. "Broken and angry."

A monster.

"He was a strong, proud man. Formidable but fair. Then he got sick." She looked at the picture. "He sure did love you kids. I hope you know that."

I looked away. My had father lost interest in me a long time ago.

"No point in getting all misty-eyed now. Think I'll go get ready for the day." Mom sighed and stood up. "Before I forget, Sheriff Buckman dropped off your rental earlier." She nodded to a set of keys sitting on the coffee table.

When my mom left to get dressed, I looked down at the photo album in my lap. I flipped through the pages, skimming over the photos of a life I could barely remember.

The last photo in the album was taken at a New Year's Eve celebration at the clubhouse. I touched the photo with perfectly manicured fingertips. An eighteen-year-old version of me smiled brightly back at the camera as if someone had just said something hilariously funny to her. Her long blonde hair swirled around her face and her eyes sparkled with youth and happiness. Her arms were wrapped around a very young Abby, who looked like Suzi Quatro, circa her *Devil's Gate Drive* days. We looked happy. So carefree.

So cool.

I looked down at my sensible black pants and polyester blouse. Somewhere in the past twelve years I had swapped *cool* for *conservative*. And instead of feeling relieved at the change, I felt a weird loss of identity.

I miss you.

I frowned and quickly closed the book.

I had left the MC to pursue a different life and to become a different person. And I did just that. I was nothing like the carefree, rebel chick in that photograph. I was grown up and responsible.

I glanced back at the album. It represented a life I had buried. One that needed to stay buried.

Pushing it aside, I stood up and collected our empty coffee cups. As I walked into the kitchen, my eyes caught on the series of dashes and dates marked into the doorjamb, and I stopped.

Childhood height charts.

I remembered standing there as a child, restlessly complaining to my mom as she recorded my height with a pencil and wooden ruler. I ran my finger up the doorjamb stopping at each age until I reached the last two. *Indy age 12. Bolt age 14.* There were none after that.

I took the coffee cups to the sink to wash. The rumble of a motorcycle broke into the early morning quiet, and when I looked out the kitchen window I saw Cade pull into the Calley driveway, wearing his Kings of Mayhem cut and looking like the devil he was in his aviators and well-fitted t-shirt.

He was just getting home.

"Old Mavis will have a field day over him revving his bike like that at seven o'clock in the morning," my mom said as she came down the stairs.

"She's still alive?" I asked. Old Mavis was the cranky old lady who lived across the street. "She was a hundred years old when I was eight."

"Yeah, that one is too stubborn to die," Mom said, looking for her keys in her purse.

Old Mavis dressed in floaty, Stevie Nicks-style clothing, circa *Tell Me Lies*, and had lashings of greying dark hair. When we were kids, Bolt convinced me she was a witch.

"Does she still think she is married to a three-hundred-year-old pirate?" I asked, remembering the stories about her. Old Mavis was batshit crazy and honestly believed she was married to a ghost. *A pirate ghost.* Some nights you could hear her arguing with him, although it was very one-sided.

Mom laughed. "Yep. They're still together and just as much in love as the day they met via a Ouija board." She dug deeper into her purse for her keys. I smiled and felt a sudden pang, knowing that my mom was going to be just fine. I took in her black pants and *Sticky Fingers* pastry shirt.

"You're going to work?"

"Life goes on, Indy." She gave up on finding her keys in her purse and sighed. I leaned over and grabbed them off the ceramic pineapple key holder on the counter and handed them to her.

"It's Bob Ellis' sixtieth birthday celebration tomorrow and he still needs his cake," she said. Bob Ellis was the town mayor. "Plus, it's Joker's birthday celebration at the clubhouse tonight, and who else in town is going to make him a cake with a burlesque girl popping out of the top?"

A cake of a stripper bursting out of a cake. *Of course.*

"Do you want to come with me?" she asked. But we both knew it was a question asked out of obligation. I was a disaster when it came to baking, and my mom had given up teaching me years ago. I might be great with a suture, but I was a nightmare with an icing bag.

Plus, once she got to her shop, I knew she would lose herself in her work for hours, and that was exactly what she needed. If I hung around, I would only distract her.

"I might drop by and see Bolt," I said.

My mom smiled softly. "It'll do you some good to see your brother."

I wasn't sure about that. It hurt to see Bolt. But I returned her smile, because God knows she didn't need something else to worry about. "It's long overdue."

"Sure, baby girl." Mom paused at the door and turned back to me. "Are you okay going to see him by yourself?"

"Yes, of course," I said. It was a lie. I didn't know how it was going to feel standing in front of my brother after all these years.

"It's been a few years," she said.

I gave her a reassuring smile. "Then we'll have a lot to catch up on."

She nodded. "Okay, baby. I'll see you here later and we'll go to the clubhouse together, okay?"

We shared a smile before she walked out and closed the door behind her. My mom may be small in stature, but she was a tough cookie. She was no stranger to grief. She knew how to cope. I watched her hop into her Mercedes convertible and disappear down the road. She was going to be just fine.

I didn't go to see my brother because I wasn't ready. Or I was a coward. Either way, it wasn't time. Instead, I headed to the morgue to drop off the photo of my father. As soon as I entered the little building beneath the hospital, the hairs on my arms stood on end. It was funny how I could see death everyday, but the moment I had to step into a morgue or a funeral home, I got the creeps.

They asked if I wanted to see my father. Figuring it was better to get it over and done with, I agreed, but when it came time to walk into the room, I couldn't. I hesitated, apologized, and then fled.

Outside, I ran into an old face I hadn't seen in twelve years.
Abby Calley.
She was Cade's cousin.
And Isaac's twin sister.
And at one time, my best friend.
Abby was pure biker chick. Except she was the blinged-up version. She didn't wear a leather cuff on her wrist, she wore a cuff made of black Swarovski crystals. Her tank top wasn't cotton, it was sequined and glittery, and her jeans weren't a simple blue or black, they were a pair of bedazzled awesomeness. She didn't do vanilla, and she didn't do bland. She did dazzling. With a side serving of biker cool.

But today she was in scrubs. Mom had mentioned she was a radiographer at the hospital.

We stopped a few yards away from each other.

"Abby," I said, feeling an immediate awkwardness radiate between us.

"Well, I'll be goddamned," she breathed.

In high school, we had been inseparable. We did sleepovers, smoked pot, and dreamed big. We also hung out with Cade and Isaac, and the four of us were the popular kids you didn't fuck with. She was there from the very beginning when Cade and I finally hooked up, and she was by my side when it all fell apart.

We had tried to stay in touch. Well, actually, that wasn't true. She had tried; I didn't. After moving to college, I went quiet, forgetting to reply to emails and text messages. I was always too busy to answer her phone calls. Eventually she gave up trying and stopped contacting me. I told myself it was what happened. Lives moved in different directions and friendships faded. But the truth was, I had pushed her away. I had pushed all of them away because I wanted to put it all behind me. The club. My father. Cade.

"You're back," she said.

Twelve years of silence filled the space between us. Loudly.

"I got in yesterday."

She nodded. Then, like she didn't know what else to do, she said, "I'm sorry about your daddy."

I nodded back. Just as clueless. "Thank you."

Being Isaac's twin sister, she shared his blonde Viking looks. Long hair. Ice blue eyes. Flawless skin.

And like her cousin Cade, she had the same shadow of resentment in her eyes.

"You're wearing scrubs," I said, because stating the obvious seemed to be all I was capable of doing.

"I'm a radiographer," she smiled awkwardly. "It's not as fancy as a doctor, but you know, it pays the bills."

I didn't know what to say. It was a dig at me. And I deserved it. Abby probably suspected I thought I was too good for her. I couldn't blame her. When I'd turned my back on Cade, I'd turned my back on her, too.

"Well, I guess I'll see you tonight at the clubhouse," she said, keen to get away.

"Sure." I gave her an awkward smile. I wanted to go to the party as much as I wanted to be thrown into a tank full of piranhas. "It will nice to see everyone."

But she didn't say anything.

She just nodded and walked away.

CHAPTER 16

INDY
Now

The party was in full swing when we arrived at the clubhouse. I came with my mom and Caleb in the *Sticky Fingers* van, and after helping them get the mammoth cake into the clubhouse kitchen, I made my way to the bar.

Bob Seger's *"The Fire Down Below"* cranked out of the speakers as I came face to face with a past I'd left behind years ago. *A clubhouse party.* Dressed in sensible black pants, polyester blouse, and flat shoes, I belonged here as much as a vegan at a keto party. I looked around me and took it all in. The smoke. The music. The sound of pool. The smell of beer, hard liquor, and poor choices.

So far it looked like a typical clubhouse celebration.

Later, a band would bring on the night with songs from Rose Tattoo, Led Zeppelin, The Stones, Credence Clearwater Revival, and Deep Purple. There would be fires lit and a barbecue, and the stripper poles would see more than one or two girls wrapped around them.

As if on cue, a woman with short blonde hair and a sleeve of tattoos walked into the room dressed in nothing but bikini bottoms and began to twirl on the pole.

Yep. Things hadn't changed.

I perched myself on a barstool. I didn't really want to hang out, but I had a feeling it was important to my mom that I was here.

"Well, hello there, lil' lady," came a voice from behind me. A pair of strong Viking arms wrapped around me for the second time in two days. *Isaac*. He grinned as he put me down. "Didn't think we'd see you at one of these parties again."

"You and me both."

I glanced around feeling way out of my depth.

"Let's get you a drink." He smacked his hands together like a man ready to party.

I sat back on the barstool and shook my head. "No, thanks."

I was going to stay for thirty minutes and then get the hell out of there. Hanging out at a motorcycle gang's clubhouse was the last place I wanted to be.

Isaac looked surprised but let it go and accepted a beer from a girl behind the bar. She was wearing the tiniest pair of Daisy Dukes I'd ever seen.

"Is it just how you remembered it?" he asked, taking a sip.

"There's a lot of familiar faces, but also a lot of new ones," I said, looking around the room.

"Well, Vader you know . . ." Isaac nodded to the good-looking, Mike Patton lookalike with the *Star Wars* T-shirt under his cut.

When I left for college, Vader was a club prospect. Now he was well into his thirties and a manlier version of the baby-faced kid I remembered.

"And of course, you'd remember Joker and Maverick," Isaac continued, pointing his beer bottle at two club members playing pool. Joker looked like the lead singer of Metallica, right down to the long, strawberry blonde hair and goatee, while Maverick was a giant wall of muscle with big arms and a mass of tangled hair pulled back into a ponytail. Watching them was a skinny girl in a too-short skirt and a too-tight top. She leaned against the pool table, looking bored.

"Who is that," I asked, pointing to a handsome redhead talking to a tall mountain of a man I knew as Freebird.

"That's Irish. Been in the club about eight years now." Isaac swung around on his chair to search the room. When he spotted whom he was looking for, he nodded toward him. "And that scary looking sonofabitch over there in the camouflage pants is Grunt. He is our current Sergeant In Arms."

Grunt looked straight out of the Marines. Tall. Broad. Shaved blond hair. He was handsome in an *I wouldn't think twice about killing you* kind of way.

"And that sonofabitch over there is Tully. Looks like your class nerd, but don't let those Coke bottle glasses fool you, the kid doesn't miss a trick."

Tully looked like he'd walk a thousand miles and fall down at your door.

"And ol' blue eyes over there is Cool Hand," Isaac said, pointing to a young Paul Newman leaning against the bar doing shots with a very made-up blonde with big assets pouring out of her dress.

"I saw Tex as I walked in," I said, folding my arms across my chest. "Is he still as crazy as a cut snake?"

Isaac grinned. "He's a bit tamer now that he's married. But I think the old Tex might show up once the other charters get here."

I thought about the arrival of the other charters and what that would mean. They were here to honor my father. To honor one of their fallen. There would be a big wake, followed by an even bigger party. And when the Kings of Mayhem originals hosted visiting chapters, things got wild. There would be liquor and women. *Lots* of liquor. And *lots* of women.

Before I could stop myself, I thought about what it would feel like to see Cade with another woman. And maybe it was the emotions of the past forty-eight hours fucking with me, but I had a feeling seeing him with another woman wouldn't be as easy as I thought.

I shook my head as if I could shake the craziness out of my mind.

Cade could do whatever the fuck he wanted.

Across the room, I noticed a bearded, dark-haired biker standing with a beautiful woman by the jukebox. The woman was stunning with caramel hair and skin that looked like toffee. Dressed in an off-the-shoulder summer dress, there was something calm and elegant about her. Almost graceful. Her lips were full, and when they parted into a big white smile, it was devastating. She looked like she belonged here about as much as I did. "Who are they?" I asked Isaac.

"That's Jacob and Mirabella. Totally loved up, if you couldn't tell. They're getting married soon."

I watched Mirabella stand on tiptoes to kiss her man. He looked at her with so much affection, my heart squeezed tight.

Just as the song on the jukebox changed to The Rolling Stones "*Gimme Shelter*" an older man in a wheelchair rolled over to us.

"And you remember this old bastard," Isaac said with uncharacteristic fondness.

"Of course, I do!" I said, affection swelling in my chest. It was Isaac's father, Griffin Calley. He was Garrett's older brother. Cade's uncle. I leaned down and kissed his cheek. "It's so nice to see you again."

"Indigo Parrish. Look at you," he said with a big smile. He patted my face. "Still a beauty. When are you going to ditch the young fellas and learn that us older men is where the real action is?" He laughed, a big throaty chuckle. "You look beautiful."

Griffin had muscular dystrophy, and the disease had taken the use of his legs from him years ago. How he was still alive was beyond all rhyme and reason.

"You don't look so bad yourself," I said with a wink.

He grinned. "Don't I know it."

At that moment, the club's current President, Bull, walked into the club, followed by his sister, Ronnie Calley.

Bull was one of the most attractive men I'd ever seen. Tall. Broad. And with a face like a model. If it wasn't for the leather cut, black boots, and wallet chain hanging at his hip, he could easily pass for a wealthy tycoon, or billionaire CEO.

He had the same blue eyes as his sister, Veronica. Not that you ever saw them. They were always hidden behind sunglasses, thanks to his acute color blindness, which made his eyes incredibly sensitive to sunlight. As a result, he always wore tinted glasses no matter what time of the day it was, and the presence of those dark glasses only added to his imposing power.

When he saw me, his face lit up with his amazing smile.

"Indy Parrish." My name rolled off his tongue like sugared honey. His strong arms came around me and pulled me to his broad chest, immediately engulfing me in a scent of pure man.

"It's good to see you, Bull," I said, pulling back. Somewhere in his forties, he was too good looking for words.

Ronnie leaned in and gave me a kiss. "Where's your mom?"

"Last I saw, she was in the kitchen with Red. Doing last-minute touch-ups to the cake," I said.

Ronnie nodded. "And my son?"

"I haven't seen Cade."

Ronnie smiled, giving me the same knowing look that Sybil had given me the day before. "I mean, my other son, Caleb. The one you came with."

Right.

Before I could answer, Caleb appeared and dragged his mom and uncle away to help him deal with some kind of problem they had with one of the strippers.

I looked away, hating myself for wanting to know where Cade was. He was probably ten inches deep into someone, and that wasn't any of my concern.

I turned around and signaled to the barman.

"Give me a shot of tequila and make it a double."

CHAPTER 17

INDY
Now

"Well, will you look at this tall drink of water sitting at the end of my bar!"

The voice came from behind me.

I was still perched on my stool, counting down the minutes before I could leave. The tequila shot I'd slung back earlier had done nothing, and I was still figuring out my escape plan. I swung around, ready to throw some shade at my admirer, but stopped when I came face to face with a familiar pair of green eyes.

"Randy?" I asked with disbelief. "Randy Ronson?"

"The one and only!" He grinned, and it was the same charming grin I remembered from high school. Randy had always been a nice guy. He was the kind of boy who made everyone feel welcome. In school, his friendliness made him popular with the girls, especially the cheer squad—and I mean the *entire* cheer squad. Somehow, he had managed to date them all, some of them at the same time, without the other knowing.

But he was so confident and persuasive, he had gotten away with it.

It didn't hurt that he was good looking either, with his strong jaw, smiling eyes, and charismatic grin.

"You're a King now?" I asked, surprised. Randy had never shown any interest in the club.

"Just their barman." He looked around the bar. "I look after this for them."

Randy was a bit rough around the edges now, but still handsome. My eyes dropped to the space where his left arm was missing.

"Bike accident," he said.

"I'm sorry."

He shrugged. "It's the nature of the beast, lil' lady. Riding too fast, too stoned, too drunk . . . took a hard corner and high-sided straight into an oncoming car. Woke up with no arm, a missing spleen and feeling like the world had stopped."

"That's rough, Randy. I'm sorry." I saw a lot of physical devastation in my job. Amputation was always a game changer.

"It was my own stupid-ass fault. But I'm in a good place now."

"So, how did you end up here?"

"After the accident, I didn't see much point to life anymore. It cost me my job. My home. My girl. I couldn't ride a bike no more. I was on a bender when I ran into Cade and Isaac one night. Ran into them at about the right time, I'm figuring. They offered me this job and it saved my life."

"And you enjoy it?"

"Honey, I'm the fucking Thor of mixology."

I grinned. Randy was charming.

"Well then, I think you'd better show me." I gestured to a row of glasses gleaming behind him. "You know how to make a martini?"

"Only the best damn martini you've ever tasted."

I raised an eyebrow at him. "We'll see."

"Oh, a challenge!"

I watched him mix my cocktail with the fast, impressive moves of a showman. Despite only having one arm, Randy's skill as a bartender outdid his two-armed rivals.

He slid a dirty martini across the bar to me.

"I'm impressed," I said. "You got the moves there, Randy."

He winked. "Baby, you have no idea."

As I took a sip, Deep Purple's *"Woman From Tokyo"* bled through the speakers.

"Goddamn, that's good!" I said, smacking my lips together.

"Drink up, little lady. I got a whole bunch of panty-dropping cocktails up my sleeve." He held up his one hand and winked. "Imagine if I had two of them."

I took another sip, this time a big one, and a sweet warmth spread out from my chest. My body instantly heated and I began to relax. I noticed Randy watching me. "What?"

He smiled. "Just thinking how strange it is seeing Indy Parrish sitting at the end of my bar."

"You and me both." I took another sip of my martini and reminded myself to take it easy. Too many of these and I'd be on my ass.

"Be careful, girl. You might actually start to enjoy yourself."

I gave him a pointed look. "This isn't my scene anymore."

"Oh, really? Let me guess, your scene involves those fancy cocktail bars in the city with some suit in a fancy label, and not a cut in sight."

"One out of three ain't bad," I said, taking another sip of my drink and almost finishing it.

"You want another?"

"Sure. Why the hell not." I watched him mix another drink. "You look like you're in your element."

"You could say that. I love it here." He winked. He nodded wistfully and then gestured around us. "This place, its family. We're lucky to be a part of it."

"I'm only visiting." I reminded him.

He slid the second cocktail across the bar to me, and then leaned down on his one arm. "So you keep saying, beautiful lady. Funny thing is..."

I raised one eyebrow at him. "What?"

"I just don't believe you."

He winked at me before making his way down to the other end of the bar to serve Vader and a girl in a PVC dress that left little to the imagination.

As Deep Purple became Clapton's "*Layla*" I felt a tap on my shoulder. It was Mirabella, the beautiful girl Isaac had pointed out to me earlier. Up close, she was even more stunning.

"Indy? Hi, I'm Mirabella. I just wanted to come over and say I'm sorry about your daddy."

She offered me a smile and it was breathtaking.

"Thanks."

"If there's anything I can do, please just let me know."

Mirabella had a comforting presence about her, and I had a sudden desire to open up to her. About what, I wasn't sure.

"I appreciate that. But really, there's no need." Keen to change the subject because I didn't want to talk about my daddy or his funeral, I added, "I hear you're getting married soon."

Mirabella's face beamed at the mention of her wedding. "Yes ...well, we were due to be married this weekend."

"*Due* to be married?" I asked.

"I wasn't sure if it was the right thing... the timing is just awful. We thought we might postpone it—"

"Postpone? No way."

"It's a horrible thing... a funeral one day and then a wedding three days later."

Mirabella was as sweet as she was beautiful. There was no way I was letting her postpone her wedding.

"Seems like perfect timing to me. A sad event followed by a happy one." I gave her a warm smile. "Don't postpone your wedding. Not because of this."

"Are you sure?"

"Of course." I looked around the clubhouse. Vader was now making out with the girl in the PVC dress, while the girl on the pole was busy making out with the pole. "Although, personally I think you're crazy marrying into all of this."

Mirabella's smile faltered for just a moment. But then she smiled brightly, obviously too polite to question what I had just said.

"I appreciate you being so kind about this," she said. "Are you sure your mom won't mind?"

"Of course, she won't. Mom would insist—"

"What would I insist?" Mom asked, swooping in and plunking a box of serviettes and paper plates onto the bar behind us.

"Mirabella was talking about postponing the wedding," I said.

"Postponing? Hell no!" Mom turned around and put her hands on her hips. "I've already started the wedding cake!"

CHAPTER 18

CADE—Aged 9
Then

I was wearing a tie. And I looked like a goddamn idiot. But Indy said that you have to look respectable when you get married. She said the woman always wears a pretty white dress and the man always wears a suit and tie. I don't have a suit, so we settled for the tie. Anyway, I'm not sure Indy was right about the whole dress and suit thing. Because last month, when Viper married a girl called Cinnamon—Daddy said she worked at a club in town—she didn't wear a pretty dress. And it wasn't white either. It was bright red, tight, and very short. Daddy said the color suited her on her wedding day, on account of her lifestyle. I didn't know what that meant. Maybe she was a firefighter or a Redwings fan, or something. I don't know. But that dress made me feel weird. Mr. Mason, the old guy who owns the mechanics garage just out of town, I don't think he liked the dress either, because a few hours later I saw him trying to wrestle it off her. I had been playing in the cellar with Indy when they had stumbled down the stairs, giggling and kissing. I was kinda confused on account that she had just married Viper, and yet here she was, kissing Mr. Mason. But then I didn't rightly understand a lot of what adults did. It seemed to me they overcomplicated an awful lot of things. So, I didn't try to work out what was happening. I just knew I had to protect Indy, because if they knew we were watching them, they would get angry and we would get in trouble.

When Mr. Mason pushed his hand up Cinnamon's skirt and she gasped the same gasp my mama does sometimes when she is in the bedroom with my daddy, Indy almost yelped. We both knew we were watching something we shouldn't be watching. So I slid my hand over her mouth and pressed my lips to her ear. "Stay quiet," I whispered. "We don't wanna get in trouble." When Cinnamon undid Mr. Mason's belt buckle, I began to feel a little weird and I got scared. They were talking real dirty to one another, touching each other and stuff. Indy squirmed next to me and I began to wonder what was going to happen. Thankfully, someone called out Cinnamon's name and she quickly pulled away from Mr. Mason, straightened her short dress and tried to fix her messed-up hair.

When they left, both Indy and I let out a big sigh of relief.

"Adults are weird," she said, dusting off her knees. "I ain't ever growing up."

"You can't stop growing up, Indy. It happens to everyone."

"Well, then I ain't ever getting married," she said stubbornly.

"You gotta get married, too," I said. "It's the law."

She pouted and folded her arms. "I don't want to get married." She raised those big brown eyes to me. "Do you want to get married?"

I shrugged. "Maybe."

"Maybe what?"

"If I get to marry you."

Her eyes widened. "You want to marry me, Cade Calley?"

Kings of Mayhem

"Of course, I want to marry you, Indy. You're my girl."

So, there I was, on my wedding day. Standing in the warm August sunshine wearing a tie, my favorite jeans and the cleanest t-shirt I owned.

"You nervous?" Bolt asked. He was Indy's older brother. He was eleven. I liked Bolt. He had a big comic collection—way bigger than mine—and he let me read them whenever I liked. Today, he was wearing a bow tie and his hair was slicked back with some of his daddy's hair gel, or something. And he was wearing cologne. A lot of it.

"Nah," I said nervously.

Bolt was marrying us. He didn't own a Bible, so he held a Spiderman comic, instead.

"Are you ready, Cade Calley?" Came the bossy hollering of my future wife from the treehouse above us. She was hiding up there, waiting for the ceremony to start.

"Ready when you are, Indigo Blue."

I nodded to Bolt who pressed the start button on the old CD player we had borrowed from his daddy's garage, and Lynryd Skynrd's *Sweet Home Alabama* filled the Parrish's backyard.

Indy appeared at the railing of the treehouse dressed in a white summer dress that was a little too big for her, with rows and rows of pearls around her neck. Except the pearls weren't white pearls, they were all different colors, like the ones my daddy brought back from a ride to New Orleans.

As she grabbed onto the rope ladder and slid down to the ground, I nervously loosened my tie. I wished Isaac and Abby weren't visiting Aunt Peggy's sister in Tennessee. Maybe then I wouldn't be so damn nervous. I wasn't sure why I was nervous. Indy was the best human I knew and I wanted her to be my wife. So, I figured it had less to do with me actually being nervous, and more about me having seen a lot of MC weddings and watching grown bikers turn green at the gills when they waited for their old lady to join them at the altar.

Indy did an awkward wedding march from the treehouse to where Bolt and I stood under the sycamore tree because her heeled shoes kept sinking into the soft ground. When she made it to where we stood, she and Bolt started to giggle, while I nervously adjusted my tie again.

"We are gathered here today..." Bolt began, his voice a much deeper, and louder version of his own. "To join these two kids in matrimony."

I glanced over at Indy. She was already looking at me, smiling, her sweet face alive with happiness and her large brown eyes warm with child-like joy. She was holding a bouquet of wild bluebells and daisies she had stolen from Mrs. Wilton's backyard. Mrs. Wilton lived across the road and was as mean as a goat. She was old and wrinkly, and this one time she had been yelling at us and her false teeth had fallen out of her mouth and broken on the ground. Mama said she was lonely and mean because Mr. Wilton had run away with Mrs. Wilton's sister long before me and my brothers were born.

"Does anyone here have any good reason why these two shouldn't be married?" Bolt asked.

The three of us looked around the empty backyard.

I had invited my mama, but she had taken Caleb to the doctor on account of his sore throat. They thought he might have laryngitis. Chance was at his friend's house, and Daddy, well, Daddy didn't do much of this stuff with us kids.

"Then I'll have the rings, please," Bolt said.

Indy hit him with her bouquet. "You can't go straight to the rings, you doofus. You have to ask if we take each other in marriage." She was smiling, but when she turned back to me she rolled her eyes as if Bolt was crazy to have forgotten.

He chuckled. "I know that. I just wanted to see if you was paying attention."

"Of course, I'm paying attention, it's my wedding day!" she cried dramatically.

Bolt pulled a face and then cleared his throat. "Cade, do you take my sister as your awfully wedded wife?"

Again, Indy rolled her eyes. "It's not *awfully* wedded wife! It's *lawfully*."

"No, it's not. It's awfully. You ask anyone."

Again, we all turned to look around the empty backyard.

"Whatever. Let's move on," I suggested. I turned from Indy to look at Bolt. "And yes, I do."

Bolt turned to Indy. "Indy, do you take Cade to be your awfully and lawfully wedded husband?"

She grinned across at me. "I do! A thousand times, I do!"

I grinned back at her.

"Then let's do the ring bit," Bolt said.

I pulled the plastic skull ring out of my jeans pocket. It had come with the motorcycle model kit my Uncle Bull had given me last Christmas. It was painted grey and had two red eyes that looked like rubies.

Indy's eyes lit up when she saw it.

"Your skull ring!" She gasped.

I wasn't sure if I was supposed to say anything as I put it on her finger because none of us could remember how this bit of the ceremony went, so I stepped back and watched Indy hug her hand to her chest with girlie excitement.

"Cade Calley, you are the best husband in the world!" she declared.

Bolt cleared his throat to get her attention, and then gestured toward me with his head.

"Oh, yes! Of course!" she said gaily. She dug into the ribbon wrapped around her flowers and pulled out a daisy ring.

I raised an eyebrow at her and then frowned. A daisy ring? What boy wears a daisy ring?

"I got it in the lucky dip at the school fete," Indy explained, her face bright with pride. "It's real pretty. It's made of real metal, and look, it's got a big plastic diamond in the middle. See? June Nicholls was real jealous when I got it because all she got was a set of coloring pencils. So I let her borrow it one afternoon at school and she broke off one of the petals. She said it was an accident, but I'm pretty sure she meant to do it because she can be mean like that. My mama had to use some smelly glue to fix it back together again."

Indy could talk.

A lot.

"It's real pretty," I said, feeling bad about not wanting to wear a daisy ring. It obviously meant a lot to her and she had given it to *me*.

Her face beamed with happiness. "You think so?"

I smiled back at her. "Yeah. I do."

She squealed. "And now it's yours."

She slid the daisy ring onto my right hand. Indy said we had to wear our rings on our right hand, because if we put them on our left hand then we would really be married and the law said we would have to live together. I would have to leave school and get a job so I could put food on the table. Wearing our wedding rings on our right hand showed people we were married but that we were too young to live on our own just yet.

"I suppose this is the bit where I say youse is husband and wife," Bolt said. He shrugged. "I guess you can kiss the bride."

Kiss?

I had forgotten about the kiss.

I tried to swallow but my stupid tie was too tight.

I glanced at Bolt who was grinning, and then looked back at Indy who was standing there with a big smile on her face.

Waiting for me to kiss her.

My heart went stupid in my chest. I stepped forward and rested my hands awkwardly on her hips. I could feel my pulse pounding against my neck. I had never kissed a girl before, but I wanted to kiss Indy more than anything in the whole world.

Quite suddenly, the unexpected sprinkle from a sun shower rained down on us. Indy's face lit up in wonderment. She looked up and laughed, then dropped her big brown eyes to look at me again. Rain glittered in her hair like beads, and sunlight glinted on her lips just as she leaned in and pressed her mouth to mine.

I closed my eyes and my stomach tightened. Her lips were warm and soft, and I could smell the cherry flavor of her lip balm. The world seemed to stop, and all I knew was the gentleness of Indy's lips on mine.

She pulled away and looked up at me with a big smile.

"You are the best kisser, Cade Calley."

My cheeks flushed and I licked my lips, tasting her lip balm.

"Can I kiss you again?" I asked.

Indy's eyes widened and her face was bright with happiness. "We're married, Cade. You can kiss me as much as you like."

I stepped in and pressed my lips to hers again, closing my eyes and losing myself to the softness of her mouth. Happiness burst in my chest and I smiled against her lips, thinking how good it was to be married to my best friend.

You can kiss me as much as you like.

Our kiss lingered and in that moment I vowed to be the best husband in the whole world.

And to kiss Indy every chance I got.

CHAPTER 19

CADE
Now

I saw her as soon as I arrived. I was late because Bull asked Elias, Davey, and me to take care of some business out at *Spank Daddy's*, and it had taken longer than we'd anticipated. So, by the time we got back to the clubhouse things were getting messy, including Indy. But she wasn't just messy, she was almost fall-down drunk. Sitting on a barstool, surrounded by Mirabella, Jacob, Abby, Isaac, and Vader, she was slinging back a shot of something clear as I approached. When she saw me, her eyes narrowed and she gave me a smile that was anything but warm.

"And so the man of the hour returns!" she slurred, raising her empty glass at me.

"This should be interesting," Jacob murmured to Mirabella as I walked past them.

I glanced at Isaac who gave me a *you should probably run* look. But I ignored him and focused on the stranger in front of me who had once been my very reason for breathing.

"It looks like you're having a good time," I said, ignoring how she swayed on the stool.

"You know what, I am! I am having a great time," she slurred again. She banged her glass on the bar, almost slipping off the stool, and then slapped her hands onto her knees. "And who would have thought! I mean, I didn't. Not in a million fucking years." She looked around her, screwing her nose up as she took in the clubhouse and everyone in it. "I mean . . . I *really* didn't!"

I eyed Randy, not impressed that he'd let her get this drunk.

"Two cocktails and two shots," he said, raising his arms at his side. "That's all it took."

"So why are you so late?" Indy demanded with the obnoxious confidence of a drunk. "No, wait, lemme guess . . . you were with some hottie you couldn't tear yourself away from . . . no! You were with two hotties . . . two hotties with big boobs, tight pussies, and no self-respect."

"Jesus," Vader muttered and turned away.

Mirabella stepped forward. "Indy, maybe we should go get some fresh air." But Indy ignored her, because clearly, she wasn't done yet.

"Or, maybe, you've got yourself a little lady stashed away somewhere. Someone whose heart you haven't managed to stomp all over . . . yet."

"What is wrong with you?" I asked.

"What is wrong with me?" She stood up and would have fallen on her ass if it wasn't for Isaac catching her. She shrugged him off as if it was no big deal and came straight for me. Her eyes narrowed. Her cheeks turned pink. When she reached me, she shoved a pointed finger at my chest. "What's wrong with me, what's wrong with *you*? Who do you think you are, treating women like that? Does she know what you're capable of? Does she know how you like to fuck club skanks behind her back?"

Indy was making a point. Even if the woman I was apparently cheating on didn't actually exist.

"You don't know what you're talking about," I said calmly.

She leaned in as if she was going to tell me a secret. "You forget, I know first-hand how you treat women."

I always knew this confrontation was going to happen. But this . . . this was a train wreck. And very public.

"You've had too much to drink," I said, standing very still while she wobbled on her feet.

"I haven't even started drinking," she slurred. She swung around to Randy. "Another shot, barman!"

"I'm taking you home," I said grabbing her wrist. But she wrenched it free.

"Don't you tell me what to do!" She glared at me. "You don't ever get to tell me what to do."

"We're not doing this here," I said.

"No. You're right. We're not doing this at all."

She stumbled off.

"I'll make sure she is okay," Abby said, brushing past me. "Crazy-assed bitch."

I turned back to Isaac who handed me a shot of whiskey.

"Here, I think you've earned it."

I slung it back and signaled for another.

Something told me the trouble had only just started.

CHAPTER 20

INDY
Now

I was drunk.

And you know what, it felt fucking great.

I hadn't had this much fun in for fucking ever.

I stumbled against the jukebox and pressed my palms against the glass to hold me up. I admit, I had trouble focusing on the playlist. The black letters swam in front of my eyes before slowly coming into focus.

"Okay, you fucking drunk," Abby said, walking up beside me. She leaned a hip against the jukebox and folded her arms across her chest. "I think you need to go home and sleep it off."

I sighed dramatically. "What is it with everyone thinking they can tell me what to do?"

"You've had enough, Indy."

"That's where you're wrong, I haven't even started to let down my hair."

"Oh, is that what you call that?"

I ignored her and kept reading through the playlist. It was taking me a while because the words would go in and out of focus.

"You just attacked Cade in front of his friends."

I looked at her and narrowed my eyes. "Whoos'ide are you on anyway?"

"*His*. I'm on *his* side because you're acting like a crazy bitch."

I pulled a face at her and then shrugged it off. "Whatever."

Twelve years' silence was a lot of time to separate alliances.

"You both have some talking to do, but here is not the time and place."

"I've got nothing to say (hiccup) to him..."

"We both know that's a load of shit. You two need to sit down and talk about what happened and find some kind of peace with it."

When I looked at her I saw two of Abby. I swayed as I tried to focus on just one of them. "Want to know a secret?"

She didn't look impressed. "Not really."

"I don't care what he... (hiccup)... has to say. I'm burying my monster of a father in four days and then... I'm gone..." I pretended my hand was a plane taking off and flying away. I even made the sound. Because apparently after four drinks I was five years old.

"Just like that? You come back and then just leave?"

"Yup. Just like that." I tried clicking my fingers but they didn't work.

Abby pushed off the jukebox and shook her head. "What happened to you?"

The way she said it—with disgust—got me pissed. I narrowed my eyes.

"You were my best friend. Why are you not sticking up for me?"

"Best friend? You've ignored me for twelve years," she snapped. But then her face softened. "You can't just show up here after twelve years of nothing and expect me to feel sorry for you. *He* hurt you, Indy, not *me*. Yet you abandoned me when you left him and it hurt. So, forgive me if I'm not rushing to your defense. I did that a lot in your absence but your continued silence kind of dampened my loyalties."

Abby had never been one to show her emotions. She was tough. Stoic. But even in my intoxication I could see how my actions had hurt her. It made me feel bad. And because I was drunk, it made me defensive.

"I got out of this shithole and made something of myself. You should be happy for me. I'm not that brokenhearted girl anymore."

Abby's eyes narrowed. "Yeah, well whoever that girl is now, she can kiss my southern ass."

I watched her walk away, then turned back to the jukebox. Closing one eye in a pathetic attempt to focus, I found the song I was looking for and pressed the button.

CHAPTER 21

CADE
Now

I found her standing in the doorway to my bedroom. *Standing* being a generous description. In reality, the doorjamb was holding her up. And she was staring into the room as if it mesmerized her.

"What are you doing?" I asked, even though I knew exactly what she was doing.

She swung around and her eyes narrowed. "Thought I'd check out the scene of the crime."

I inhaled deeply. This was always going to go down. But I had hoped it would be when she wasn't behaving like an inebriated asshole.

"Fine. You want to do this now—here I am, Indy. In the flesh. Give me your best shot."

She huffed. "I've got nothing to say to you."

"Of course, you do. You have twelve years of *pissed* to fling at me."

"You know what, you're right. I am pissed at you. And it's fucking insane because it's been twelve years and I really shouldn't give a fuck. But now that you bring it up, fuck it. You're an asshole."

I nodded. "What I did was a dick move."

"Oh, it was more than a dick move, Cade."

"I know. And I've always owned it. I was drunk. My asshole father drugged me, and yes, I fucked someone else. But I thought she was you. It never once entered into my head that it wasn't you in bed with me—"

She put her hand up to stop me.

"I don't give a fuck what excuse you think you have. You did what you did and it drove me away."

"That's bullshit, Indy, and you know it. Me fucking up was the perfect excuse for you to run and stay away. You hated the club. You wanted a reason to stay away without owning it."

"Oh, that's just rich! Is that really how you spin it in your head? You cheat on me at the clubhouse party with some club whore and I'm the one with the problem?" She shoved her hands on her hips but they slipped right off because she was drunk. "I catch you sticking your dick into another woman and I'm the one who is the asshole?"

"No. I'm the asshole. You're the coward."

Her eyes rounded. "A coward!"

"Yes! A coward! You turned and ran. And it was easier to blame me than to be honest. You wanted an out. And my stupidity gave it to you."

"So it's *my* fault you cheated on me?"

"No. But you turned your back on everything. Your family. Your friends. The club. And I'm tired of you blaming me for it. I may have given you a reason to leave, Indy. But you chose to stay away."

"Why *wouldn't* I choose to stay away? I'd rather be gone than hang around with a bunch of backwater hillbillies on Harleys, who treat their women like shit."

"And I suppose you're so fucking perfect!"

When she scoffed, I lost my patience.

"You want to be gone. Fine! But them out there. You owe them your respect. They're your family." I pointed to my chest. "*I'm* your family."

"They're not my family and neither are you," she yelled, her eyes burning right through me. "You're nothing to me!"

Her words inflicted the pain she intended. Right into my heart. But I didn't have time to react, because one minute she was looking at me like she hated me, and the next minute she was vomiting all over my boots.

"Brilliant," I said, stepping back. Without hesitation, I threw her over my shoulder and walked her through my bedroom to the small bathroom attached to it. She struggled but was no match for me in size or strength. When I let her down beside the toilet she threw up again.

And then again.

I left her to get some club soda from the clubhouse kitchen.

But by the time I got back to the bathroom she had passed out with her arms wrapped around the toilet and her face pressing against the seat. Drool dripped from the corner of her mouth.

"I guess some things don't change," I said, using a wet washcloth to wipe her lips. I smoothed away a lock of hair from her cheek and felt an all-too-familiar ache in my chest. Even passed out, she was the most beautiful girl in the world.

Lifting her into my arms, I carried her to my bed and carefully laid her down. She stirred and moaned, but then settled into my pillow. She wore a heavy bauble on her ring finger, but it had moved so I could make out the tattoo underneath.

I smiled. My heart suddenly hopeful.

It was still there.
After all these years, my name was still there.

CHAPTER 22

INDY
Now

What the hell happened to me?

I attempted to open one eye but immediately closed it again when sunlight assaulted my retinas. My face was mashed against a pillow. Drool had dried in the corner of my mouth and I was desperate for water. But I wasn't going to move. I wasn't going to move ever again. I would just lie here, wherever here was, until the pain subsided, or I died.

Which seemed like a really good idea until my stomach decided otherwise.

Feeling sick, I pushed up on my hands and looked around me through squinted eyes. "What the hell?"

I was in Cade's bedroom in the clubhouse.

But I didn't have time to wonder how the hell I got there, because a few seconds later my stomach tried desperately to escape my body via my mouth. I made it to the small bathroom just in time to throw up violently. Not once. Not twice. But three times.

"Oh God, let me die. . ." I moaned. Sweat beaded on my brow and I wiped it away. When I was sure I wasn't going to throw up again, I shakily rose to my feet and stumbled to the bathroom sink. I splashed water on my face in an attempt to pull myself out of my nightmare, then rinsed out my mouth and stared back at the pale mess in the mirror. I was a mess. A big, hungover mess.

What happened to me last night?

And then it all came flooding back. The party. The shots. The cocktails. The slurring. The insults. The harsh words I had flung at Cade and my meltdown that followed. *Don't kid yourself, Cade, I never belonged here. Who would want to belong here?* As more fractured memories rushed at me, I swung back to the toilet and vomited again.

Of course, I look down my nose at them. Everybody does!

Tears rolled down my cheeks. Christ, what was wrong with me? Alcohol hadn't just made me mean, it had made me a complete bitch. I was angry at Cade but I had taken it out on everyone around me.

You're nothing to me.

Overwhelmed with regret and embarrassment, I leaned against the wall and closed my eyes. I would have to apologize to them . . . all of them. And I wouldn't blame them if they never forgave me. I had behaved like an ass.

I got up and had a shower, combed my hair with what I assumed was Cade's comb and found a clean t-shirt large enough to cover the top of my thighs. It was strange being around Cade's belongings. Touching his things. Smelling the scent of his deodorant still lingering in the air. Feeling his shirt against my skin. I sat on the bed and let my fingers slide through his sheets, imagining him lying naked amongst them. Twelve years ago I had made love to him right here in this very bed. My body tingled, and for a moment I let myself wonder what it would feel like to be in this bed with him. Feeling him kiss me. Feeling him touch me again. Feeling him run his tongue along the edge of my throat and thrust my hands above my head as he slowly and powerfully made love to me. I closed my eyes and felt the longing reawaken in me.

I wanted to check out the scene of the crime.

My eyes sprang open and I pulled my hand back. Twelve years ago I had walked in on him fucking someone else in this bed. I wasn't the last person he had made love to here. There had been many, probably hundreds of women tangled amongst these sheets since then, moaning and calling out his name as he fucked them.

I stood up. But I wasn't going to be one of them. Not ever again.

Searching for my handbag and finding it on the bedside table I scooped my clothes off the floor and fled the room.

I was hoping for a clean getaway. But that was never going to happen in an MC clubhouse. Despite the early hour, I could hear voices coming from a main room off the hallway. From memory, it was a room the old ladies used for meetings or events, sometimes kids' birthday parties. Unfortunately, if I wanted to avoid going out via the bar, which would be littered with passed-out bikers, I would have to pass through it to get to the back door. Either way, I was going to have to face someone.

I clutched my clothes against my chest and made my way toward the sounds of the voices. When I walked in the room, Mirabella, Abby, Cherry, and Anna all looked up from a table covered in what looked like some kind of paper craft. Going by the lack of smiles on their faces, it was obvious I had some serious apologies to give. Without a word, they looked away and resumed making paper streamers.

"I really don't know what to say," I said, my voice raspy. "Other than I am very sorry. My behavior last night was unforgivable and I can only hope you ladies forgive me."

They all looked up again. Mirabella gave me a soft smile. Cherry and Anna looked at her and then did the same. Abby, however, looked uncomfortable, almost as if she was ashamed to look at me.

"Being back here is a bit of a mind fuck," I continued. "But that doesn't excuse my behavior, and I really am sorry. I said a lot of shit that I didn't mean."

When no one said anything, I felt crushed. And ashamed. But I couldn't blame them. I was a bitch. And MC women didn't forgive easily. There was an awful silence as if I wasn't in the room, and I had a feeling I had blown it. Not that I should care. I told myself that I didn't but in reality, I did. I wasn't an asshole but I had certainly behaved like one.

I turned to leave.

"You know, we could use an extra pair of hands with these paper streamers," Mirabella said. "The wedding is less than a week away and you can never have too many decorations."

I turned back to look at them.

"We have a lot of wedding buntings to make, too," Cherry said, holding up a handful of triangle cut-outs.

"And you look like you could use a strong cup of coffee," Anna said, rising out of her chair. "Sit down and I'll get you a cup."

I breathed a sigh of relief. They were going to give me another chance. But when I looked at Abby, I realized it was going to take more than an apology for her. She and Cade were family, and I had slayed her cousin with insults in front of the entire club.

I sat down next to her, and Anna placed a cup of coffee in front of me.

"I'm sorry for all those things I said to Cade last night," I said to Abby.

"You know, I think I saw some pretty cool decorations in the storage locker outside," Anna said to Mirabella and Cherry. It was an obvious attempt to give Abby and me some privacy.

"Let's go check them out," Mirabella replied.

But Cherry didn't catch on. "Really, I was in there the other day and I didn't see—" She stopped when Anna kicked her chair, and then slowly nodded. "Of course, we should go and have a look."

Once they were gone, Abby looked at me.

She was pissed.

"You've changed," she said. "And not in a good way."

"Abby, I'm sorry—"

"It's bad enough that you just left. Just turned your back on all of us. But then to come back here and treat us all like we're trash? Who the fuck are you?"

"Good question." I raked my hands down my face and sighed. "I thought I knew the answer to that very question. But I'm more confused now than ever." I shook my head as if I could somehow shake my confusion free. "I'm sorry. I made a complete fool of myself and I said a lot of things I didn't mean."

"What Cade did to you was shit. And you've gotta believe how much shit we gave him for what he did. We gave him hell. We were your best friends and he hurt you, so we rallied around you. But you weren't here and you wouldn't answer our phone calls or our messages." Her eyes welled with tears. "Isaac loved you. *I* loved you. We were here to help you through it, but you just turned your back on us. It fucking hurt. It fucking hurt like hell."

"I'm sorry," I whispered feeling lousy. I remembered all the text messages from Abby and Isaac and how I had ignored them. Not because I wanted to but because it hurt. They were a direct vein to Cade, and he was my kryptonite.

"Good. If you're really sorry, you'll go and sort things out with Cade. Until then, you and me don't have anything to say to one another." Her ice-blue eyes found mine and I could see the pain on her face. "What happened between you and Cade affected more than just the two of you. Isaac may have forgiven you, but I'm still a little pissed. I'm still trying to work out why I was so easily cast aside. So, go and sort it out. Then maybe you and I can talk."

My heart sank but I nodded. "Fair enough."

"And go home." She stood up. "You look like hell."

CHAPTER 23

INDY
Now

I decided to take Abby's advice and go home, have a second shower, and pull my shit together. When I was feeling more human, I would find Cade and apologize for my behavior. I would be honest with him and let him know how mind fucked I felt.

But I needed another cup of coffee, and some greasy food before I faced him.

Unfortunately, fate had other ideas. As I was leaving, I ran straight into him walking out of his room.

We paused a safe distance from each other.

"Nice shirt," he said, his eyes sweeping up and down the length of me.

I had forgotten I was wearing one of his t-shirts.

Feeling embarrassed, I clutched my bundle of clothes tighter to me, painfully aware of how short the tee was.

"I don't know what to say," I said, awkwardly.

He leaned against the doorway and folded his arms across his chest. "Seemed to me you had an awful lot to say last night."

I tried to swallow the knot of shame in my throat. I hated being wrong. But worse, I hated being an ass. And something told me Cade wasn't going to let me off easily.

"I'm so sorry, Cade. I was such an ass."

"Yeah, you were."

"Clearly I'm not a good drunk. I didn't mean what I said."

"Which part? Where you accused me of cheating on my non-existent girlfriend or when you called me a slut?"

I cringed.

I hated that word.

"Or do you mean when you called everyone here a bunch of backwater hillbillies on Harleys?" He continued. "Or that memorable moment when you told me I meant nothing to you right before you puked all over my boots?"

My cheeks burned with embarrassment. Boy, when I messed up, I made sure I did it in spectacular form.

Christ, I was such an asshole.

"All of it," I said, shifting uneasily on my bare feet. "I can't apologize enough . . . to you, the girls, the club. I was being an ass—"

"Ride with me," he said suddenly.

"Excuse me?"

"You want me to accept your apology? Come ride with me."

It was natural for me to want to argue with him, but I thought better of it and relaxed.

"Where?"

"It's a surprise."

"I hate surprises."

He leaned in and looked a little smug. "I know. See you back here at ten."

I watched his broad back as he started to walk away.

"Be here or the deal is off and I won't ever forgive you." He called over his shoulder before disappearing around the corner.

I stared at the empty corridor and dropped my hands to my side wondering what the fuck had just happened.

Outside, I ran into Davey, the club's treasurer. Somewhere in his forties, he was a big teddy bear of a man.

When he saw me, he pretended to duck for cover.

"I'm sorry," I said sincerely. "Seems I'm a bad drunk. I have this murky memory of saying you have Neanderthal hands."

At some point during the night he had walked in. I had a vague, fractured recollection of me shoving my finger into his chest and telling him to lose weight.

Why I had told him he had Neanderthal hands was a complete mystery to me. I didn't even know what that meant.

He took pity on me. "Wanna hug it out?"

Normally I'd say no. Davey could be an old pervert.

"Come on," he said, his arms out wide.

Davey was a good guy. I couldn't believe I'd been such a dick to him. So I accepted his hug.

But of course, he squeezed my ass.

My near-naked ask.

"Just kidding," he said, releasing me.

I smacked him on the arm for the butt feel. "You're incorrigible."

"Admit it, if I didn't, you'd be disappointed."

I tugged on the hem of Cade's tee wishing it covered more of my thighs.

"Come on, sweet face. Let me give you a lift home. I don't want you getting into a cab with some stranger leering all over you."

"Why do I get the feeling that a cab is probably the safer option here?" I asked, cocking an eyebrow at him.

Davey winked as he opened the car door for me. "You couldn't be more safe with me, honey. Don't think for a second that Cade wouldn't kill any man who tried anything with you."

Because I had messed up my pants by puking all over them, and because my other clothes weren't back from the dry cleaners, my options were limited. I still had another pair of black pants from McGovern's, but let's face it, they weren't really my style. And as I looked at them laid out on my bed I wondered how long I was going to keep trying to convince myself that they were.

Still wrapped in my towel from the shower, I opened my wardrobe to see what I had left behind all those years ago. It was pretty sparse. There was a jacket, a pair of jeans, and a few shirts.

Everything smelled like the patchouli fragrant discs I'd left hanging next to an old Led Zeppelin T-shirt.

I stared at the jeans. Would they even fit me after twelve years? I reached out to touch them and the worn denim felt familiar against my palm. Did I even want to know?

Apparently, I did, because two minutes later I was bouncing up and down to get them up and over my thirty-year-old thighs before zipping them up.

I slipped on a tank top and an old pair of knee-high boots I found at the bottom of the closet, and then stood in front of the mirror.

"They look good," came a familiar, female voice behind me.

Startled, I turned around to see Ronnie standing in the doorway.

"I wanted to see if they still fit," I explained.

Knowing, hooded eyes gleamed over me.

"The jeans?" Ronnie asked, her wild curls gently brushing her face as she tilted her head to the side. "Or the old feelings between you and Cade? I heard he was taking you for a ride today."

This was typical Ronnie Calley—the straight-shooting biker queen. She wasn't one to beat around the bush.

I looked away.

"Those days are long gone, Ronnie," I said, studying my reflection in the mirror.

"Sure, sugar. But seems to me you and my son have a lot of unfinished business to tend to before either of you can move on... if last night was anything to go by."

Again, my face burned with embarrassment.

I looked at her. "I behaved like an ass. I get it."

She shrugged. "There was a lot of emotion behind it. Seems to me there are a lot of things left unsaid between the two of you."

"Cade has moved on. So have I."

She pushed off the door frame and walked in. "Oh, he says he has. He says a lot of things because he is a man, and just like his daddy, he can be a damn fool. But I know my boy. The torch he burns for you is as bright as any torch is going to get." She slid my leather bolero jacket from a hanger in the closet and put it on me. And because I was so lost in what she was saying, I let her. "If you're going to say goodbye to that girl for good, best you know who you are saying goodbye to."

She turned me to face the mirror and my heart stalled. The girl standing in front of me was the same girl who had walked away from Cade and Destiny twelve years earlier. Oh sure, she was slightly older, and hopefully a hell of a lot smarter, but other than that, not much had changed.

I frowned at my reflection. I didn't know what startled me the most.

How these clothes still fit me after all these years.
Or how good it felt to be wearing them again.
Confusion knotted in my chest.
I needed to clear my head. Get my emotions straight.
I needed to see my brother.
Talking to him always helped.
I needed some brother-sister time.

An hour later, I walked through the immaculate green lawns of Grenville Park, our local cemetery. It had been twelve years, but not a lot had changed and I had no trouble finding Bolt's grave. He was next to our grandparents, Connie and Jude Parrish, and our Uncle Samuel who'd died at nine years old from acute leukemia.

On Sunday, my daddy would join them in the shade of the willow tree.

I walked toward Bolt's grave and immediately felt an all-too-familiar feeling of pain and regret spread through my chest. I used to visit every week, but hadn't been back since leaving for college.

I knelt before his gravestone and drew in a deep breath, exhaling slowly as I let the feelings of grief and loss engulf me. Bolt had died young. One minute he was here, and the next minute he was gone.

And I was alone.

I reached out and traced his name carved into the fieldstone.
BOLT HANK PARRISH

Sadness wrapped itself around my heart. It had been eighteen years since I had seen my brother. Eighteen years since I'd heard his voice and his infectious laugh. Eighteen years since he had put his arm around my shoulders and told me everything was going to be okay.

My heart ached. Tears spilled down my cheeks.
My brother.
I had left him behind, too.

CHAPTER 24

INDY—Aged 12
Then

I hated the smell of the hospital. Mama said I would get used to it, but I didn't think I would, not even if I worked there every single day. And why anyone would want to work where it smelled so bad and people were so unhappy was beyond me. The only good thing about the hospital was getting to hang out with Bolt and watching TV while eating Jell-O and ice cream. The nurses were kind and gentle, and they would bring me little tubs of it when they brought Bolt's dinner to his room. And half the time, Bolt didn't feel like eating, so I got to eat his, as well. Lately, Bolt hadn't been eating at all, so they had him hooked up to a bag that fed something into his arm, but the nurses still brought dessert for me.

Bolt got tired a lot. Even watching TV was tiresome for him, so he'd ask me to read to him instead. He loved *Harry Potter* and we were half-way through book three. I liked reading out loud to him because he would close his eyes and his face would look peaceful, and I wondered if me reading to him was the only time he was able to block out the pain. It made me feel helpful, which was good, because watching his illness eat him from the inside out and not being able to do anything made me cry into my pillow every single night.

Not that I let Mama know. Or Daddy—especially not Daddy, because he had become so stressed and mean lately. He didn't smile anymore, and there was a harsh edge to his voice, so I stayed away from him. One night, I found him sitting in the treehouse with his legs dangling over the side. He had a bottle of liquor in one hand and his face was buried in the other. He was sobbing and it made me feel real weird because I had never seen my daddy cry before, but this night he was really letting his tears get the better of him. I watched him sob, then take a swig of liquor, and then sob again.

He didn't really come to the hospital very much anymore, either. But today he did, although him being there didn't seem to comfort my mama much. She was crying a lot, more than usual. Ronnie, Garrett, and Cade were there, too, and even they looked torn up and scared, and I didn't understand why. They'd seen Bolt lots of times, but for some reason today they were taking it real bad. I went to the water fountain for a drink, and when I walked back to Bolt's room, Garrett Calley brushed past me muttering, "It ain't right, God taking them so damn young."

Alarmed and confused, I watched him disappear down the hallway and out of view. When I turned back toward Bolt's room, Ronnie and Cade were walking out.

"Go see your brother, baby girl. Go spend some time with him," Ronnie said softly.

Cade took my hand in his and squeezed my fingers, but he didn't say anything. Feeling a sense of urgency bubble up from deep within me, I pulled my hand free and pushed open the door to Bolt's room.

Inside, Mama sat beside his bed, holding his hand, while my daddy stared out the window that looked out over the parking lot. Neither glanced up when I walked in, and Bolt looked like he was asleep.

A strange mood hung in the air.

They weren't telling me something.

I cleared my throat and mama looked up at me.

"Hey, baby." She forced a smile. She looked sad and tired, the type of tired where people look sick to their bones.

"You want me to get you some coffee, Mama?" I asked.

She shook her head. "No, sweetheart."

"Well, I feel like one." My daddy turned away from the window to look at mama. "Irish. Hold the caffeine."

Mama looked weary. "Not today, Jack. Please, let's just get through today without whisky."

"I'll do whatever the hell I want, woman," my daddy replied darkly, and turned back to stare out the window. "I'll do whatever I goddamn want to."

My mama and daddy fought a lot lately. I remember how he used to touch her with such tenderness. A gentle stroke on the cheek. A small squeeze of her hand as he walked past. Now he barely looked at her.

"I can go get you something if you like, Daddy," I said. But he just ignored me and kept staring out the window like I wasn't even in the room.

Mama reached for my hand and squeezed it. "You're a good girl, Indigo."

I heard my daddy growl and then storm out. Mama looked worn out and sad.

"Sit with your brother, Indy. Maybe read him one of those books he likes."

I nodded and Mama got up and went after Daddy.

I looked at Bolt. For the longest time. I just stared down at him lying in the hospital bed.

"Will you quit lookin' at me like that, Indy." He opened one eye. "Anyone would think you ain't seen someone dyin' before."

"Is that what you call it, Bolt Parrish? I thought you was just lazyin' around." I sat on the edge of the bed. "Don't think I ain't noticed how I've been picking up your slack around home with chores and stuff."

"You got me." He forced a weak smile. "This is just some ploy to get outta chores."

I chuckled. "I was figuring."

"I would give anything to be home right now."

"You'll be home soon enough."

His smile faded. "I'm never going home, Indy."

My smile faded, too. "Don't say that," I whispered.

"It's true. Why'd you think Mom and Dad are so upset. Why'd you think the Calley's are here. I'm dying, Indy."

"You're fourteen, Bolt. Fourteen-year-old boys don't die."

"They think I don't know. But I do. I hear stuff. They think I'm asleep or passed out on pain medication, but I hear their conversations. I know that it's only a matter of days, maybe even hours—"

I stood up. "Don't you speak like that! It's not true. You hear me?"

"It is true." He lifted his head off the pillow. But it must've been too much for him, because he grimaced and winced, and fell back into his pillow. He looked so weak. I felt a horrible tingling at the base of my stomach and looked away from my brother. I couldn't let him see the truth in my eyes. That I was terrified for him. That I was terrified that he may be right.

"Where do you think we go when we die?" he asked, looking up at me from his pillow.

I didn't want to have this conversation with him. But I knew he needed to talk.

"I don't know. But I bet it's real nice."

Again, he smiled weakly. "When it's time for me to go, I'm going to soar like an eagle. I'm going to fly over town and people will look up and go, 'There goes Bolt Parrish, flying like an eagle, flying free at last'. And I will be free—free from this pain." He sighed and his breath left him slowly. His lashes brushed his cheeks as his eyes closed. "How I want to be free."

Tears spilled down my face. I didn't want my brother to die. But he was dying, and no matter how much I didn't want it to be true, he was ready to go.

"Bolt . . ."

He opened his eyes and reached for my hand. Then he gently shook it. "Don't you go getting all soppy on me, girl."

I smiled weakly and wiped the tears from my cheek. "As if! I was going to suggest I read you some more *Harry Potter*."

He smiled up at me. "Please . . ."

I opened the book to where we last left it and began reading. Ten minutes in and I glanced over at Bolt. His eyes were closed and he looked still. Very still. I swallowed deep. My heart pounded in my chest.

"I'm still breathing . . ." he croaked out. A small smile curled on his pale lips, but his eyes remained closed. "You can quit your starin', Indy."

I couldn't help but smile. "I know that, silly. I was just taking a breath."

I took a sip of water from the cup beside his bed, and started reading again. I glanced at the clock: 4:39 pm. I turned the page and continued into the next chapter.

At 4:43 pm, I looked over and Bolt was sleeping again. I bit my lip. Again, he looked very still.

Was his chest moving?

I drew in a heavy breath and leaned in closer.

"Bolt?" I whispered softly.

There was silence and a terrible tingling began to unfurl in the base of my stomach.

"Bolt?"

The *Harry Potter* book dropped from my grasp as I went to him and shook him.

"Bolt, wake up." Another shake. "Bolt."

But he didn't wake up.

"Wake up, please!" I cried.

The door opened and Mama walked in carrying a cup of coffee. When she looked at me and then to Bolt, the paper cup in her hand fell to the floor and coffee spilled like blood across the linoleum.

"No," she cried, and raced toward the bed.

Everything seemed to move in slow motion from that point on. A nurse ran in, followed by a doctor, followed by my father. My mama grabbed onto Bolt's pajama shirt and cried for him to open his eyes. She pulled him toward her, but his arms were floppy at his side. The nurse and the doctor struggled with her, trying to get her to free her grip on his shirt.

"No," she kept crying. Over and over. And finally, she fell into the arms of the nurse while my father stood there like a helpless toy soldier.

"I'm sorry, Mrs Parrish," the doctor said, winding his stethoscope around his neck. "I'm so sorry."

Mama screamed then, like a wild animal. She unleashed her pain and heartache into the small hospital room. My daddy fell forward and dropped to his knees by the bed.

"Time of death . . . 4:45 pm," the doctor said.

I stepped back, one foot behind the other until I reached the door.

Time of death.

I turned the doorknob.
My brother was dead.
I opened the door and ran.

CHAPTER 25

CADE
Now

My jaw hit the floor and I had to check myself to make sure I wasn't dreaming when she walked in. Sure, she looked like Indy. But she was nothing like the conservative, angry girl who had walked back into my life after twelve years. No. My ex-girlfriend was back. Tight jeans. Leather jacket. Knee-high boots. An attitude in her hips as she walked in the room. A real MC Princess.

I smiled to myself.

Would she complain if I called her that?

Nah. Seeing her look so fine, I had a feeling my soul mate had just walked back into my life for good.

Whether she knew it or not.

Wolf whistles echoed around the room and I couldn't help but grin when Indy shot down each and every one of them with a few choice words and some rather suggestive hand gestures.

Yeah. My MC Princess was back.

I stood up as she approached.

"Nice to see you got your dress sense back," I said with a grin.

She raised an eyebrow. "What can I say, I ran out of clothes."

"And your accent? I see that's back, too."

She shrugged. "You can take the girl out of the South…."

I licked my lips and leaned in. "Does that mean you're thinking of hanging around?"

She pressed her hand into my chest to keep me at a safe distance. "I'm here under duress, remember?"

"Oh, yeah, that's right. Because you were an ass to me last night."

She gave me a pointed look. "You told me to be here at ten. Its five minutes past. *Now* will you tell me where we're going?"

"Not a chance. You're not getting off that easily." I pulled my bike keys out of my back pocket. "You ready to ride?"

With a roll of her eyes, she followed me outside to the parking lot. As we walked to my bike, a car barreled up the driveway and came to a screeching halt next to Indy's rental car. An angry looking blonde climbed out and slammed the door.

It was Genevieve.

Davey's ex-old lady.

Her eyes zeroed in on Indy, but as she came closer they narrowed in on me.

I nodded to her. "Genevieve."

But she ignored me and yelled, "Davey, you fucking asshole!" as she disappeared inside.

"Friendly," Indy said.

I handed her a helmet. "You have no idea."

"Friend of yours?"

"Davey's ex-old lady." I secured my helmet and slid my legs over my bike. "Totally unhinged."

We could hear her screaming at him, even when I started my bike. I reached around and guided Indy onto the back, securing her arms around my waist.

"Ready?"

"Ready."

I smiled, and with a flick of the throttle, we roared off into the warm, Mississippi sunshine.

CHAPTER 26

INDY
Now

The Destiny Watermelon Festival had been a big deal for as long as I could remember. Mom and Ronnie used to bring us here every year. Now, apparently, the club were a part of it. They ran a barbecue cookout stand to raise money for the local hospital. It was a silent payoff for building a strip club across the road from their Emergency Room.

It was busy. Being a Saturday, the showground was packed with families. Parents pushed strollers while kids ran around hopped up on cotton candy and corndogs. Teenagers hung in groups, while lovers strolled hand in hand. There were tantrums. There was laughter. There was a festive vibe in the air as the town gathered on the small showground to celebrate their biggest export: the watermelon.

Here you could get it all. Watermelon cotton candy. Watermelon slushies. Watermelon ice cream. Fresh watermelon. Juiced watermelon. Watermelon cut in the shape of your favorite Pokémon. Watermelon socks. Watermelon stress balls.

At midday, there would be a watermelon-eating contest, followed by a seed-spitting competition.

Yep. A seed-spitting competition.

Because we did that here.

It had been a long time since I'd been to the festival and I had almost forgotten about it. The last time I'd visited it, I was with Cade and we'd just become official boyfriend and girlfriend, and he had won me a gigantic soft toy in the shape of a donut.

I stopped walking. "Why did you bring me here?"

Cade turned around. Two dimples deepened in his cheeks. "Something tells me you need to be reminded how to have a good time."

I put my hands on my hips. "What is that supposed to mean?"

"It means you need to lighten up and have some fun."

When he started to walk away I stomped after him.

"I know how to have fun!"

"I don't think you do."

I had to walk quickly to catch up to him. Cade was tall. His stride was twice the size of mine.

"Just because I don't want to hang out at some stupid watermelon festival, doesn't mean I don't know how to have a good time."

"Yeah, it does."

"My friends all think I'm fun," I insisted. "Anyway, I have things to do. More important things than hanging out at some fruit carnival."

He stopped walking and turned around. "Fine. Just let me kick your ass at Shootout and then we'll go."

He started walking again.

"Kick my—I don't think so!" Again, I had to walk fast to keep up. "My aim is on point, I'll have you know!"

"Still not as good as mine," he said, stopping beside the Shootout booth.

I knew he was baiting me to play, but I couldn't help myself. And he knew I wouldn't be able to resist the challenge. Because he knew me so well.

Even when he paid for the both of us to play, I still resisted.

"If you beat me, we'll go home," he said, picking up a wooden air rifle and loading it. "If I win, we stay and ride the wheel."

"There is no way you're getting me up on that thing."

"Oh, that's right, I forgot. You're afraid of heights."

"I'm not afraid of anything," I said raising my chin. "I just don't trust their safety standards, is all."

"Sure, you don't." He cocked his gun. "We got a deal?"

For a moment, our eyes locked in battle.

"Fine," I snapped, picking up a rifle. "You win, we ride the wheel. If I win, we aren't leaving right away, I'm going to pick out the biggest soft toy there is and make you walk around the park with it all morning."

CHAPTER 27

CADE
Now

She kicked my ass.

I mean, she really mopped the floor with me.

When she won the first game, I insisted it was the best out of three. When she won all three, I talked her into game four.

Which she won.

And I had to admit, watching her handle that rifle like a badass made me hard as fuck.

Now I was walking around cuddling a gigantic soft bunny with the biggest floppy ears known to man.

And Indy was enjoying every second of it.

The upside—she wasn't running away from me. Or telling me what an asshole I was. She wanted to stay and make me walk around with this damn thing attached to my hip all morning as some kind of payback.

The downside . . . well, there wasn't one. Hanging out with Indy was turning out to be the best day I'd had in a long time. She was relaxed. And she laughed . . . a lot. I missed that laugh.

And the way she tilted her head back and half closed her eyes when she found something hilarious.

Being with her was easy.

And a turn on.

Because I had a hard-on that wouldn't quit.

"What should we do next?" I asked as we walked down Sideshow Alley, eating corndogs smothered in ketchup.

When I looked at her, she was already looking at me. She had a smear of ketchup at the corner of her mouth, and when I reached over to wipe it with the pad of my thumb, I found myself resisting the sudden urge to lean down and brush my lips against her mouth. Everything in my body begged me to touch her. To lick the sweet sauce from her skin. To part those luscious lips with my tongue and kiss her to hell and back. To reach for her and crush her body against me so she could feel everything she was doing to me. She lifted her lashes and smiled, but it slowly faded as the moment deepened and something shimmered between us. Her lips parted and said *kiss me*. While her eyes darkened and said *don't*.

"How about the wheel?" she said, breaking the spell.

I pulled my hand away.

"You hate the wheel," I reminded her.

"You walked around with a massive toy bunny attached to your hip all morning. It would be poor sportsmanship if we didn't." She shrugged and took my hand. "Come on. Before I change my mind."

The line for the Ferris wheel was short so we didn't have to wait long. But when it came to our turn, Indy hesitated.

"No need to be afraid, *Princess*," I teased, winking at the young ride attendant who was watching us. In her late teens, she had blonde pigtails and freckles, and a t-shirt that read, *Sorry I wasn't in church, I was busy practicing witchcraft and becoming a lesbian.*

"I'm not afraid," Indy protested. She turned to the ride attendant. "Really, I'm not."

The girl grinned and held out a bucket of candy. "Some of the parents find it helps to preoccupy the little ones if they're, you know . . . afraid."

Indy gave the girl a traitorous look but took a lollipop from her anyway.

"What about the bunny?" she asked me, unwrapping the lollipop.

"Bunny's coming with us."

She raised an eyebrow at me. "It's okay, Cade. Torture time is over. You can get rid of the bunny."

I covered the giant bunny ears with my hands. "Get rid of him? No way!"

I couldn't wait to see the look on Brax's face when I gave it to him. Or the look on Isaac's face when he realized the ears squeaked every time you tugged on them.

Every. Single. Time.

Indy rolled her eyes and climbed into the bucket. After securing the oversized, soft toy between us, I sat down next to her.

"Ready?" I asked as we started moving.

She nodded but gripped the safety bar so hard her knuckles were white. She could deny it as much as she liked, but she fucking hated heights.

Growing up, Indy was fearless. She was always getting into mischief. But heights were her kryptonite. The one fear she couldn't hide. Or conquer.

When I looked at her, she was biting her lower lip and I felt like a real dick for teasing her. An all-too-familiar rush of protectiveness came over me and I slid my hand over hers. She turned her head, her large brown eyes gleaming in the light of the early afternoon, and a slow smile tugged at her lips as her gaze rolled over my face. When she didn't pull her hand away, a spark ignited inside me. Her scent. The heat of her skin. They engulfed me.

Slowly, the town of Destiny came into view below us, but I couldn't drag my eyes away from her. She slid the lollipop between her luscious lips and my cock hardened even more. I knew how they felt wrapped around me and my body ached to feel them again. I wanted them on me. I wanted to be in them.

"I'm sorry about what I said last night," she said.

"You already apologized," I replied, trying not to notice the way she sucked at the candy in her mouth. Or the fact that I was falling in love with her all over again.

Her eyes softened with regret. "I know. But I need you to know that I didn't mean those things."

"Some of them you did."

She blinked and nodded regretfully, then turned her head to look out at the view. Golden sunlight danced on her beautiful face.

"This place . . . coming back. It's been strange." I could see the remorse in her expression. She looked sad. *Lost*.

I gently turned her chin to look at me. "I know."

She licked her lips and I had to fight the craving to cover them with mine.

"Thank you for being so nice," she said, a small smile tugging at the corner of her mouth.

Heat flared in me. There wasn't one nice thing I was thinking in that moment. My eyes were focused on those lips. On that milky, smooth throat and how I wanted to bury my face in there and cover it in my kisses. I held back a moan. In my mind, I was already kissing her. Touching her.

And that was when I realized.

I wasn't falling in love with her all over again.

Because I had never stopped.

I never would.
And I was fucking doomed.

CHAPTER 28

INDY
Now

We didn't leave the festival until after lunch. The hours just flew by. Before I knew it, the sun was getting lower in the sky and our *date* was almost over. As I climbed on the bike behind Cade, I couldn't help but feel a little disappointed. Today had been surprisingly fun.

We rode back to the clubhouse and my heart began to sag a little. My hangover was finally catching up with me. I felt strange and reasoned it was because of all the alcohol my organs had marinated in the night before. Alcohol was a depressant and I'd had enough of it to make me depressed for a week.

When we pulled up to the clubhouse I wasn't sure if I was ready for today to end.

And that confused me.

"Thanks for today," I said.

Cade held up the giant bunny. It had ridden home between us, its big ears flopping about in the wind.

"Want to come with me to give this to Brax?"

I grinned. Yes. Yes, I did.

"He's over at the playground." He gestured toward the clubhouse. "He and Vader's little girl have a play date every Saturday afternoon."

As we made our way up the driveway, I looked up and came to a sudden halt.

Across the parking lot, a large coffin was being unloaded from a truck and carried into the workshop of *Shadow Choppers*, the custom motorcycle shop co-owned by the Kings. Next door to it, was their tattoo shop called *Sinister Ink*.

"Is that my daddy's coffin?" I asked.

It was a lame question, because of course it was.

All fallen Kings were buried in a custom-sprayed coffin, usually to match their motorcycle paint job, and always with the Kings of Mayhem patch on the sides.

"Ah, yeah . . . sorry, Indy. Picasso is getting it ready for the funeral."

I watched the coffin disappear inside the workshop, hating the feeling of sadness that swept through me. My daddy didn't deserve my grief. He was lucky I was even here.

"I'm sorry, Indy," Cade said again.

"Why?" I looked at him, my eyes narrowed. "You didn't kill him."

I stalked off. I didn't know why I was suddenly so angry. Only moments ago, I had been fine, and now—now I hated everything about this Godforsaken hick town and this stupid motorcycle club.

"Hey . . ." Cade called after me. When I ignored him, he caught up to me and gently turned me around. "Come on, Indy. I know you're hurting."

My anger—or whatever the hell it was I was feeling—peaked.

"That's where you're wrong." I folded my arms. "I'm not hurting. I'm not hurting at all. My daddy was a mean sonofabitch who cheated on my mom, and put a fist in her jaw more than a couple of times. He was a bad husband and an even shittier father. So, no, I'm not hurting. I'm nothing. So spare me the apologies. And let's just get this shit done so I can get out of the fuck out of here."

I had no desire to be back in the Kings of Mayhem compound. I wanted to go home. Get as far away from all of this as possible. But as I stomped toward the timber fort and playground, the sight of it made me come to a quick halt. Garrett Calley and my daddy had built the playground for us when we were kids, and twenty-five years later, it still looked the same. Two little blonde kids played on the timber fort and they could have easily been Cade and me when we were little. They were laughing as the little boy chased the little girl around the swing set, and when the little girl fell down, the little boy rushed to her and helped her up.

How many times had Cade done that for me? Picked me up when I had fallen down.

Cade stood directly behind me.

"The very first time I kissed you was on that fort," he said, his voice husky and his breath warm against the back of my neck. "We were five years old. Do you remember?"

I nodded and tears sprung to my eyes as my anger started to wane.

Hell. My emotions were all over the place. Stupid hangover.

"Yes, I remember," I whispered. My heart pounded in my ears as those happy memories rushed at me all at once. We had spent hours playing on that stupid playground. And he was right; the very first time he had kissed me had been behind the timber fort when we were five, and it was the first of many. Although, by the time we were teenagers, the kissing was a little less innocent and involved a lot more tongue.

My heart ached and my chest felt heavy. They were happy times, but again I felt at war with myself. I sighed. Exhausted. It was time to stop running from my past and face it head on.

Without turning around, I asked, "Can you take me to see my father?"

Cade's voice was deep and strong. "Of course."

CHAPTER 29

INDY
Now

Dead people don't look like they are sleeping. They look dead. Gone. *Empty*. My father was no different. His eyes were closed. I mean, he looked like my father. Beard. Longish hair. A face marred by grief and the torment of losing his son. Not to mention the drinking and drugs. But he also looked dead.

Not sleeping.

I stared down at him, my chest tight. It was real. It was over. There would be no more stalemate between us. No more unanswered phone calls. No more missed birthdays, Thanksgivings and Christmases. No more *nothing* between us.

The end.

I felt even further away from him than ever before.

"Excuse me, Miss Parrish?" The morgue attendant approached us. "These are your father's personal affects. He had them on him when he passed."

He handed me a plastic envelope. Inside were his chunky silver rings, the watch Bolt and I had given him for his thirty-fifth birthday, his wallet, and one other item that surprised me. It was a handmade friendship bracelet I'd made for him when I was ten.

"He was wearing this when he died?" I asked.

The attendant nodded. "We weren't sure if you wanted it back or if you'd like him to wear it."

My heart swelled unexpectedly. He'd kept it all these years.

I looked down at him lying still on the stainless-steel stretcher, the sheet pulled up to his chest. I reached for his wrist, momentarily stunned by how malleable it was, and secured the leather bracelet around it. If he'd worn it all these years, then it had meant something to him.

Maybe I had meant something to him too.

As I child, I thought my father's meanness was my fault. That I'd done something wrong to make him angry at me. Then, as a teenager, I told myself it was because he was a monster who just didn't care about anyone anymore. Then, as an adult, my perspective was different again. I understood his grief had taken him. Changed him. Made him mean. He hadn't abandoned me. He had hidden from me. Protecting himself from further heartache. And he had let it destroy us.

Losing his son had shattered his marriage, his relationship with his daughter, and his mind.

Now the tears rolled down my cheeks as I whispered my last goodbye to him.

"I hope you're happy now that you're finally with Bolt," I whispered.

I felt something in me weaken.

I turned to Cade.

"Take me for a ride. I don't care where, let's just ride."

CHAPTER 30

CADE
Now

I kept a journal.

I know. Big tough biker dude, right?

But the truth was, after I'd returned home from chasing Indy to Seattle and behaving like a complete psycho, my mom forced me to see a counselor. My head was out of control and she was worried I was going to really lose my shit. It was a good move, because the counselor—a youngish guy called Donnie from San Francisco—really helped to pull me out of the pit I'd fallen into.

One of the things Donnie asked me to do was to keep a journal. To write down the things that happened throughout the day and how they made me feel. He said it would help put things into perspective, and he was right. Writing it all down helped calm my craziness because it made me stop and take a breath. I was able to vent. I was able to get it all out of the tangle in my head and put it together on the page.

Even as life moved on without Indy, I continued to write in my journal. It helped with all of life's sharp turns, like when my father died in a bar brawl less than a year after Indy left, and Donnie's death in a car accident only a few months after that. I kept writing about everything. When Caleb went to prison for assaulting a college kid who was raping an underage girl, because he'd beat him so bad he put him in a coma. When Krista thought she was pregnant and the relief I had felt when she wasn't—because having a baby with another woman would make me feel even further away from the one true love of my life. When Travis Hawthorne was released from jail and the devastation that followed. I had written it all down and it had helped, kind of like some literary Prozac.

Tonight, it was all about Indy. About how she was back in town. How she had asked me to take her to see her daddy. How she had stood over his coffin and stared down at him with tears in her eyes. How her wall of anger had finally come down and she'd reached for my hand. How my heart had longed to take her in my arms and hold her to me so I could absorb all the pain from her body. It all tumbled out of me and onto the page. About the ride we went on afterwards and the sapphire blue sky above us as she wrapped her arms around my waist and held on tight. About longing to feel her lips against mine just one last time.

Afterward, we'd gone to *Billy Joe's* in town and eaten burgers and fries, washed down with cherry colas. Her walls were down and we had talked for so long our asses stuck to the vinyl booths when we got up to leave. It was almost as if the years had peeled away. As if the old Indy was back.

When we got home, she wrapped her arms around me and whispered, "thank you" against my neck, before disappearing inside.

Now, I sat alone in my room, my body aching for my girl.

A sudden ping against the window made me look up. I stopped writing and waited. *Ping*. It was a sound I hadn't heard in years. I put down my journal and went to the window, and there she was standing in the moonlight. *Indy*. Still dressed in her jeans and boots, her arm paused in mid throw as she prepared to throw another stone at my window. I leaned down on the windowpane and couldn't hold back the smile.

"You know, you can use the door. I'm pretty sure your mama ain't gonna holler at you for being out after dark."

She smiled and shrugged. "Now where would the fun be in that?"

I grinned. I was so pleased she was back. "Want to come up?"

Her smile faded and something in her body language changed. She nodded. "Just for a bit."

She hoisted herself up, and I guided her through the window like I had a thousand times when we were kids.

"You okay?" I asked. I could see in her face that she wasn't. Her eyes were sad and there was a vulnerability to her that I hadn't seen before.

"Thank you for today," she said. "I'm pleased I went and saw him. It was good to get things off my chest."

She smiled awkwardly and wrapped her arms around her chest as if she didn't know what to do.

"You feeling okay about it?" I asked, refusing to acknowledge how beautiful she looked. Or how her tank top and tight jeans clung to her perfect body.

"I just want to forget for one night, you know. About what he did. What he became. The things he said. But I constantly bounce between missing the man he was and hating the man he became… and I'm tired, Cade. I'm tired of hating him. He was a good dad. A good husband. And then he wasn't." She tried to act like it was no big deal, but she could barely keep her tears back. I stood up and took her in my arms and held her tightly as she finally stopped fighting her emotions and sobbed into my chest. "I miss the man he was. Before he beat her. Before he cheated on her. Before he gave up on me—"

She trembled in my arms. And I longed to take the pain from her.

"He never gave up on you," I said. "He gave up on himself because he was broken hearted."

I smoothed down her hair and savored the warmth of her, closing my eyes as her scent engulfed me.

She pulled away and looked up at me.

"I'm sorry," she whispered. "I should go."

She turned to leave, but I reached out to stop her.

"Don't go," I said, my voice rough with desperation. "Stay."

She looked unsure and glanced around the room as if the answer was hidden there somewhere.

"Nothing weird," I said, trying to reassure her. "Like you said, let's just forget for one night how fucked up it all is."

She hesitated but then relaxed. She looked exhausted. "Okay."

It was weird having her in my room again. But at the same time, there was something so right about it.

It was like we were kids again.

She curled up on my bed and I sat a safe distance from her at the desk. I'm a grown man, and let's face it, I'm a fucking mountain of a human being. Not the type of guy who did sleepovers like a teenage girl. But having Indy in my room was like the old days. Before life fucked with us.

We talked for hours. About everything. Well, almost everything. Nothing about our breakup. And we laughed as we remembered all the good things, and nothing about the bad things.

Sometime after midnight, we found ourselves on the bed together. Close, but not touching. Our eyes heavy; our words muffled and sleepy.

She yawned and relaxed farther into the mattress. When she finally fell asleep, I didn't wake her. It felt good. *Right*. And I can't lie; I had a raging boner that would be pretty hard to hide. But I had no intention of getting close enough for her to notice. Too close and I didn't trust myself. If I touched her, it wouldn't be enough. I would kiss her. Undress her. And plunge so deep into her she would have no choice but to moan my name.

No. I wasn't going to fucking touch her.

Because the ice beneath us was thin, and I didn't want to risk it breaking and lose her forever. Today had been good and I wasn't going to fuck it up.

Feeling content just to have her close, I fell asleep listening to her soft breaths, but wishing more than anything that my girl would come back to me.

CHAPTER 31

CADE—Aged 14
Then

My window shuddered as it was pushed up. A few seconds later, Indy climbed through and crossed the room to my bed. I opened up my sheets and she climbed in, nestling her face into my shoulder as I secured my arms around her.

"Are you okay?" I asked when she was settled.

"I hate him," she said. "I hate him and I wish he was dead."

I released her and sat up, turning on the lamp.

"He's your daddy, Indy."

She looked at me, her eyes dark and her jaw set.

"You saw what he did, Cade. He hit my mama, right there for all the MC to see." She sat up. "And not one of them did anything to help her. Except for you."

"They were surprised."

"They were cowards!" She glared at me. "They think it's okay to do that to their women. Because they're scum and I hate them all."

"They're not all like that."

"Why are you sticking up for them?"

"Because they're good people."

"Hitting women is not okay, Cade."

"Hey, I know that. I'm not saying it's okay to hit women. Ever. I would never raise my hand to a woman. And neither would most of them."

"Oh, yeah? How would you know? Huh? How do you know what goes on behind closed doors?"

I tilted my head to the side. "Are you telling me this has happened before? That your daddy is hitting your mama."

"You live next door, Cade. How can you not know?"

I reached for her hand. "I didn't! I swear. When did it start happening?"

She looked away and shrugged. "A few months back. I mean, he'd come close a few times when they argued. But he actually went and did it last fall. I didn't see it. Just saw the bruise on her cheek the next day. I had heard them fighting the night before and put two and two together." She shook her head. "I confronted my mama but she denied it. Said she'd walked into a wall." Her shoulders sagged, and when she looked up, I saw the tears welling in her eyes. "They used to be so in love—so crazy for one another. So affectionate. So happy. But my daddy has turned mean, it's like I don't even know who he is anymore." She shrugged and looked away again. "Now it seems all they do is fight."

I took her hand in mine. I had noticed how different Jackie Parrish had become since Bolt's death. He had turned mean.

I reached for her but she stiffened.

"Hey, I would never . . ." I stopped when she lay back down and turned away.

"As soon as I can get away, I'm leaving this goddamn town," she said sharply.

I didn't know what to say. I didn't want Indy to leave. I lay down beside her and wrapped my arm around her waist. If she wanted to leave, then I wanted to leave, too.

I pulled her close and murmured into her hair. "Then we'll leave together."

She didn't say anything. She just reached around and pulled my arms tighter around her. I could feel her heartbeat against my arm and it made me sleepy again.

"Good night, Indy," I whispered.

We fell asleep, like we had a thousand times before, wrapped up in each other and safe.

But when I woke up, something was different. My body felt strange, and as I slowly came out of my dreams, I came to a sudden realization.

I'd had a wet dream.

Alarmed, my eyes flew open as a fleeting pleasure receded and stark humiliation took over.

"Are you okay?" Indy asked sleepily.

She felt for me, but her hand brushed the soggy sheet. I lurched away.

"Cade?" She sat up, confused by my reaction and the sticky sheet.

Humiliation ripped through me. It would only take her a few moments to realize what had happened.

I raced to the bathroom praying I didn't run into my mom or dad, or worse, my brothers. But it was early and the house was still and quiet.

I closed the door behind me and leaned against it, squeezing my eyes closed.

Did I have wet dreams often? No. Not if I jerked it. But Indy had been hanging out with me more and more and the opportunity never . . . arose.

There was a small tap on the door and I knew it was Indy.

"Go away," I whispered harshly, my cheeks still burning with embarrassment.

"Please open up," Indy begged softly.

"No. Go away."

I wanted the floor to open up and suck me down to hell.

"Please, Cade. Talk to me."

"I said go away."

There was a pause. Would she do as I asked and leave me alone?

Of course not.

"Cade Calley, if you don't open this door, I'm going to start hollering."

I sighed. Great. Just what I needed. Indy waking up the entire house.

I grabbed a towel off the side of the bathtub and wrapped it around my waist, then opening the door, I hustled her in.

"Quit your hollering," I whispered, closing the door behind me.

"Well, you wouldn't let me in."

"Of course, I didn't. Because I needed . . ."

"What?"

"Space. I needed space."

Indy folded her arms and she raised an eyebrow at me. "We're best friends, Cade, and best friends don't lie. I know you had yourself a wet dream."

"I did not!"

"I don't know why you're so embarrassed. It's natural." She shrugged. "Isn't that what you told me when we went to the movies last summer and I got my period. Remember? It stained my skirt and I was so embarrassed. You told me it was only natural so I shouldn't be embarrassed."

Of course, Indy had a memory like an elephant. It was almost photographic.

"So?" I shrugged uncomfortably. "That's different."

"How is it different?" She put her hands on her hips, but seeing how awkward I was, her face softened and she took a step toward me. "We don't keep any secrets from each other, remember?" She reached for my hand. "You never have to be embarrassed around me. Just honest."

The softness of her skin on my hand made my body jerk. I pulled my hand free and exhaled deeply, wondering what the hell was wrong with me.

"It's okay. I know it didn't happen because . . . well, you know . . . because of me." She lifted a shoulder and then let it drop. "It's just somethin' boys do."

She was wrong. It did happen because of her. Because she was warm and soft, and pressed up against me in my sleep. Because the sweet smell of her lingered in my sheets and on my pillow, and in the air, and for a kid whose body was just waking up to all things female, it was just too much to take. Not that I would admit it to her because that would make things weird and I didn't want her to stop staying over.

I sighed and smiled across at her, and she grinned back.

"Come on, it's time I should be going home anyway," she said, taking me by the hand again.

I pulled her back to me. "Don't leave just yet. Let's go watch the sunrise."

She smiled, and in the early morning light I thought she was the most beautiful girl in the world.

CHAPTER 32

CADE
Now

Something pulled me out of my sleep.

"Indy?"

I sat up and let my eyes adjust to the darkness and saw Indy standing at the window, staring across at her house. Dressed in nothing but her tank and panties, she turned her head at the sound of her name and came toward the bed. In the moonlight I could make out the smooth contour of her body. Her skin looked smooth as stone and her hair tumbled around her shoulders as she made her way slowly toward me.

"Are you okay?" I asked, my voice hoarse with sleep.

But Indy didn't answer, instead she climbed on the bed and slid her legs on either side of me.

The touch of her panties against my raging boner sent my desire into overload like I was a fucking thirteen-year-old boy. I was at her mercy.

"Indy—"

She cut me off with her mouth. And then her tongue.

And then her hands as they slid across the bumps of my abs and up along my chest. I didn't need any further invitation. I pulled her tank top up and held her by the hips, rocking her against me. Desire flared in my balls and shot up the length of my straining cock. And just when I didn't think I could want her any more than I already did, Indy moaned, a long, drawn-out moan that rumbled through me and packed extra dynamite to my orgasm. She felt for my cock and pushed her panties aside. And then I was there, the tip of me sliding through slippery flesh that was wet and warm. Hell, I was going to come before I was even inside her.

None of this made sense, but God, it made all the sense in the world to my balls.

She moaned my name. And it was raspy and desperate. She wanted me to fuck her. To make her forget.

"Are you sure?" I panted.

Her dark eyes filled with heat and the look she gave me was pure bad girl. "I want you to fuck me . . ."

I sat up with a rush. Sunlight assaulted my eyes while my cock raged in my jeans. I was seconds away from coming, but seeing the bed was empty beside me, my soon-to-be wet dream dissipated like smoke. What the fuck!

I fell back on the bed.

Indy had snuck out.

Just as she had always done.

CHAPTER 33

INDY
Now

I woke up, my body so tight and turned on it would only take the seam of my jeans to rub against my clit once and I'd lose it. It only took me a moment before I realized why. I was in Cade's arms and the heat of his body was wrapped around me like a cocoon. A big, warm, muscly cocoon.

My eyes flicked open.

Fuck.

I had slept over.

Worse, I had slept over in his arms.

This was bad.

The kind of bad that led to mind-blowing orgasms followed by a world of regret.

I looked at Cade. Christ, why did he have to look so hot first thing in the morning?

The way I saw it, I had two choices.

I could sneak out and pretend that having his body pressed up against me didn't excite me.

Or I could stay and give into temptation.

The throb between my legs begged me to stay. Especially when I saw the hardness punching against Cade's zipper.

I let my hand slide between my legs and felt the pulse flare into a relentless throb as it screamed at me to do something. Something with the six-foot-four wall of muscle lying next to me.

I hastily pulled my hand away.

Was I insane?

Regaining my senses, I carefully extracted myself from Cade's embrace, but froze when he stirred and moaned my name. His lips parted with a sigh but his eyes remained closed. For a moment, I couldn't move. I took in the image of him. The strong jaw with a hint of scruff. The dimples. The soft fan of dark lashes against his skin. The body that was nothing but muscle. He was beautiful. And sexy. *Too sexy.* A war ignited inside of me. Both my heart and clit pleaded with me to stay. To touch him. To wake him up with my tongue. To slide my thighs on either side of him and ride his hard cock until I was moaning his name. But my head yelled at me to leave the room and to keep running.

Before I could do anything I'd regret, I climbed off the bed and quickly left the room.

Memory lane was too tempting.

Get in and get out. No distractions. That was the plan.

"I see," my mom said as I let myself inside the house via the patio door. She was standing at the kitchen sink drinking a cup of coffee.

"No, you don't," I said rushing past her. "Nothing happened."

"That's why you're walking in here dressed in the clothes from yesterday." She took a sip of coffee and winked at me over her cup. "I'm surprised you didn't try slipping in through your bedroom window like you used to as a teenager."

I stopped. "You knew about that?"

She raised an eyebrow at me. "Oh, baby girl, please."

"Just don't read anything into it," I said, walking over to the coffee pot and pouring myself a cup.

Mom raised her hands in innocence. "Wouldn't dream of it."

Thankfully, the doorbell interrupted us and I went to answer it before Mom could say anything more about my sleepover with Cade.

It was a man from the airline, and he had my missing suitcase. Somehow it had ended up in Anchorage. And then Colorado. Then back to Seattle. Now the damn case had been to more cities in the US than me.

I thanked the airline man, tipped him twenty, and then dragged my suitcase up to my room. Five minutes later it was open on my bed, and I was staring at the clothes I had packed four days earlier. I shook my head. It was like they belonged to a stranger. Designer labels. Sensible shoes. Respectable pants. Modest shirts. I held up a floral blouse. It was designer and incredibly high quality. Not to mention, expensive. But it was also boring as hell. So were the black slacks I had packed to wear with it. And the safe leather shoes. And the patent leather belt.

"Who are you?" I whispered to myself.

My mom walked in and stood next to me. She looked at the clothes and then back to me. "Time to go shopping?"

I closed the suitcase and smiled at her. "I'll grab my purse."

She grinned. "Welcome home, baby girl."

CHAPTER 34

INDY—Aged 15
Then

I sat on the steps leading to George Jones's porch with my elbows on my knees and my fists pressed into my cheeks. Farther along the step, George Jones sat looking the other way, refusing to make eye contact with me while I shot bullets at him with my eyes. George Jones was two years older than me. He was a junior while I was a freshman. He thought he was God's gift to girls. I didn't. He thought that because he was a boy, and bigger than anyone else in our school, he could harass girls. He was wrong. And I just happened to be the one to tell him.

With my fist.

In front of us, his father, George Jones Sr., was talking with Sheriff Buckman.

It was Sunday and I was at George Jones's birthday pool party. Behind us, hidden by a tall, wooden fence, George's seventeenth birthday party was buzzing with the arrival of the police.

"I want the little troublemaker charged," George Jones Sr. said with his hands on his hips.

Above us, dark clouds rumbled with promising rain and I watched a single drop fall onto the bald spot at the back of George Sr.'s head.

"Now calm down, George. We're waiting for Veronica Calley to get here, and when she does, we will sort this out."

Ronnie was coming because my mom and dad were in Florida visiting my mom's parents. Things hadn't been good at home lately.

"Sort it out? What is there to sort out?" Mr. Jones exclaimed. Perspiration glittered on his shiny forehead. "She gave my son a black eye!"

George Jones Sr. owned the only men's clothing store in town. He wore a fancy suit jacket over a crisp white shirt and suspenders, and shoes that were so shiny you could almost see your reflection in them.

He glanced over his shoulder and gave me a foul look. I didn't know if he was waiting for me to show a hint of remorse or not, but he could wait all he wanted, I wasn't going to give him any. When he turned away, I rolled my eyes.

"I told my son not to invite her. I know who her parents are. What they do. Where she comes from. What white trash nonsense they bring to the town."

My fists tightened against my cheeks, and my nails dug into my palms. George Jones Sr. was a douchebag just like his son.

"Veronica is on her way, and once she gets here, we'll settle this," Buckman said calmly, ignoring his comments.

As if on cue, a sporty Mercedes pulled up to the curb and Ronnie climbed out. Dressed in a pair of tight blue jeans, a loose, silk top, and knee-high boots, she exuded a cool authority and commanded everyone's attention. I watched her throw her tasseled leather bag over her shoulder and close her car door. As she walked toward us, her long, curly hair swung around her shoulders and down her back.

"So, what's this about?" she asked as she came toward us, adjusting her bag over her shoulder. She looked calmly at the two Georges and then over to me.

"Indy assaulted my son," Mr. Jones said before Sheriff Buckman had the chance to explain. "And I want charges pressed."

Despite the threat, Ronnie looked unfazed and calmly folded her arms. She swept her heavy-lidded eyes over George Jones Sr. with cool disdain before slowly turning to Sheriff Buckman.

"Is this true?" she asked evenly.

"I'm afraid so," Buckman said. "She hit George in the face. Close fisted. Clocked him right in the eye."

Ronnie's expression didn't change. "And what was George doing at the time?"

"That's hardly the point," Mr. Jones snapped, turning his sweaty face red. "The little shit hit my son!"

Ronnie slowly turned back to him.

"It's been my experience, Mr. Jones, that there are always two sides to every story, and sometimes those sides vary greatly. We've heard your son's version, now let's hear Indy's."

"Version!" Mr. Jones raged. "My son's *version* is all over his fucking face!"

"Mr. Jones—"

"It's okay, Sheriff," Ronnie said coolly. She nodded to me. "Go ahead, Indy."

I looked at the three adults and then to George—who still wouldn't look at me. But his face was turned and I could see the beginnings of the shiner over his left eye.

"He was behind me when I was at the barbeque table getting a plate of food. He tried untying my bikini top. When I turned around to confront him, he and his friends laughed. I turned back to my plate of food and he did it again. I knew what he was doing. He'd done it to Mallory in the pool so her boobs fell out. He was trying get my bikini loose. So I turned around, and I warned him. I said, "I know what you're trying to do, George Jones. I don't care if this is your birthday party or not. If you do that again then I am going to lay you on your ass." That's when he reached over and tried to yank down my bikini top. He wouldn't quit." I looked at George, who finally looked at me, and I narrowed my eyes at him. "So, I made him."

George looked away.

"So you admit to hitting him?" Buckman asked.

"Of course, I did."

"Charge her!" Mr. Jones roared. "You heard the little shit, she admits it."

Ronnie's voice broke into the melee. "You want to talk about pressing charges? Go right ahead. In fact, I insist on it. Let's talk about how a seventeen-year-old boy continued to touch a fifteen-year-old girl after she told him to stop. I'm pretty sure that's the very definition of sexual assault."

Mr. Jones thrust his hands on his hips. "Now wait just a minute..."

Ronnie raised her eyebrows at him. "Wait for *what* exactly, Mr. Jones?"

"It was a prank. They were just fooling around."

"You see, that's where you're wrong. Your son was physically harassing Indy and she fended him off with reasonable force. Isn't that right, Sheriff?"

"Sounds about right, Ronnie," Sheriff Buckman said as he wrote on his notepad.

"Let's discuss the charges I want pressed on your son for trying to take the clothes off Indy without her consent."

"Take her clothes off—wait, you can't press charges! He'll never get a football scholarship to A&M. You'll ruin his life."

"Maybe your son should have thought about that before he went all grabby on a fifteen-year-old girl."

"That's not what happened—"

"I beg to differ."

"You're overreacting," Mr. Jones muttered, still refusing to see that what his son had done was inappropriate.

"Indy told him to stop," Ronnie said. "And he didn't."

"Well, maybe if she wasn't wearing such a tiny bikini . . ." Mr. Jones let his sentence trail off when we all gave him a filthy look. Well, all of us except George Jr., of course. He was too busy trying not to cry. Stupid ass.

"Don't embarrass yourself with that old chestnut," Ronnie said with a cocked eyebrow.

George Jones Sr. shifted uncomfortably on his feet. His comment had been spoken with misogynist fuckery, and he knew it.

"It's about time we start looking at bad behavior for what it really is and stop brushing it off as harmless playfulness." Ronnie raised an eyebrow at Mr. Jones. Again, her hooded eyes took him in with unflappable contempt. "How would you like it if I reached into your pants and tried to pull them down, grabbing your balls along the way?"

"What the fuck—?" Mr. Jones's eyes went so round I thought they were going to bulge right out of his head.

But Ronnie remained unfazed.

"What? Because it's a pair of balls it's somehow different than a pair of breasts?" Ronnie leaned forward. "Open your eyes. Inappropriate touching is inappropriate touching." She straightened and turned to Sheriff Buckman. "Are we free to go?"

"Free as a bird," Buckman replied, with a ghost of a smile tugging at his lips. "What about the charges against George Jr., here?"

Ronnie looked at George Jr. and he withered beneath that look because Ronnie was not someone you fucked with. "I ever hear about you touching another girl inappropriately again, there'll be trouble. Do you hear me?"

"Are you threatening my son?" Mr. Jones gawped.

"No. I'm warning your son to stop putting his hands on other people without their consent." She looked at me. "Come on, Indy. Let's go."

I walked behind Ronnie and climbed into her car. Behind me, George Jones Jr. started to cry.

"You know those charges probably wouldn't have stuck," I said, once we were inside her car. For all of my fifteen years, I knew how things worked. You didn't grow up an MC kid and not know a thing or two about prison sentences and criminal charges.

"Maybe. Maybe not," Ronnie said, pulling onto the street. "People are starting to take this kind of situation a little more seriously nowadays. And so they should. Because stop means fucking stop."

"You certainly scared them."

"Serves them right."

We pulled up to a set of lights.

"You think George had his lesson scared into him?" I asked.

"If anything, I think he will think differently before he touches someone inappropriately again."

I sighed. "The sad thing is, if Cade were here, then it would never had happened."

Ronnie looked at me and raised an eyebrow. "If Cade were here, George Jones Jr. would be in a body bag."

CHAPTER 35

CADE
Now

I didn't see Indy until after lunch because I was busy at *Spank Daddy's*. The police had been called. Apparently, one of the dancers—a feisty redhead called Bronte—stabbed her ex-boyfriend with her stiletto when he climbed on stage and tried to drag her off. By the time I got there it was fucking chaos and the club was lit up by the lights of an ambulance and a patrol car.

Something like this would usually shut us down for the night. But one call to Sheriff Buckman, and the situation was handled. The blood got cleaned up, everyone was treated to a round of free drinks, and we were back up and running like nothing had happened.

When I got back to the clubhouse, Indy was waiting out front. She stood up when she saw me, and Christ, she looked incredible. Silk shirt. Black, thigh high boots over a pair of blue jeans I wanted to undo with my teeth.

She walked toward me and all I could think about was how good it had felt falling asleep next to her last night. But I knew, *fucking knew*, if it happened again, I wouldn't be able to keep my hands off her. There was only so much a man could take.

"I wanted to thank you for last night," she said, digging her hands into her back pockets. She seemed nervous. *Cautious.* Her walls were down but she was definitely still reserved.

"It was good to hang out," I replied, trying not to notice the subtle hint of her nipples pressing against the silk of her shirt. Or the way her jeans clung to her firm thighs.

"I mean, for not taking advantage of the situation," she explained. "You know, in your bedroom last night."

Her words wiped the smile off my face.

Who the fuck did she think I was?

Some douche who couldn't get a girl to fuck him willingly, so he took advantage of her when she was emotional?

Did she really not know me?

"It's not my style," I said, pissed.

I walked past her toward the barbecue tables.

If Indy noticed what her words did to me, then she didn't show it.

"I was wondering if you had any plans?" she asked. "I thought maybe we could go for a ride to the lookout."

I turned around. At the mention of the lookout, my stomach burned with pain. I didn't go to the lookout anymore. Not since … not since losing her.

"The lookout?"

She grinned. "Yeah. Can we?"

I gave her a forced smile. "I haven't been out there for years."

"Really?"

The lookout had been one of our places. As teenagers, we'd lost hours there. Drinking. Stargazing. Watching the glittering skyline of Destiny. Making love.

My heart warned me not to go.

Spending so much time with her was a tease.

"I only have a couple of days left in Destiny. I thought it would be nice to go and see some of the old hangouts."

"You not staying for the wedding?"

Disappointment and something close to alarm spiraled through me.

"I don't think so," she said softly. "I don't belong here anymore."

I wanted to grab her and tell her that yes, yes, she did belong here. But Indy's walls had only just started to come down. I didn't want to scare her off. The tortoise won the race. Not the fucking rabbit.

"The lookout, huh?"

"Is that a yes?" she asked with a grin.

The way she smiled at me, I'd say yes to anything she wanted.

"Whatever you want."

Her grin was big.

"I just need to get something from my car, okay?" she said.

Her rental was parked across the lot. She ran toward it while I grabbed a second helmet from inside the club. As I came back outside, I saw Genevieve storm into the lot.

When she got close enough to Indy's car, she pulled a handgun out of her bag and aimed it at the tires.

Alarm ripped through me.

"Genevieve!" I yelled.

Indy looked up at the sound of my voice, and when she saw the gun in Genevieve's hand, she ran for cover.

The first bullet took out the front tire. The second pinged the front panel and echoed across the lot. The third bullet got one of the windows, the fourth lodged in the rear passenger door.

Hearing the gunfire, Davey, Isaac, Vader, Maverick, and Joker ran onto the lot.

"Genevieve, you fucking psycho fuck!" Davey screamed at his ex-old lady.

She swung around to Davey, aiming the gun in his direction. Everyone ducked for cover. "Is this why you left me, Davey? For this stuck-up city whore?" She swung back toward Indy's car and fired another shot, killing the rear tire.

"No, I left you because you're a crazy bitch," Davey yelled back, NOT helping the situation.

"I saw you. And her." She pointed the gun at Indy and I instinctively stepped in front of her. "I saw her half-naked and draped all over you yesterday morning."

"You've completely lost your mind!" Davey yelled. "She's Cade's old lady, ain't nothing to do with me. I was just giving her a lift home, is all."

"You lying piece of shit!" Genevieve screamed at him.

While she was preoccupied slinging insults across the lot to her old man, I rushed at her. She struggled but I managed to wrench the gun out of her hands without having to drive my fist into her like I wanted to. I didn't hit women. Not even crazy bitches like this loose cannon. But part of me wanted to because she had pointed a gun at Indy, and that made me see fucking red.

I pushed her away from me and I was quickly forgotten as she stormed over to Davey.

"You forget you got two kids at home? You prefer to hangout and fuck whores?"

She lunged at Davey with clawed hands but he pushed her away and she fell to the concrete.

Indy knelt down to help her up. God knows why. Considering the psycho had just pointed a gun at her and shot up her car. The old Indy would have knocked her on her ass. But this Indy was more in control.

"He's telling the truth," she said, placing a hand on her arm to help her up. "He was just giving me a lift home."

But Genevieve shook her off and gave her a scowl full of pure venom. "Why don't you go fuck yourself, you fucking city piece of shit."

I wanted to kill her. I'm not kidding, the rage was blinding. She had just pointed a gun at Indy. Shot up her car. Called her a whore.

I stepped toward her to tell her to mind her mouth, but Indy put a hand to my chest to stop me. "We're going for a ride, remember?"

I wasn't doing a very good job at hiding my wrath. My fists curled at my side as I tried to calm my temper. When I lost my mind to my rage, I was like a fucking freight train. Indy was trying to stop me before I reached that point.

"Let's not waste any more time on this," she said.

I fired a dark look at Davey. "You take care of this mess." I gestured to Indy's bullet-riddled rental car. "Get it fixed and let me know when it's done."

"Come on," Indy said, taking my hand and leading me over to my bike.

Climbing on, I helped her onto the back and secured her arms around my waist and roared out of the compound. It was the best fucking feeling in the world. My girl. On the back of my bike. With her arms wrapped around me.

Fuck the craziness happening at the clubhouse.

Nothing mattered but this.

CHAPTER 36

CADE
Now

It was late afternoon so the traffic was light. I took it easy, not wanting to rush our time together, and if I was honest, being out on the road with my girl on the back of my bike was pretty much my idea of heaven.

As we made our way up Calvary Hill to the lookout, we left the world behind us.

There was a space for parking at the top and I pulled my bike up near the edge, overlooking Destiny in the distance. Streetlights twinkled like diamonds in the dying light of dusk and stars started to appear in the indigo sky.

Indy slid off my bike and walked over to the edge, taking in the glittering view below. As I joined her, her subtle scent engulfed me.

"You okay?" I asked.

She smiled. "Let's see, I've been back in town for three days and I've already had a gun pointed at me twice. I've performed crude surgery on the side of the road to save the life of a guy who may or may not have been deliberately run off the road. And I've managed to alienate an entire motorcycle club because I'm a nasty drunk. Hmmm ... let's see, I guess my rental being riddled with bullets by a psycho ex-old lady seems ... *expected*?"

When she put it like that, I couldn't help but grin. The old Indy was back. And she seemed more relaxed. She was smiling and *goddamn* it was beautiful.

"I really am sorry," I said.

"For what? You didn't make Genevieve crazy." She gave me another smile before turning away to take in the view of Destiny sparkling below us. I watched her stretch her arms up and inhale the twilight air, fascinated by the way her face looked in the fading light. She was more beautiful than anything I'd ever seen. "I always loved this view," she said. "I used to love coming up here. With you."

She looked at me and something shimmered between us. I felt a pull so strong toward her that all I wanted to do was take her in my arms and kiss her. But I wouldn't. I couldn't scare her away from me now. If I had to, I would take all the time she needed.

"I haven't been up here in years," I admitted.

"Really? I thought this would be the perfect spot to bring all your girls."

I hated that she thought I was some kind of biker man whore.

"Indy..."

"I often thought about this place." She cut me off. "The twinkle of the city lights. The smell of the wild lavender." She turned away from the sunset, her brown eyes gleaming like dark stone in the dusk light. "You really don't come up here?"

I shook my head. "Not since ... this is where I read your letter."

At the mention of the letter, she cringed.

"It's okay," I said quietly.

Indy took a cautious step toward me, nervously shoving her hands in her back pockets. "About that—"

"It's okay." I cut her off. "I understand why you wrote it. I was crazy. I had lost my mind."

When Indy had taken off for college without me, I had followed her. Despite her demands to *stay away*. I had ridden two days to get to Seattle and then proceeded to terrify her with my craziness. I mean, I really lost my shit. I turned into a real emotional psycho. For the first time in my life, I was out of control and desperate, and completely unsure of what to do.

I was so in love with her and terrified because she didn't want me anymore. I begged her. Stalked her. Pleaded with her. I didn't sleep. Drank too much. And combined with my extreme emotional state, I became a desperate wreck who did crazy shit that frightened her. Like begging on my knees on her front stoop, with my fists pounding against her door.

In the end, she had called her father and both Jackie and my dad had turned up and dragged me back to Destiny. Back in the clubhouse, Jackie had handed me a letter from Indy. The long version was two pages of anger and disgust, peppered with swear words and some rather creative name calling. The short version: *stay away from me, you psycho—I don't want you anymore.*

It had killed me inside. But it was more than warranted.

"I was angry," Indy said softly. "I'm pretty sure I didn't mean half the stuff I wrote in it."

"Yeah, you did." I looked at her. "But it was deserved. I was an unreliable jerk who fucked up our future."

She didn't argue.

I looked across at the fading sunset, feeling regretful, feeling sad that life hadn't turned out how we had planned.

"Do you ever wonder?" I asked.

"What?'

"Where we'd be now if I hadn't gone to that the clubhouse that night?"

"Cade—"

"Do you think we would still be together?" I asked. I looked into her beautiful eyes, wishing more than ever that I had never lost this amazing woman. "That we would've followed through with all our plans?"

"Do you mean, would we be married with two-point-five children and living normal, happy family lives?"

Inside, my heart collapsed against my chest cavity. That was the future I had hoped for us before I had fucked it all up.

"Yeah."

She looked wistful. "I work long hours. Who knows if we would've survived the craziness of my residency."

I'm pretty sure we could've survived it.

There was only one thing we couldn't survive and it was the one thing I had done.

Looking at her in the fading light, my heart ached for another chance. She smiled softly but then her expression changed, like she was suddenly aware of what I was thinking and she stood back abruptly.

"I can't do this, Cade."

I took a step toward her so I was standing close. *Intimately close.* "Do what?"

"This. You. *Us.*" Her eyes dropped to my mouth and she licked her lips. The way she was looking at me sent all sorts of crazy through me.

The time was right.

I took a step closer so only a breath separated us. "Tell me you don't still love me and I will take you home."

Her big brown eyes slid up to meet mine and she hesitated long enough for me to know that she did still love me, and it filled me with hope.

"Tell me you don't love me," I whispered.

I didn't give her a chance to answer. I took her face in my hands and pressed my mouth to hers, opening those luscious lips with my tongue and kissing her hard. Caught by surprise, she resisted, but within seconds her hesitation vanished and her kiss became just as hungry and as needy as mine.

A low moan escaped me. A moment ago, this was all I had wanted. But now I wanted this and more. I wanted Indy back.

I pulled back to look in her eyes, searching for signs of how she was feeling. "I'm still in love with you."

She resisted me then and struggled to free herself from my embrace. But I wasn't having any of it. "I know you don't want me anymore, Indy. But I still love you. And after seeing you this week, I don't think I will ever love anyone like I love you. I've tried. Believe me, *I've tried*. But you're too much to get over."

For a moment, she looked alarmed. But then the old Indy turned up, and her eyes narrowed, and with a flash of anger she pushed me backwards, and slapped me hard across the face.

"Fuck you, Cade," she snapped. "What am I supposed to do with that bullshit?"

She slapped me again, harder. And I had to grab her wrist to stop a third blow.

"Stop hitting me would be a start." She tried to slap me again, but I had a firm hold on her wrist and it was enough to settle her down.

She yanked her hands free and turned her back on me.

"I'm sorry," I said, not sure what the fuck I was supposed to say.

She swung back to me. "I loved you! Do you get that. I loved you. It wasn't some teenage puppy love. Not some mild infatuation. Not some sweet, young love. You were my life. My entire fucking life. And then you went and broke me—do you understand that, Cade? You broke *me*. Not my heart, but my *everything*. Now you think you can just kiss me at sunset, tell me you still feel the same way about me, and I will fall into your arms? Are you fucking kidding me?"

Her words were like a sword plunging into my chest. But I knew she needed to do this. To vent. To get it all out. Apart from her drunken, verbal assault at Joker's birthday party, we hadn't spoken about what happened. Not sober, anyway.

We needed to get it out in the open.

She stomped forward and pushed me in the chest.

"I fucking hate you for what you did!"

When she began to pound me with closed fists I wrapped my arms around her to ward off the blows and to calm her down. She struggled, but I held her tight until her cries died down. She stopped fighting me and buried her face into my chest.

"I'm so sorry, baby." And I was. I was so fucking sorry. If I could take away her pain, I would. If I could turn back time to that night and never go to that party, I would. I kissed the top of her head and she sank her fingers into my chest, twisting them in my shirt. "It rips my heart out to know that the one thing I couldn't protect you from was me."

The night of the clubhouse party I had gotten drunk and my asshole father had spiked my drink. I ended up fucking a girl I didn't know. I was so intoxicated and high, I thought she was Indy. Never for a moment did I think I was inside of someone else. Unfortunately, I worked it out at the same time as Indy. She walked in on us when I was in the middle of coming inside a girl whose name I didn't even know. I squeezed my eyes shut at the memory. Indy broke up with me and moved away to college. Alone.

In one night, I had lost everything.

She relaxed against me and I felt her body shudder. Knowing she was calmer, I loosened my hold around her arms and pulled back to look at her. Her large, brown eyes were wet and full of pain.

My thumb brushed over the plump slickness of her lips. "I don't deserve you. Not in a million years. But tell that to my stubborn heart. It's not ready to give you up. Not now, not ever." I tucked her hair behind her ear and her eyes glittered up at me.

She frowned as she whispered, "I loved you so fucking much."

"I know." I tangled my hands in her hair and held her as close as I could. "I just hope one day you'll forgive me."

She pulled away, just slightly, so our bodies were still together, and looked up at me through her damp lashes. Christ, she was beautiful. Blinking, she raised up on her tiptoes and slowly pressed her lips to mine. It was a soft and uncertain kiss. Slow and hesitant. And I felt her breath leave her as she fisted her hands in my shirt again. With a moan, I broke it off.

"Indy—"

But Indy wasn't done. She pulled me back to her warm, soft mouth. But this time she kissed me like she couldn't get enough, and it was all I needed for my body to respond in all the usual ways.

Before I realized it, she was undoing my belt buckle and grabbing at the zipper of my jeans. Urgent hands tugged at denim and then slid between me and my boxers.

But this wasn't right.

This wasn't the way I wanted this to happen.

I wasn't going to make love to my girl for the first time in twelve years like this. No matter how hard my body was begging me to.

I pulled back, hesitating, but Indy wasn't interested in any hesitation. She wanted exactly what her hand was about to touch and... *oh, goddamn...* I groaned as she wrapped her warm fingers around me. The man in me knew I had to stop her. But my cock in her hand had other ideas.

"Wait..." I breathed.

"I'm not interested in waiting," she said, her mouth crashing to mine again.

I wanted to do the right thing, but damn, I wanted her.

Gently, I pushed her back to hold her at arm's length. We looked at each other. "This isn't going to happen," I breathed.

Her eyes darkened and her grip on me loosened. I felt her shoulders sag. "You don't want this?"

"More than you could ever know." My breathing was ragged and my cock hated me. But I had to stop her. "Not like this."

She pulled away and turned to look at Destiny in the distance. The way she bit her lower lip made me want to say *to hell with it* and give her what she wanted. Right here. Right now.

But when I reclaimed what was mine, it wasn't going to happen in the parking lot on the side of an old cavalry fort, rushed and frantic. I wanted to take my time with her. Make sure it was what she really wanted and not because she was having some emotional response to her daddy dying.

"I thought—" She stopped herself from talking and her beautiful face settled into a frown. She thought for a moment, and then nodded. "Will you take me home?"

Either she thought I was rejecting her, or she had already convinced herself that it would be a mistake. I couldn't be sure.

When we climbed on my bike, I secured her hands around my waist and she became a sweet warmth wrapped around my body.

Time to take my girl home.

And to take back what was mine.

CHAPTER 37

INDY—Aged 17
Then

Grass tickled the back of my arms as I lay with my face tilted toward the sun. It was an unusually hot day for February. The sky was clear and the sun was shining brightly. The smell of freshly cut grass drifted across the football field on a warm breeze. Spring was coming.

"You're lying!" Mallory Massey's husky voice broke into my sun-lulled daydream.

"I swear to God it's true," Abby protested. "He slid his arm around my neck and said, 'Come here, beautiful.' And then slobbered his kiss all over my mouth. It was like making out with a slug."

The three of us were lying on the grass embankment overlooking the field where a group of kids from our high school played a game of football. It was an informal game. Most of them didn't even have shirts on. Abby was filling Mallory in on her date with Jamie Brown, captain of the debate team at school. She liked his ability to argue, but apparently his make-out skills were less than satisfactory.

Mallory giggled again. "Slug kissing is the worst!" She sighed and then made a noise like she was devouring a big chocolate brownie that was the most delicious thing she'd ever tasted. "Now there is someone who wouldn't slug kiss you. I imagine his lips and tongue would kiss you all the way into nirvana," she said and then sighed again.

"Who?" Abby asked.

"Cade," Mallory replied.

I opened my eyes and sat up at the mention of Cade's name.

"You want to kiss, Cade?" I asked.

"Oh, finally, she's awake," Abby said. "Welcome back."

I poked my tongue out at her and then continued to question Mallory. "As in Cade Calley?"

"Of course, Cade Calley, silly." Mallory shivered as if the mere mention of his name was enough to excite her. "That boy has muscles in all the right places."

I followed her gaze to the football game on the field. Cade had hold of the ball and was running for the imaginary line. He wore jeans but no shirt or shoes, and sweat gleamed on a well-developed torso packed with muscle and power. When had Cade gotten so big? I had lived next to him nearly my whole life and I couldn't remember him transitioning from a boy to . . . to that.

"You're ogling my cousin like you're going to eat him," Abby said to Mallory, pulling a face. "That is so gross."

"He's so fine. I know you can't agree with me—"

"I *don't* agree with you. *Don't.* Not can't. Don't."

"—but what about you, Indy? Don't you think he is just as fine as spun gold?"

I watched as Cade powered across the field, his muscles pulling and flexing as he ran. When he touched down, he thrust two muscled arms above his head and something inside me began to tingle.

I looked at Mallory. I guess you could call her the more-experienced girl in school. She wore tight clothes, lots of makeup, bright jewelry—including big hoop earrings she never took out, and lots of bangles. She also chewed a lot of gum, which she was doing now. I watched as she blew a big pink bubble and then smacked it against her bright red lips.

The idea of those red lips brushing against Cade's suddenly irritated me.

"I don't even know what that means," I said, annoyed. I wasn't sure what annoyed me most. Mallory and her stupid metaphors. Or the idea of her putting her red lips all over him.

If Mallory sensed my irritation, then she didn't show it.

"I'm going to ask him out," she said, eating him with her eyes. She turned to me, "I think he likes me. Do you think he'll go out with me?"

Jealousy coiled in the pit of my stomach. "How would I know?"

"Because you guys are like the biggest BFFs," Mallory said with a dramatic eye roll.

"We're not as close as we used to be," I said softly. And it was true. Lately, something had changed between us. He was a little distant. Moody. Busy. Sometimes I just didn't understand him. It was almost as if I irritated him.

"Well, I'm going to ask him out," she continued. "And I'm going to kiss him."

That sealed it. The idea of Mallory devouring him with those experienced, scarlet lips made me want to punch her in the mouth.

I looked away and picked at the grass.

"Hey, girls," came a familiar, baritone voice.

I looked up. Cade was walking off the field, looking too delicious for words as he approached us. Sitting cross-legged, I shifted uneasily.

"Hey there, yourself," Mallory replied, popping another pink bubble against her red lips and looking at Cade through her long lashes. He stopped at her feet and grinned down at her when she offered him a bottle of water from our cooler.

"You're an angel," he said, taking the bottle from her and twisting the cap.

I watched him bring the bottle to his mouth and my breath stopped short in my chest as his lips parted and he began to drink down the cool water. My stomach tightened and then flared with the strangest of sensations. When he pulled the bottle from his mouth, water dripped from his beautiful lips and slid down his throat to mingle with the sweat on his chest. My throat felt like sandpaper and I struggled to swallow. He smiled and it was like the world suddenly slowed and everything in it went in slow motion. The thud of my heartbeat. The whirl of my blood in my ears. Even the birds seemed to lumber in the sky above us. He turned to me and when those beautiful blue eyes found mine, his smile grew bigger and two dimples appeared on either side of his beautiful mouth.

That was when it became crystal clear. Right there in that moment.

I had fallen in love with my best friend.

CHAPTER 38

INDY
Now

It was official. I was crazy.

What the fuck had I been thinking, kissing Cade like some love-sick moron? Had I completely lost my fucking mind?

On the ride home I replayed my foolishness over and over in my head, so by the time I arrived home I felt stupid.

The house was dark when we pulled up. Mom had messaged me earlier. She was at the clubhouse with Ronnie and Bull, which was a relief because I wanted to drown my embarrassment with a shit load of wine.

And I wanted to drown alone.

I climbed off the bike and mumbled a pitiful goodbye to Cade, fully expecting him to leave. But he didn't. Instead, he followed me up the tidy driveway and waited for me to unlock the front door.

I made a second attempt at a goodbye, which involved absolutely avoiding any kind of eye contact with him and pretending I hadn't just launched myself at my ex-boyfriend like a psycho.

But Cade wasn't having any of it.

"I'm making sure you get inside," he insisted.

I didn't want him to be so chivalrous. Mentally, I'd already sought out my first bottle of wine. I just needed him to leave. I was embarrassed. Hurt. Angry at myself for kissing him and wanting more. From this moment on, I would be immune to his charm and bullshit sexual aura. I didn't care how big and sexy he was. I was done.

Reluctantly, I opened the door and we stepped inside. Trying to avoid eye contact, I turned around to tell him he could leave. But as soon as he closed the door behind us, he grabbed my wrist and pulled me to his powerful chest, crashing his mouth to mine and holding me tightly against his hard body. Completely taken by surprise, I whimpered and then, like the sucker I am, gave into the eruption of desire crashing through me.

With a rush, he pushed up against the door and kissed me fiercely, moaning into my mouth as he captured my lips and thrust his tongue in.

Remember the girl who was going to be immune to his potent charms and overwhelming sexual aura?

Yeah, that girl—she was gone. But what the hell. I had a throbbing need to travel down memory lane...just once.

With that thought, any reservations about what I was about to do turned to ashes and fluttered away on the cool, twilight breeze.

Tonight didn't count.

I reached for the top of his jeans and slid my hand across the hardness behind the zipper, ripping at his belt buckle and pulling it free. Cade returned the favor and had me out of my jeans faster than you could say *I'm a ridiculous human being and I really shouldn't be doing this.*

He hoisted me up into his arms, effortlessly, and I wrapped my legs around his hips, his hard cock seeking me out like the pussy-seeking missile it was.

Like I weighed no more than a feather, he carried me down the hallway to my bedroom, kissing me wildly as he walked, turning me on more than I thought was possible.

I'd forgotten how glorious Cade was at kissing. How perfect our mouths fit to one another's and it was robbing me of all my common sense.

I was so turned on. Every part of me was a piston firing heat and pleasure to the one magical spot that would erupt with little effort if he kept kissing me the way he was.

We paused only long enough for Cade to slip on that all-important layer of latex. And I had to admit, all types of crazy went off inside of me as I watched him take his cock in his hand and roll the condom down the impressive shaft. I remember him being big, but in reality, he was so much bigger.

He sat on the edge of the bed and I slid my legs on either side of him, kneeling slightly above him as he took my mouth with his.

"I want you so badly . . ." He moaned between kisses. His hands slid up and down my thighs and cupped my naked ass. "I've wanted you for so long."

"Then allow me to oblige," I whispered in his ear at the exact time I sank down onto him.

Pleasure blasted through me, and my moan was so powerful it forced my head back. He filled me, stretched me, his cock searing through the slickness of me, and making me feel so deliciously full of him. I reached for his shoulders, which were hard and broad, to help steady me as I rode his cock with fervor. He was so physically powerful. Strong. Formidable. I ducked my head to kiss him, slowing my hips to grind hard and slow against him, making my body swell with sweet tension.

Cade responded with noises that sent fireworks off through every nerve and fiber of my being. He gripped my ass with his big hands, driving his hips up as I rode him.

"You feel so good…" he moaned, his face showing the pleasure spiraling throughout his body. "I've missed you so much … so … . damn … much."

The feeling was mutual.

I had forgotten how good his cock felt to ride. I kissed him greedily, deep and ravenous. It wasn't going to take me long because it had been months, *years*, since I'd had sex this hot.

That, and the fact that when it came to sex we were a perfect fit.

Cade's big hands slid up my body to my neck and cupped my jaw as he took our kissing to a new level of hot. His big hands held my face to his while his lips and tongue set my mouth on fire with fierce kisses. Lust roared through me. His cock was so big, so hard, and at this angle it was hitting every erotic spot deep inside of me, stirring the growing arousal.

Oh God. This was too good.

Nothing good was going to come from this, but damn if I cared.

"You're going to make me come so hard," he moaned into my mouth.

My inner muscles clenched around him at the thought, tightening against his erection as I rode him slowly, *deeply*. The pleasure was insurmountable but there was something else. A strange emotion buzzed around us.

But I refused to think about it. This was nothing. What we were doing … was nothing. I needed fucking and Cade had always been good at the task. It was a one-time thing.

But as my climax swelled in me, our eyes locked and neither of us could look away. What we were doing, it was spellbinding.

The look on his face. It sent me over the edge and his name fell from my lips.

We came together and it was blinding. Ecstasy burst inside of me. I shuddered, and collapsed against his warm chest, certain my legs had turned to liquid.

Cade's heart thundered against my cheek and we both struggled to catch our breath.

I climbed off him and was immediately aware of the emptiness. My muscles clenched as if looking for the fullness of him. But it was done. Memory lane was closed.

I sank into my bed and closed my eyes, and let the haziness take me away.

CHAPTER 39

CADE
Now

Once was never going to be enough. I'd already made up my mind before drowning in the pleasure of my first orgasm.

The first one—that was to release the tension of twelve years of separation.

The second one—that was going to be a reminder of just how perfect our bodies worked together. When I finished with her, Indy was going to remember all the reasons why we *should* be together and none of the reasons why we *shouldn't*.

She lay on her stomach, her eyes closed and every glorious inch of her naked.

In the hazy stillness, I reached for her, my fingertips finding the smooth planes of her shoulder and trailing an invisible line along the curve of her throat to tuck a lock of hair behind her ear. A soft sigh escaped her parted lips as she stirred.

A strange feeling hung in the air. A thousand different emotions soared through me.

She opened her eyes but didn't say anything as she looked at me. And man—my dick hardened as soon as I saw those long lashes lift and those beautiful brown eyes focus on me.

I could spend forever looking into them.

She slid her fingers through the sheets until they reached me, then skimmed them down the length of my body until they curled around my already hard cock.

There was no need for words.

I rolled her over and slid between her legs, kissing her slowly as I pressed my pelvis into her, slowly waking her up. I coaxed her out of her sleepiness with my mouth and reawakened her body with the heat of my own. She whimpered beneath me and tightened her legs around my hips, wanting me in her, wanting me to make love to her, shifting her perfect little butt so her pussy was right there for the taking.

I pulled away, barely able to hold back from entering her bareback, and reached for a condom. She watched with hooded eyes as I tore the foil package open with my teeth and slid the layer of latex over my cock. She licked her lips and it was all I needed. As I leaned down to kiss her, I put myself right where I needed to be and with my mouth moving over hers, pushed deep into her tight body, right to the very hilt. She moaned into my kiss and dug her nails into the muscles of my back, her hips moving in a leisurely rhythm to meet every stroke as I slowly made love to her.

I couldn't stop kissing her. Loving her.

Our bodies and panted breaths were all the guidance we needed as we made love, long and slow, deep and hard.

When I knew she was close, I slowed down, grinding my pelvis into hers, my arms holding me up so I could look into her beautiful face as I moved deep and slow into her body. And she didn't look away, so I knew she could feel it, too. What we were doing, what was happening between us, we were awakening fires that not even twelve years could extinguish.

I wanted to tell her I loved her. But words would break the spell. So I showed her with my body, with every deep thrust of my hips, with every moan and kiss into her mouth, with every stroke of my tongue against hers.

Christ, I love her. I love her so damn much.

"Cade..." she moaned breathlessly.

She was going to come. Her sweet, sweet pussy clenched tightly around me, pulsing as her orgasm consumed her, and Jesus Christ, there was only so much one man could take. This was bliss.

Pure. Fucking. Bliss.

I moaned into her mouth and she gripped me tighter with her legs and rocked harder. It took everything I had not to come. I had waited a long time for this and wanted it to last all night. But she felt too good—*this* felt too good—and out of nowhere, the ecstasy overcame me.

"Oh God, Indy..." I grabbed her face between my palms, and kissed her as hard as I could. I let go of my restraint, and spilled hard into the girl I had lost once, but who I would never let go of again.

CHAPTER 40

CADE
Now

"Why are you in such a cheerful fucking mood?" Bull asked when I put a beer down in front of him. We were about to start chapel. "Got something to do with an old flame being back in town?"

"Maybe," I shrugged, taking a seat at the table. "Or maybe I'm just a happy guy."

"I think he lost his virginity last night," Isaac piped up, reaching into his pocket for a cigarette.

"You finally pop your cherry, son? Good on you." Joker patted my shoulder as he joined us at the table.

"Can't a guy smile without all you dicks thinking something of it?"

"That smile has pussy written all over it," Bull said.

"Literally, has pussy all over it," Isaac added.

I gave all of them a good look at my middle finger. "Jealous, ladies?"

"Hell yeah!" Joker said, sliding into his chair and dancing his beer bottle around on the table with one finger. "If I had a woman like that, man—!"

I stopped Joker from finishing his sentence with a look. If he started talking smack about my girl the way he talked about his club girls, then I was going to put that damn beer bottle right where the sun didn't shine.

"Right, let's get down to business," Bull said. "Is everything organized for Jackie's send-off tomorrow?"

Grunt leaned forward. As SIA, it was his responsibility to oversee the funeral arrangements with the family.

"It's all good. Everything is organized," he said. "And I gotta say, man, Mrs. Stephens is one awesome chick. She organizes things with military precision."

Mrs. Stephens was like a personal assistant to the club. She helped out with organizing events, took care of the finer details when it came to ensuring things went off without a hitch, and was even known to help Tito out with events at Head Quarters. You knew things were done right when she was entrusted to do them.

Somewhere in her forties, she was nothing like the women of the MC. She dressed in knee-length skirts and cardigans, and looked like she was going to teach math class. But while she looked conservative, she didn't bat an eyelid at ordering six girls and a Jell-O wrestling pool for a night's entertainment.

Grunt stood up. "Being that it's the day before the funeral of one of our fallen…" The door to the chapel opened and Mrs. Stephens appeared carrying a tray of shot glasses, Cubans, and a bottle of Chivas Regal whiskey. She put a shot glass down in front of each King and filled it with the $5,000 whiskey, placed the Cuban beside it, and then left without a word.

She was a strange one, but I was willing to bet a million dollars that there was a wildcat somewhere beneath those layers of tweed.

Bull lit his cigar and the sweet aroma of fine tobacco filled the room as we all followed suit. We all stood and raised our glasses.

"To Jackie," Bull said.

"To Jackie!" We threw back our whiskey. It was warm and smooth, and the room rippled with twelve grown men sighing in satisfaction.

"Let's make sure tomorrow goes without a hitch," Bull said, looking around the table. "Thankfully, this isn't something we have to do all the time. So let's make it a good one."

With a smack of the gavel, chapel was over.

I didn't stick around at the clubhouse for any longer than I needed to. The entire time I was away from her, all I could think about was Indy and how I wanted to get back to wherever she was. I ran into Lady talking to Mrs. Stephens, and she said Indy was at home watching old movies. That there was an 80's movie marathon on. I knew they were her guilty pleasure. *Breakfast Club. Pretty in Pink. Some Kind of Wonderful.* She would be glued to that TV screen all night.

I grabbed some Chinese takeout and a bottle of wine on the way, looking forward to spending some time with my girl.

Except when I got to her house, Indy wasn't alone.

She was with a guy.

And he had his arms around her.

I saw them through the open curtains when I pulled my bike up to the curb and climbed off. They were on the couch and he had his arm draped over her shoulder as she leaned forward, her face in her hands.

When she heard my bike, she raised her head and looked out onto the street in my direction.

I just stood there like a dick, watching some guy rub her back as she stared out the window at me. When he leaned forward and planted a kiss on that exquisitely tender spot between her ear and jaw, the bottle of wine dropped from my hand and smashed to the ground. Red wine splattered like blood across the concrete. Last night I had buried my face in that exact spot when I'd come inside her, and now he was kissing it?

Anger tore through me. My initial reaction was to rip open the front door and pull him away from her, and then beat the absolute fuck out of him so he would never touch her again. But an overwhelming sense of betrayal froze me to the spot. Indy wasn't fighting him off.

She wanted him to touch her.

Gutted, I watched her stand up, say something to him and then disappear from the room. The front door opened, and after closing it behind her, Indy made her way down the driveway to me.

"What are you doing here, Cade?"

I wasn't one for beating around the bush, so I basically got straight to the point.

"Why is he touching you?" I asked, feeling so full of anger and grief I had no idea how I was going to contain it. "Is he your boyfriend?"

My nostrils flared and I couldn't keep the sharpness out of my voice.

Indy sighed. "He's not my boyfriend, Cade."

I relaxed a little, letting the relief flood through me.

But it was short lived.

"He's my fiancé."

It was like a bomb went off inside of me.

Heart. Obliterated.

"Your fi—are you fucking kidding me?" Rage tore through me. My anger was ferocious and knew no bounds. I kicked the already broken bottle of wine across the driveway and punched the Chinese takeout sitting on my gas tank, across the yard.

Indy just sighed. "Can we not do this here? Not now."

"Yes, here. Yes, now!" I strode right up to her, but she didn't flinch. She would never flinch. Because she knew that no matter how angry—how volatile I got—I could never hurt her. And I was as pretty volatile as I had ever been. I was ready to go medieval on someone's ass.

She put her hand on my chest and pushed me back. "I will talk to you tomorrow."

She was trying to get rid of me.

So she could spend the night with *him*.

The pain that shot through me almost blinded me.

"Are you fucking him?" The words launched themselves out of my mouth before I could stop them. And then the realization hit me. Of course, she was fucking him. He was her goddamn fiancé.

Indy stopped walking away and turned back to look at me.

"Go home, Cade."

But I couldn't let it go. I stepped into her, grabbing her hand to stop her from turning away from me again.

"Indy, please—" I was ready to fucking beg.

What the fuck was going on?

"I didn't know he was coming," she said. "But he is here now. And he is here for me."

My stomach muscles clenched and pain flared out to my chest, squeezing my heart.

"So, that's it? We're done?" I asked incredulously.

Her dark eyes found mine. "Yeah. We're done."

CHAPTER 41

INDY
Now

My father was buried with all the fanfare of an MC funeral. Kings of Mayhem charters from California, Nebraska, Tennessee, Oklahoma, and as far as North Dakota descended on the small town of Destiny. You could hear the rumble of Harleys for miles. Some of the townsfolk lined the streets. The Kings had a lot of friends in Destiny and there was a strong feeling of support for one of their fallen.

I drove to the church in my daddy's restored Impala with my mom, Ronnie, and Anson. We followed the hearse that carried my daddy's coffin. Bull, Cade, Isaac, and Caleb led the funeral procession, while the rest of the club and other charters followed behind us. It was an ostentatious display of club power. Rumbling Harleys. Somber-looking bikers. Charter flags proudly displaying the club's insignia and the state from which they came.

When we arrived at the church, Cade pulled up beside us and parked his bike. He opened the door for my mom but barely looked in my direction, his jaw fixed and rigid. I knew he was hurting. I knew he was confused. And I felt bad. Because I had lied to him.

Anson wasn't my fiancé. Or my boyfriend. *Not anymore.* Once upon a time we had talked about marriage. There was even a ring. But now we were just friends. His surprise arrival was the handbrake I needed to slow down what was happening between Cade and I. He was the shield I needed while I tried to work out my tangled emotions because things were racing out of control and I needed to catch a breath.

But now I felt guilty. I had hurt Cade and it was the last thing I wanted to do.

But we would both have to suck it up because today wasn't about us. It was about saying farewell to my daddy and being there for my mom.

Inside, the church overflowed with mourners. Mainly bikers, but other family members and friends, and people from town, as well. I sat in the front row, my face rigid with unshed tears. I felt sick and had to keep swallowing mouthfuls of spit. The last time I'd sat in this church had been eighteen years ago when my brother had passed away.

Tears welled in my eyes when I thought of Bolt. And then my dad. And then Bolt and my dad playing baseball in our front yard. They had been close. Even so, I didn't think Bolt would have ended up in the club. He had dreams of being so much more than a club member. He was a curious soul. He wanted to explore the world. He loved ancient history and archaeology. He would have travelled the world and his life would have been rich in knowledge and interesting experiences.

But he was gone now. Nothing but dust.

I wondered if he and our daddy were playing baseball up in heaven.

The thought brought on another wave of emotion. I glanced around me in an effort to keep my tears at bay. Unfortunately, I looked straight at Cade, who was already looking at me, and for the longest moment, neither of us could look away. His face was set, his strong jaw firm. He was fighting back emotion but doing a good job at concealing it.

I turned away and focused on Father Murphy in front of me. Anson slid his hand over mine, but I pulled my hand away and wiped a non-existent tear from my cheek.

My mom wept quietly throughout the service, then openly sobbed into a tissue as six pallbearers—including Cade—picked up my daddy's coffin and carried it back outside the church to an awaiting hearse for his final journey to the cemetery.

Daddy's coffin was lowered into the ground as the bright Destiny sun warmed our backs and a gentle breeze blew in from the south. Mom knelt by his grave and cried while I stared at my toes. I felt empty. I wanted to run back to Seattle, to my safe, comfortable life.

Ronnie touched my elbow. "Come on, honey. Let's get your mama back to the clubhouse for your daddy's farewell."

In the back of the car, I curled into my mom like I used to as a kid, and she wrapped her arms around me. I felt her sigh and her breathing calmed. We didn't talk, but the affection was comforting and warm. Anson sat in front with Ronnie, quietly taking in the landscape of Destiny as it rolled past.

"Are you okay, Mama?" I asked when the car pulled up at the clubhouse.

She smiled softly. Her tears had dried and she was composed. It was typical of my mom. She had done what she needed to do, allowed herself to feel the pain and emotion of her loss, but now she would square her shoulders and get on with things. She wouldn't wallow in her heartache; she would take that first tentative step in moving forward. It's what the women of the MC did.

"I'm going to be fine." She squeezed my hands. "And so are you."

Our shared smile was warm and my heart swelled. I missed her. I couldn't even remember the last time we'd been this close. My chest tightened. Maybe running home to Seattle the following day was a bit too soon. Maybe I could stay just a few more days and get in some much-needed time with my mom. Plus, Mirabella had been pretty insistent about me staying for the wedding.

The clubhouse was already bustling with activity when we walked in.

I sat with my mom and made idle chit-chat with everyone who stopped by our table to offer their condolences. I was determined to keep my mind off Cade and the things that had happened over the past couple of days. But that was a lot easier in theory than practice. I couldn't help but seek him out in the crowd of Kings of Mayhem cuts, and every time I saw him, my stomach flared with longing.

Twelve years apart had done little to ease the affect he had on me. I could accept that now. I just needed to keep myself at a safe distance from him before I fucking fell into bed with him again and lost another little piece of my heart.

When he approached the table, my mom took one look at Cade's face and she knew. She glanced at me, and then back at him again, and I saw the realization flicker across her face. She squeezed my hand and then excused herself with some bullshit about using the restroom.

"Thanks for helping organize all of this," I said to Cade once we were alone.

He nodded curtly and his jaw ticked. "It's what family does."

An awkwardness hung in the air.

"How are you?" I asked, feeling uncomfortable.

"I'm fine." But he wasn't, he and I both knew that. "What about you? Are you okay?"

I could see he was struggling with his feelings toward me and about Anson not just being my boyfriend, but my fiancé. He was hurt. Confused. Angry. And I got it. Actually, I depended on him feeling all that stuff. Because then maybe, just maybe, he would stay the fuck away from me like I needed him to.

I nodded, avoiding his handsome face by studying my toes. "Yes. Thank you."

But when I looked up and saw the hurt and thinly veiled heartache, I couldn't bring myself to look away. He was clenching his jaw and barely containing his emotions. His blue eyes glittered like sapphires. "Well, I guess I'll leave you to it."

I struggled to swallow the giant lump in my throat. And in that moment, I wanted to say and do so many things. I wanted to throw my arms around him and inhale his familiar and comforting scent deep down into my soul. I wanted to trust that I could fall in love with this man, be with him, and know that without a doubt, my heart was safe with him. Safe from hurt. Safe from aching. Safe from being ripped out of my chest by him when he fucked another woman.

But that would never happen. Because Cade was the object of desire for almost every woman he met. They wanted him. They wanted to touch him. Flirt with him. Fuck him. And while he barely glanced at them now, I couldn't live with the threat that one day he might.

My heart hardened and I raised my chin. Yeah, one day he might just do that. *Again.*

"Thanks," I said, deciding in that very moment that no matter how much I wanted to be in his arms again, I would do whatever it took to keep Cade at a safe and unfuckable distance.

And with that I stood up and walked away.

CHAPTER 42

CADE
Now

I made sure I avoided them throughout Jackie's wake and then left early, taking off into the dusk on my bike. I rode for hours—in no real direction, with no real destination. I just couldn't be around them. *Indy and Anson.*

Engaged. She was fucking engaged. To that preppy fucktard!

I felt gutted. My dream of a future with Indy was not just out of my reach, it was blown to smithereens like a fucking car bomb.

I wasn't sure how long I rode for. But when I pulled into my mom's driveway later that night, the moon was high and the stars were bright, and apart from the streetlights that lined the sidewalk, the street was cloaked in darkness.

When I climbed off my bike I glanced over at Indy's window. It was dark and there were no signs of life. But she was there. With him. And knowing she was sleeping in his arms on the other side of that glass was torture. Pure fucking torture.

I could've slept at the clubhouse. I should've. But there was that pathetic need in me to at least be close to her while I could, even if she was with another man. In a few days she would be gone and I would have to learn to live without her all over again.

Feeling that all-too-familiar ache in my chest, I turned my back and made my way inside my house, and headed straight to the bottle of Jack in the liquor cabinet.

Drinking her off my mind had never worked before. But damn if I wasn't going to give it another try.

The following day, the club held a memorial barbecue for Jackie. I didn't want to go but I couldn't avoid it. All members were expected to be there.

It wouldn't be a somber affair like the wake. This was the opportunity for everyone to celebrate, drink, listen to music, reminisce, and get messy. There would be booze, barbecue, live music, and women. When it came to hosting visiting charters, the Kings of Mayhem Originals knew how to put on a good party.

I was in the bar of the clubhouse when Indy and Anson walked in. I told myself to look away, but there was a serious communication breakdown between my brain and my eyes. So I just stood there, like a dick, beer bottle half-way to my lips, unable to tear my gaze off them.

It took Joker patting me on the back to pull my attention away from them.

"Looks like Indy traded up in her absence," he joked, shaking his head and flipping open a beer bottle. As he walked past, I gave him a special salute with my middle finger.

I took a long pull of my beer, draining it before banging it down on the counter. I stole another glance at Indy and Anson as they made their way in the opposite direction, stopping so Indy could introduce Anson to Isaac and Cherry, and Cherry's sister, Ashlee.

My heart ached at the sight of them. I just didn't get it. What the hell was the other night all about? I thought I had my girl back. Then I saw the look in Indy's eyes and I realized the other night wasn't about reconnecting at all. It was her saying goodbye.

I watched Anson slide his arm around her waist. Fury tore through me and it took everything I had to restrain myself from throwing him against the wall and fucking him up for having his hands on my girl. For touching her. For loving her. For offering her the life she deserved—the one I couldn't.

Indy didn't even glance my way, but she knew. I could see it all over her face. She knew what was taking place inside me and she didn't even flinch. *Payback's a bitch, Cade.*

With my fists at my side, I drew in a deep breath and nodded. I had broken us all those years ago, but Indy had just closed the book on us for good.

I took one final look at the girl I would never have, and without another word, I walked away.

It was more than an hour later when I caught up with Indy at the bar. I couldn't see where Anson was, but I didn't give a fuck and took advantage of the moment alone with her.

She was flipping the tops off a couple of beers when I came up behind her.

"Does he know how well I know you?" I said, standing right behind her so she had nowhere to go, my lips brushing her ear as I leaned in and asked, "Inside and out?"

She swung around to glare at me.

"That's none of your business," she snapped.

"See, that's where you're wrong." My eyes burned into hers. "It became my business the moment you climbed on my cock and cheated on him."

She barely flinched at my words. I'd just accused her of cheating on her fiancé and her face remained completely unresponsive. She had one hell of a poker face.

Planting her palms on my chest, she pushed me back.

"You think because I fucked you that you know everything about me?" She cocked an eyebrow at me, her gaze unwavering as she said, "You know nothing about me or my relationship."

"Maybe I don't. But let's recap what I do know." My eyes narrowed slightly as I struggled to regain my temper. "I know that the night before last you wanted nothing more than to make love to me. That while your fiancé was back in Seattle, you were loving me. Touching me. Begging me to make love to you. And it wasn't fucking. So don't try to deny it. You made love to me because you still fucking love me. Just like I love you. So why don't you quit fucking lying to me and admit it."

She took a step toward me and stared right into my eyes. "So what if I do. It wasn't enough last time, so why in the hell would it be enough now?"

And then pushing past my shoulders, she walked away from me.

CHAPTER 43

CADE—Aged 17
Then

I lay on my bed and tried not to look. I tried not to feel what I was feeling. Tried to ignore the physical yearning and pleading of my body when I thought of her. But I couldn't. And even though I knew it was wrong, I turned my head to look out the window and across into Indy's bedroom and watch as she stepped out of the sundress she'd been wearing and let it drop to the floor. My body ached for her and my heart longed to feel her in my arms. I wanted to do the things to her that I did with Mallory Massey, Cathy Winters, and Jane Peters.

And Kelly Brunton from PE class.

And Julie Anderson who was a grade above us and who liked to sneak me dirty notes when we passed each other in the school corridor between classes.

But this was Indy we were talking about. *My Indy*. My best friend for as far back as I could remember. I had no business wanting to do those things with her. I loved her too much.

Yet lately, every time I saw her, my stomach would twist like a tightly coiled spring. And at night, my body would heat up and harden with thoughts I usually saved for Mallory, Cathy, Jane, Kelly, and Julie. And every other goddamn female, because let's face it, I was a seventeen-year-old boy and all of a sudden, every feeling, every sensation I had was heightened like I was on some kind of mind-blowing drug.

But I didn't act on my feelings toward her. I hid them. I tried to distance myself from her, and I would keep distancing myself from her until I felt normal again. But it had been weeks—months, and my longing for her was only getting stronger.

So, I resorted to this, sitting here on my bed in the dark like a fucking freak, staring across the yard at her bedroom window, watching her undress.

Call me perverted.

Call me a fucking psycho.

But it was better than confessing to her that I was in a permanent state of longing for her. She would laugh at me. Hell, she'd probably put her fist in my jaw and call me a fucking weirdo.

She wouldn't be wrong.

If it weren't for the fact that Mallory was coming over later, I'd probably have to take care of what was raging in my jeans.

But for now, I would have to settle for silently watching the girl I had fallen in love with but could never have.

She disappeared from view and I waited, wondering what she was up to. When she reappeared, she was wearing jeans and a simple tank top. Even from this distance I could see the muscle tone of her arms, and the smooth tan she had gotten over the summer. I watched, mesmerized, as she brushed her long blonde hair and pulled it back into a ponytail. Desire tore through me. In my mind, she smelled like sunshine and jasmine, and her skin felt like velvet to touch. In my mind, her lips were like wine and I longed to drink from her.

Oh Christ.

What. The. Fuck. Was. Wrong. With. Me.

I heard a car pull up. Even though I couldn't see from where I sat on my bed, I knew it would be Mallory. She was early. But when the knock on the door didn't come to my front door, I leaned forward to get a better look out the window, and saw Tommy Baker standing on Indy's front step.

Alarm lurched through me.

What the fuck was Tommy Baker doing at Indy's house?

I rushed to the window and gripped the windowsill until I was white knuckled.

Seconds later, Indy's front door opened and Jackie Parrish filled the doorway.

Relief flooded through me. No way in hell Jackie would let that preppy little fuck anywhere near his daughter.

Yeah, Jackie. You stop that sonofabitch from being anywhere near your daughter. He's a skeeze, Jackie. A real skeeze.

But relief turned to panic when I saw them shake hands and Jackie invited him inside. Granted, Jackie didn't look impressed, but then, Jackie never did. It didn't mean he saw Tommy for the douche that he was. I gripped the windowsill even tighter until the tips of my fingers stung with pain.

Indy's light turned off and I watched in misery as the front door opened again, and she stepped into the dusk with Tommy Baker at her side.

They were going on a date.

Heat prickled at the base of my skull.

If he touched her, I was going to break every bone in his dweeby little body.

I grabbed my phone and texted Mallory. *Sorry, babe, have to cancel tonight.*

I couldn't hang out with Mallory now. Not when Indy was out with that douchebag. Last week he had bragged in the locker room about finger fucking Mindy Carlton. Last month it was about Laura Hope, and how he'd fucked her in the back seat of his daddy's Ford. If he bragged about Indy that way...

I turned around and punched a hole in my wall. Pain glowed in my knuckles but I couldn't care less. Not when my girl was out with a maggot.

I waited until they left, then knocked on her front door.

Jackie answered almost immediately. "What can I do for you, son?"

"Is Indy home?" I asked, knowing full well she wasn't.

"Just missed her. Gone to the movies with some preppy kid from school."

There was only one cinema in Destiny, so it would be easy to find them.

I played it cool. "Okay, no problem. Guess I will catch up with her tomorrow."

Jackie's eyes glittered across at me from his heavily bearded face. And something told me that he knew what was going on. "They didn't go to the movies in town. Said they was going to see some early release over in Humphrey."

Yeah, Jackie knew, all right. He knew exactly how I felt about his daughter. Hell, he had probably known longer than I had.

"Thanks," I said.

I didn't even bother waiting until I was out of sight before running to my car. I jumped in and took off toward Humphrey.

Two hours, two sticks of gum, and almost a full packet of cigarettes later, I watched Indy finally emerge from the cinema with Tommy. It was dark out. A light rain had started to fall, and as they made their way along the boardwalk toward his car, Tommy pulled off his jacket and wrapped it around Indy's shoulders. Jealousy twisted in my gut. The way he had his arm around her. The closeness of his body to hers. My heart felt like it was stuck in a vise and someone was tightening it.

I lit another cigarette and watched as he opened the door to his car—the very car where he had fucked Laura Hope last month—and then scooted around to the driver's side. For a while, they didn't go anywhere. They just sat and talked—only talked. I could see from where I sat, my eyes glued to his car, as I kept dragging on my cigarette. After about ten minutes, he gunned the engine and they pulled out of the parking lot and drove away. I followed them through the rainy streets, my gut stirring, my heart thumping, my anger slowly simmering beneath my skin when I realized he was taking her to Cavalry Hill.

The number one make-out spot in town.

CHAPTER 44

INDY
Now

The plain and simple truth was this: Anson and I had broken up a couple of months before my father's death.

A brilliant trauma surgeon, Anson had been offered a position in a world-renowned Swiss medical facility almost a year into our relationship. He had asked me to marry him because it would be easier for me to follow him to Switzerland as his wife, so in one afternoon I had agreed to be his wife and to follow him half way around the world. But I had agreed to marry him for all the wrong reasons. Because I needed more time to think about the offer, and agreeing to it seemed like a better option than turning him down and breaking his heart in one fell swoop.

Two months later, and I'd had all the time I needed. I wasn't going. And I wasn't going to marry him either.

So, we had broken up in a surprisingly un-painful and calm manner, and I remember thinking at the time how bizarre it seemed, breaking up with my fiancé and feeling completely and utterly ... *relieved*.

Then two months later my daddy died.

When I had weakened and given into my traitorous urges toward Cade, Anson and I weren't together. But he had shown up, unannounced and uninvited as a show of *friendly* support, and seeing him was exactly what my confused and battered emotions needed. He was my safe house. I felt emotionally bruised by Cade and my father's death, and seeing something so safe and familiar in Anson I had grabbed onto him for dear life so I didn't have to face my feelings toward the other things going on around me.

Why did I tell Cade that Anson was still my fiancé?

The truth? It wasn't planned. But when Cade showed up looking so damn beautiful and my stupid heart went all achy for him, I realized I'd fallen back in love with him.

And that was bad.

Like super bad.

Because where my heart was concerned, Cade Calley was my kryptonite.

So, my self-preservation kicked in, and telling Cade I was engaged erected a wall between us and gave me the space I needed to think about what had happened and how the pieces all fit together.

Now my safe house was leaving to go back to Seattle. We left the barbecue at the motorcycle club early so he could catch his flight home. He insisted I didn't need to drive him, but I was grateful for the excuse to get away, especially from Cade's watchful eye. I needed to catch my breath, and the drive out of town to the airport was exactly what I needed.

As we stood in the departure lounge at the airport, I wrapped my arms around him and hugged him. His warm, familiar smell was both a comfort and a reminder that we were well and truly over.

"Thank you for coming here," I said. "You didn't need to do that."

"Hey, we were friends before we were anything else. I'd like to keep it that way." He smiled warmly. "But having said that, just so you know, if you change your mind about any of it ... Switzerland ... me ... the offer still stands."

I nodded. "Thank you."

He squeezed my hand. "But I have a feeling you have some unfinished business here."

I frowned. "Like what?"

He gave me one of his *nice try* looks. "Your friend Cade."

I looked away at the mention of his name. But Anson wasn't having any of it. He turned my chin to look at him.

"By the look on his face the other day, he wasn't expecting me."

"Cade is an old friend."

"The way he looks at you makes me want to get myself a body guard," he said with a half-smile. His humor faded. "And the way you look at him makes me realize that you and I were never going to work out."

"What do you mean?"

His face was gentle. "There was always something holding you back. Something stopping you from giving everything you had to our relationship. And now I see that it was him."

I looked away because I felt guilty. He was right. I was never able to give myself to him, *wholly*, because if I was being really honest, I gave my heart to a boy a long time ago. And he still had it.

I just wasn't ready to admit it out loud.

"It's complicated," I said.

"Does it need to be?"

They announced Anson's flight and it was the perfect opportunity to change the subject. "You'd better go, or you *will* miss your plane."

He looked at me like I was a lost cause. And maybe I was. Because even though I knew what he said was true, I still couldn't admit it to anyone. It was almost as if I had spent so long running from Cade I didn't know how to stop.

"If he is what you want, Indy, then don't waste any more time." He held me by the shoulders and fixed me with one of his fierce stares. "Because life is short and you never know when it's going to end. If he is your chance at happiness, then you run to him and you be with him. Do you understand me, Indy? You run as fast as you can in his direction."

And with those parting words of wisdom, Anson picked up his overnight bag and left Destiny.

CHAPTER 45

INDY—Aged 17
Then

Anger flared in my chest and my cheeks reddened. I didn't want to go to Cavalry Hill. I mean, what the hell? It was supposed to be a simple movie date. I had no desire to make out with Tommy.

My hands fisted on my lap. When he'd asked me where I'd like to go, I hadn't been sure. I just knew I didn't want to go home because Cade would be in his bedroom with Mallory, and my stupid teenage heart couldn't stand the idea of sitting yards away from them while he kissed her.

Now I was at Cavalry Hill with a boy who looked like he belonged in a Ralph Lauren commercial.

"Why are we here?" I asked as Tommy pulled his car into a parking space.

He just grinned that big, movie-star smile that made Laura Hope swoon in gym class.

It had nothing on Cade's beautiful, dimpled grin.

"Why not? The view is incredible," he replied as he slid his arm along the back of the seat. "I thought we could talk. Get to know each other better. We don't really get to do that at school. It's nice to get you alone."

"Alone?"

"Without Cade and Isaac and Abby."

When he said it, it suddenly occurred to me that I *was* alone. Very alone. With Tommy Baker. He was a big guy. Athletic and strong. While I was petite like my mama. It was then I realized I had just put myself in a very risky situation.

"I think we'd better be getting back," I said, shifting awkwardly in my seat.

"Why? This is nice."

My chest started to tingle.

"Sure. But it's getting late."

"Come on, relax," he insisted. "It's early."

Rain splattered across the windshield.

"We can't see anything because of the rain," I said. "Let's come back another time. When we have a better view."

"Fuck the view." His voice, which had been charming up until now, suddenly had a hard bite to it. And it alarmed me.

"What did you say?" I asked.

"I said fuck the view." He turned to look at me and his eyes were dark. "I'm not here for the view."

I tried to swallow, but my mouth was too dry. I looked away from him and folded my arms in a deliberate attempt to show him that I wasn't afraid of him.

"Take me home," I demanded.

That was the moment Tommy Baker decided to take it to the next level. He launched at me, pushing himself onto me, his big arms holding me prisoner as he forced his lips to mine. I jerked my head away from his wet mouth.

"Get off me," I yelled. "Get the fuck off me!"

I struggled, but he was too strong. I felt powerless as he used his strength to hold me still.

"Just one kiss. Come on, now. Don't be a tease, girl."

"Get away from me!" I yelled again. "You're hurting me."

He growled and shoved me back. One hand wrapped around my throat while the other went for the space between my legs.

"You fucking prick tease," he growled.

I squirmed and thrashed about, bringing my knees up to stop his hand from getting between my thighs.

Stop!" I screamed.

Suddenly, the driver's door was ripped open and Tommy's hold on me disappeared as he was yanked out of the car by a big, muscular arm.

"The lady said stop!" Boomed a strong voice.

It was Cade.

I flew out of the car in time to see Cade throw Tommy up against the back door. It was raining hard now, and fat raindrops splashed against his big arms, and made his white t-shirt cling to his broad chest. Tommy's head snapped to the side as Cade put his fist in his jaw, once, then twice. Then he grabbed the front of his shirt and pulled him close so Tommy's face was inches from his.

"You stay away from her," he yelled. "You stay away from my girl."

To make sure Tommy understood, Cade smacked him right across his face again.

"Cade!" I ran around the car and put a hand on his arm. "He's had enough."

Tommy wobbled on his feet and slumped against his car.

Cade turned to me. "Are you okay?"

Rain battered against my face. I nodded. "I'm fine."

He turned back to Tommy and shoved him into his car. He leaned in menacingly, "You come near her again, and I'll finish you."

Kings of Mayhem

Slamming the door closed, he turned to me and grabbed me by the arms. "Are you sure you're okay? Did he hurt you?"

I shook my head. "No, I'm fine."

He took my hand and pulled me through the rainy parking lot. Puddles splashed beneath our feet as we ran for his car. We climbed in, and when the interior light flicked on I could see how soaked we both were.

For a moment, we said nothing and weirdness hung between us. Then Cade suddenly started to pound his palms against the steering wheel.

And for some stupid reason, I started to cry.

Cade stopped and turned to me. "Oh, Angel, don't cry. Please don't cry."

Angry at myself, I wiped them away.

"Just take me home," I whispered.

When Cade didn't move, I turned away and looked out the window. A few moments later, the car engine ignited and the lights in the parking lot began to move as we pulled away and drove toward home in silence.

A wall of anger went up between us.

I was angry at Tommy for being a rapey jerk, and angry at myself for not seeing it earlier. I was angry that he had even thought for a moment that I would give it up to him in the front seat of his father's car. And I was angry at Cade for being with Mallory, and Jane, and Julie, and God knows who else! Knowing they got to enjoy the warmth of his arms around them when he pressed his lips to theirs. But most of all, above everything else, I was angry at my stubborn little heart for falling for the boy I could never have because we were only ever destined to be best friends.

Cade was angry, too. Because Tommy Baker was an asshole who didn't understand the concept of no. And it was only a guess, but I was pretty sure Cade's head was filled with images of what Tommy would have done if he hadn't been there to stop him. He was gripping the steering wheel until his knuckles were white. And when I glanced over at him, his jaw was set and his dark brows were pulled in to a scowl.

I wanted to reach over and touch the sharp contour of his jaw. I wanted to put my lips on his and kiss him until we were both breathless. I wanted him to do the things to me that he did to Mallory, and Jane, and any other girl. I longed for his kisses. Sometimes it felt like my heart would stop beating just from the longing, and I had to force my mind to think of something else. I turned away. My heart sank. He would drop me home and then spend the rest of the night with Mallory.

To my surprise, Cade suddenly pulled over to the curb, and for a moment we sat in complete silence, many unsaid words and intense emotions filling the space between us.

"I want to kill him," he said, facing straight ahead. His jaw ticked and his fingers still gripped the steering wheel, even though we were parked. He looked at me. "Why the fuck did you go out with him in the first place?"

I looked at him in disbelief. Anger bubbled up from my achy chest and flew out my mouth. "Oh, so now I deserved it? Is that it? Are you saying I was asking for it?"

Cade's eyes widened. "What? No! That's not what I'm saying."

"Then what are you saying?" I folded my arms across my chest.

"It's just . . . if he . . . fuck, Indy." His hands balled on the steering wheel. "When I think about what he wanted to do to you..."

I felt foolish. My cheeks reddened and I had to fight off another wave of tears. I didn't know why I was so damn emotional.

"If a man ever puts his hands on you again—you go for the eyes, Indy. You go for them. Poke them. Gouge them. And then, you run."

His face twisted with anger again. He could barely control his rage. If he were a cartoon, smoke would plume from his flared nostrils.

He ran a hand through his inky hair in frustration, but managed to calm himself. For the longest while he didn't say anything, he just stared out the windshield trying to calm down. While I stared out the window hating how I was feeling. Finally, he sighed and I felt him relax next to me.

"Tommy Baker?" He scoffed. "What were you thinking?"

I snapped my head to look at him and I could see the hint of amusement on his face. I knew he was trying to diffuse the situation by making light of it, but it just made me mad.

All of a sudden, I couldn't take it anymore.

"What do you want me to do?" I yelled. "Wait around and watch you kiss Mallory, and Julie, and Kelly, and the entire female body of the eleventh grade?"

I ripped open the car door and slammed it shut behind me.

With my pulse thundering in my ears, I stormed down the street. I heard Cade climb out of the car and come after me. He called out but I ignored him and continued to stomp away from him.

When he caught up to me, he swung me around. "What the hell was that about?"

I glared at him. I knew I should turn and walk away, but I was tired of wanting him. Tired of longing for him to notice me. Tired of wanting my best friend to fall in love with me. It all bubbled up inside me until I couldn't take it anymore.

"Why are you so blind?" I yelled at him, tears of frustration welling in my eyes.

"What are you talking about?"

"Why can't you see that I'm right in front of you? Am I so friend-zoned that you can't even see me anymore?"

For a moment, he looked confused. He went to say something but then stopped. He just looked at me. Drinking me in with those amazing eyes. The next minute, my face was in his big hands.

"If I thought for one moment you wanted to kiss me, Indy, then I'd spend the rest of my life kissing *just* you."

My breathing stopped in my chest. I wanted Cade to kiss me more than I wanted the oxygen in my lungs.

"Then what are you waiting for," I whispered.

His face shimmered with surprise and his eyes searched my face for a sign. He brushed his thumbs against my cheeks and I could see in his eyes that he understood. Then, without any further hesitation, he leaned in and pressed his lips to mine. Light burst behind my closed lids as his mouth closed over mine, his lips savoring the feel of mine against his.

Tommy Baker and his grabby hands were a distant memory, and all I knew was Cade Calley and his sweet, gentle kisses.

CHAPTER 46

INDY
Now

Mirabella and Jacob married three days after we buried my father.

They exchanged vows down by the river in the shade of the poplar trees that lined the water. It was a glorious Fall day. Still and sunny, with just enough warmth left in the air. Dandelion husks floated in the shafts of dusky light coming through the trees. And the gentle wind brought the sweet, heady scent of the honeysuckle growing wild along the riverbanks.

I sat beside my mom, Ronnie, and Bull. Across the aisle from me, Cade sat with Isaac, Cherry, and little Brax. Behind us, bikers and their old ladies filled the rows of chairs, all of them sober and ready to celebrate, all of them on their best behavior. Silver rings gleamed in the late afternoon light. Long hair was brushed and gelled back. Hems were high and dresses were tight.

Together, Mirabella and Jacob made a beautiful picture. The six-foot, bearded biker with gentle eyes, and the stunning girl with caramel hair dancing around polished shoulders. Standing in front of their friends and loved ones, they only had eyes for one another.

I watched on, stiff-faced, as Jacob slipped the crown pendant necklace over Mirabella's head and secured it in place around her throat. Every King gave his old lady a crown pendant when he made her his queen. It was a Kings of Mayhem tradition that stretched back to Hutch Calley and the crown pendant he gave Sybil on their wedding day all those years ago.

Mirabella gave Jacob a dazzling smile and you could see his love for her sparkling in his eyes. My heart ached in my chest. I knew how that love felt. I also knew how it felt when it ended.

I stole a glance at Cade. He was looking at me, his eyes dark, his brow pulled together. His jaw set. I turned away. One day he would drape his crown pendant around the neck of another woman, and she would stare up at him with the same starry eyes as Mirabella. He deserved it. And I wanted him to be happy. Yet, the very idea of another woman wearing his crown made my chest ache. I closed my eyes, and hated that my heart still hurt for him. Hated that I still loved him. Hated that I couldn't come back because I was too damn scared.

I opened my eyes and lifted my head. I looked at Jacob. He towered over his slender bride. He cupped her face in his big hands and looked lovingly into her eyes. The priest pronounced them man and wife, and he bent his head to kiss her passionately. We all clapped and cheered, and confetti filled the golden light of the afternoon.

Afterwards, we celebrated by the river. Chairs and tables were brought down from the clubhouse, and candles and flowers festooned the tablecloths. Caterers brought in food and cake, and wine that was drunk out of antique crystal glasses. The paper streamers and buntings made by Mirabella and the other old ladies were looped from tree branch to tree branch, gently swaying in the mild breeze.

As the afternoon wore on, the wine flowed and we danced to the sounds of a live band set up in the shade of the tree line.

I did my best to avoid Cade. But as the sun sank lower into the horizon, and the stars scattered in a twilight sky, he approached me while I sat talking with Tex and his wife, and asked me to dance.

And I'd had just enough wine to accept.

As he led me on to the makeshift dance floor, the band started a rendition of the Eagles *"Wasted Time."* He pulled me close.

"You look beautiful," he said, his bright blue eyes roaming my face.

"Thank you." I felt awkward but drawn to him. "You look very handsome."

And he did. He looked so damn handsome my heart ached.

He gave me a closed-lip smile and his beautiful blue eyes sparkled down on me. As our bodies swayed to the music his fingers curled into mine and my head spun with longing. Our bodies were close. Crushed together so I could feel every inch of him. It was wrong. Yet I couldn't pull away.

"You smell good, too," he said, his fingers untangling from mine to trail along my throat. He tucked my hair over my shoulder and I shivered. His breath on my skin was intoxicating and I was powerless against the allure of him. Instead of stepping away, I melted into him.

"I want to kiss you," he whispered.

The gentleness in his voice tugged at my heart.

"Cade..." I breathed his name, but my own yearning cut me off, taking up a pulse at the very core of me.

"I know you're not mine but you should be."

"Please..."

He held me even tighter, his body hard and enticing, stealing the strength from me so I couldn't pull away. I longed for his touch and the wine in me told me it was a good idea.

"Tell me you didn't think about us when you watched Jacob and Mirabella become man and wife. Tell me you have no regrets."

"Don't do this," I pleaded. "Let's just enjoy tonight."

His lips brushed my throat. "Tell me there is a chance for us."

Before I could reply, Joker bumped into us and slung his arms around our shoulders.

"Bitches . . ." he cried. Too much bourbon had taken its toll on him and it wasn't even seven o'clock. "Let's dance! Whoa!"

I saw my chance to escape and I took it. I pulled away from Cade and walked off the dance floor leaving him to untangle himself from Joker.

Sitting down at one of the tables I poured myself a big glass of wine. I needed it. My heart was hopping all over the place. I downed it in three gulps and quickly poured another. I felt myself being pulled toward Cade and I couldn't stop. I had spent too long running from my past. Now it had caught up with me and was all up in my face, forcing me to look at what I had left behind. And that was all of this. All of these people.

And Cade.

Sometime between running away and now, I had forgiven him. He was a good guy. Yes, he had broken my heart. But it was time to let it go. Move on. My heart was healed. I could leave Destiny knowing I was free of all the angst I had dragged around with me for twelve years.

Yet the idea of leaving was no longer as appealing as it had been.

I glanced over to where Cade had sat down. Mirabella's sister, Cora, was talking to him and must have asked him to dance because he rose from his chair and followed her onto the dance floor. When he took her by the hips, she curled her arms around his neck and crushed her body up against his. Something close to possessiveness raced through me. I could live a million years and never be okay with seeing him in the arms of another woman. I looked away and drained my glass. *Stupid heart.* Staying the extra week had been a mistake. It was making me feel things I had buried a long time ago.

When I glanced back at them, Cora was looking up at Cade with starry-eyed affection.

Oh Christ. She didn't just want to fuck him. She had a crush on him.

"She's always had a thing for him," Mirabella said, sitting down next to me. "But he's never shown any interest in her."

"Until now." I went to take a sip, but my glass was empty. Leaning forward, I refilled it from the open bottle on the table.

"Oh, that's nothing. He's just being sweet, is all." Mirabella's beautiful brown eyes found mine. "I'm sure it would be different if you were out there dancing with him."

"We're not together," I said.

"He's in love with you." Mirabella leaned in so her shoulder nudged mine. "And I think you're a little bit in love with him, too."

I didn't get a chance to respond because Jacob appeared beside us with an open bottle of champagne in his hand, asking his wife to dance.

"You and I are going to continue this conversation soon, okay?" she said with a broad smile as her giant man of a husband swept her away.

I watched them on the dance floor. Jacob and Mirabella's love was a once-in-a-lifetime thing. They were a perfect match and I couldn't help but feel envious. Theirs would last. Mine was already over.

Abby sat down in the chair Mirabella had just vacated.

"They look great together, don't they?" she said, talking about the bride and groom.

"They're the best," I said, trying not to look at Cade and Cora still out on the dance floor. I took a mouthful of wine but felt Abby's eyes on me. "What?"

"I can't believe it," she said.

"What can't you believe?"

"How much of a coward you are."

I looked at her. "Gee, Abby. Why don't you say what you really mean?"

It was the second time in a week someone had called me a coward and I was beginning to see a trend. Unfortunately, somewhere deep inside I knew they were right.

She shrugged. "You asked."

"Okay, I'll bite. Why are you calling me a coward?"

"Because you still have feelings for him, yet here you are, sitting here like a wallflower as another woman crawls all over him." She poured herself a glass of wine. "You know, the old Indy wouldn't put up with another woman pawing her man."

"Yeah, well, the old Indy grew up."

"I don't think so. I think she is in there somewhere. Begging to crawl out and go and get her man."

"Don't hold your breath."

We were quiet for a moment, both watching Cade trying to keep Cora at arm's length.

It was Abby who broke the silence. And just like I suspected, she wasn't going to let it rest.

"Boy, you were wild once," she said, bumping her shoulder to mine. "Wild Indy Parrish. Fearless and as *cool* as a cucumber. The original Nature's Child."

"I don't even know what that means."

"You're kidding, right?" She looked at me like I was crazy. "Steppenwolf? Born To Be Wild? *Like a true nature's child . . .*"

I laughed. "And now?"

She looked at me, her eyebrows raised. "Now . . . not so much."

I looked away and sighed. "We've all got to grow up sometime, Abby."

"Yeah, but it's not just that. You're so grown up and . . ."

My eyes shot to hers. "And?"

"Some would say you've got a bit of a pole up your ass."

Her response was classic Abby. She had always been brutally honest, and I loved her for it.

I looked at her sheepishly and cocked an eyebrow. "A pole, huh?"

She grinned. "A fucking *giant* pole!"

I looked horrified. "Ouch."

We laughed and she put her arm around my shoulders. "I've missed you. Have I told you how pleased I am that you are back? Not that I understand why you left in the first place."

"You know why."

She took a sip of her wine. "No. Not really."

I watched Cora rest her head on Cade's shoulder. The one I'd grabbed onto only five nights ago when he'd given me a mind-blowing orgasm.

I looked away and focused on the floral arrangement in the center of the table.

Being in love sucked.

"It got to be too much," I said. "Being in the MC. The lifestyle, the expectation..."

When I looked over at Abby she was giving me her classic *don't bullshit me* look, and I sighed. There was no point in being anything but honest with Abby because she'd just call me out on it.

"I didn't want to become my mother, okay. A slave to the man she once loved. Tolerating his shit. Picking up after him. Putting out for him even when he'd stuck his dick into some club skank right in front of her." I chewed on my lip as the memories surged forward. "When he hit her, that was it for me. I wanted out. I didn't want to end up like that and I knew if I stayed . . ."

"Cade's not like that. He would never hit a woman. He doesn't tolerate that old-school behavior. There are not too many guys in the club who would put up with that shit."

"I know. But when you're sixteen and you watch your father crumble before your very eyes, and you watch him deteriorate into this monster who beats and cheats on his wife," I shook my head, hating the memories. "I wanted out. I wanted out and as far away from that as possible."

"And you got out. And you did everything you said you wanted to do." Abby looked me right in the eye. "But yet, here you are."

I gave her a pointed look. "My father died. I had to come back and make sure the asshole was buried."

Bad memories made me mean.

"But you're still here. A week later. Maybe that's because there is something here that is worth hanging around for?"

"I stayed for Mirabella and Jacob's wedding." I was still unwilling to admit my feelings to anyone.

But the look she gave me told me I was wasting my time.

My confusion peaked and I had an overwhelming need to confide in someone. To get my tangle of emotions out in the open for someone else to unravel.

I let out a deep, confused breath. "I don't know what I'm doing, Abby. I have this amazing life back in Seattle. And I'm happy. Really. But then I came back here and this place, and these people . . . I feel like I belong here, too." I covered my face with my hands. "I don't get it. What do I do?"

Abby peeled my face from my hands and fixed me with those wise blue eyes of hers. "You work out which one makes you more happy. Your life back in Seattle without Cade. Or a life here in Destiny with Cade. The way I see it, that boy is so in love with you it's completely your choice."

I bit my bottom lip as I digested her words. On the dance floor, Cade untangled Cora from around his neck and kissed her politely on the cheek before walking away.

The thought of living without him opened a gaping hole in my chest. But the thought of him breaking my heart again was too much to bear. Did I risk it?

"I'm so confused," I whispered.

Abby looked sympathetic. "Do you love him?"

My eyes found hers. "That's the sad thing, Abby. I never stopped."

CHAPTER 47

CADE
Now

I walked down to the river's edge, away from the party. I needed a break. I was so acutely aware of Indy and it was killing me. Not being able to touch her. Knowing she wasn't mine. I drained the bourbon from my glass and stared across the river to where the last ribbon of light was slowly sinking beneath the tree line.

It didn't matter that I wanted to kiss her. Touch her. Bury myself so deep into her I would lose where I ended and she began. Because she belonged to another man and I had no right.

Not that I gave a fuck about Anson and what he thought.

It was Indy I had to respect. And this was what she wanted.

Fuck!

I ran my hand through my hair. I wasn't too proud to admit I was fucking terrified of losing her. Fucking terrified of her returning to Seattle. But it was a fucking hopeless situation. She didn't want me anymore, and yet I couldn't imagine a future without her in it. Giving up wasn't in my nature, but that was exactly what she wanted me to do.

Kings of Mayhem

The snap of a twig told me I wasn't alone.

"Cade?"

I swung around.

It was Cora. Mirabella's kid sister who was visiting from college for the wedding.

I watched her make her way toward me. She was a cute kid. Good looking. And the pink dress she wore did little to hide her smokin' figure. But she was young. Naïve. Needy. She had a crush on me and she didn't try to hide it.

"Here you are," she said. "I've been looking everywhere for you. They're about to cut the cake."

"Thanks." I wasn't in the mood for cake. Or to see Indy. I wanted bourbon. Not that there was enough bourbon in the world to help me. But for tonight, at least I could drown my sorrows until I passed out. "I might pass on it."

Like she could read my mind, Cora pulled a hip flask out from her cleavage. "Maybe I could tempt you with this?"

I couldn't help but grin. She was sweet. And she grinned back, because she was pleased to make me happy. She unscrewed the lid and handed it to me. I took a strong mouthful and savored the heat as it travelled down my throat and spread throughout my chest. The second mouthful was just as good. Yeah, drowning my sorrows tonight seemed like a great idea.

I felt Cora's eyes on me.

"Good?" she asked.

I handed her the flask and watched as she closed her mouth over the top and slowly took a sip, letting bourbon spill on her lips as she pulled the flask away. When she ran her tongue along her bottom lip, she looked up at me through her lashes. She moaned as if it was the best thing she'd ever tasted. She was flirting.

Making sure I was watching, she slid her tongue across her lip again, this time slow and teasing... inviting.

Before I could stop it, her mouth was on mine and she wrapped herself around me like she couldn't get close enough. The flask fell to ground with a loud smack. And because I was unsteady from too much liquor, I fell, too. Cora landed on top of me, and with an enthusiastic moan she straddled me and leaned down to devour my mouth with hers.

CHAPTER 48

INDY
Now

I was a fool.

I needed to find Cade.

Maybe I was drunk. Or maybe I was just sick of pretending. Either way, my stupid head was finally ready to listen to my demanding heart. I scanned the reception for him, but he was nowhere. I didn't know what I was going to say to him.

I forgive you?

I want to kiss you?

I love you?

No.

Not *I love you*.

Even if it was the truth, I wasn't stupid enough to think that we had a future together. But I could at least put our history back in the past where it belonged and move forward. I understood now. It wasn't the club or Cade I was running from; I was running from the ugliness that my mom and dad had become. Somewhere in my teenage mind I had twisted it all around. I had blamed the club—the MC lifestyle—for the demise of their marriage. But in truth, my father had turned mean in his grief over the loss of Bolt, and in my confused teenage mind, his viciousness had manifested into a monster I identified as the MC.

I might not be able to be with Cade. But I could stop hating the MC like I had been.

"I have to talk to Cade," I said to Abby.

"I think I saw him head toward the riverbank," she replied, taking my glass from me.

I nodded. I knew where he would be. Through the trees was a small, sandy beach where we used to fish for catfish as kids. I slipped away from the wedding reception and disappeared into the darkness, navigating the uneven terrain in my Valentino Garavani heels.

Almost straight away I heard it.

The moaning.

Then a giggle.

Followed by more moaning.

I stopped. It was coming from deep within the scrub. I heard the rustle of leaves and then a gasp, followed by a muffled, "You like that, baby?" I couldn't make out the voices, but the girl gasped again, followed by a long, pornographic moan.

I thought I could sneak past them. Thought I could get by them without them knowing I was there. But when I started walking, my foot slipped on some damp bark and I yelped.

Immediately, a gruff voice called out to me. "Who the fuck is there?"

I grimaced.

Fuck me.

Now I looked like a creeper.

"Sorry! It's just Indy," I said, feeling like a voyeuristic loser. Thankfully, we were covered in darkness and this unbearably uncomfortable scene was in audio only.

"Oh, hey, Indy. It's Maple and Hawke," called a female voice.

I had no idea who Maple was.

"Hey, Maple. Hawke. Sorry, guys, I'm just on my way to the river," I called back.

"You okay, girl?" Hawke asked, like he wasn't currently inside a woman called Maple.

"All good," I called out, climbing to my feet and dusting off my knees. "I'm leaving now."

"Okay, have a good night, Indy," the woman called Maple said.

"You, too!"

I scurried off, keen to never relive that moment in my head ever again.

As I made my way through the trees toward the little beach where Cade and I used to play as kids the clanging of something metallic turned my head. I heard noises and walked toward them. It was hard to see in the fading light, but I could just make out the silhouettes of two people as they lay by the water's edge. As I walked closer and stepped through the trees and into the clearing, I could see who they were.

I stopped.

It was Cade.

And he was kissing Cora.

CHAPTER 49

INDY—Aged 18
Then

I couldn't stop kissing him. It was like the floodgates were open and we couldn't keep away from each other. Abby and Isaac teased us, relentlessly, and Mallory walked around in a huff for the first few weeks but eventually got over it and moved onto Blake Lawson. And then, Brody Meyers. And then, Chris Frost.

To most people it was no surprise we were together. Especially to our families and the MC. To them it had only been a matter of time.

It didn't take long for us to settle into a normal routine. Cade would pick me up for school and we would walk the halls of West Destiny High just as we always had, side by side and always together. But now we walked closer with our fingers tangled, and with an intimacy that everyone noticed. We were together every chance we got, losing ourselves in our newfound relationship, always touching, always kissing. And when we separated for class, Cade would hold me to his strong body and kiss the breath out of me.

Then, at the end of the day, I would fall into those strong arms and lose hours to kissing him. Sometimes things went too far and our bodies would beg for more, but Cade made it clear we should wait for when I was ready. Sometimes I thought I was, I mean, it's hard to think of anything else when the full weight of his body was on mine and he was kissing me into a stupor.

"Can I touch you?" I whispered one night when things had gone past the point of no return.

He nodded and his body trembled when I reached between us. My hand moved down his muscular stomach and slid beneath his boxer shorts. When my fingers found him, his breath left him in a sharp exhale. Desire pooled between my thighs when I felt him harden in my hand, and boy, he was big. Not that I had anything to compare it to. He shivered and his lips parted with a slow exhale. I pressed my palm harder against him, and slowly began to move my wrist in an up and down motion.

"Indy . . ." he rasped desperately.

"Let me do this," I whispered. I shifted restlessly, driven by the throb between my legs. Cade started to rock against the motion of my hand, his breathing heavy, his tortured moans strangled in his throat.

"Oh, baby . . ." He brought his hand up to cup my jaw and kissed me urgently. He rocked his hips and we fell into an erotic synchronicity. His breathing came hard and I had to clench my thighs together to stop the throbbing there.

"I'm going to come." He breathed out the warning against my lips. He moaned and I felt him pulse beneath my fingers as a warm liquid shot onto my hand.

Watching him come brought me close to my own climax. The look on his face. The rasp of his moans. It turned me on more than I could have imagined. I wanted him. I wanted all of him.

Forever.

Two nights later, I lay beneath him, my body tight with desire as he kissed me hard. Things were getting out of control. Our kissing was fierce. Cade moved against me, pressing his pelvis into mine as his desire increased. I shifted beneath him, moaning at the sensation of his zipper rubbing against my panties. I was so turned on I was desperate to take things to the next level.

"Make love to me," I breathed desperately between kisses.

Cade's denim-covered erection ground into me. But he said nothing. He just kept kissing me.

"Please..." I begged.

He pulled back. His blue eyes dark as they roamed my face.

"It's a big move," he breathed.

"I know that," I replied.

I felt him throb against my panties.

"I'm ready," I urged.

Cade frowned. "You want to do it now? Don't you want something a little more special? Something planned?"

I dragged his hand between us and guided his fingers beneath my panties. When he felt how wet I was, his face shimmered with need.

"Oh God," he rasped.

"Yes, I want to do it now," I said. "And yes, I want to do it with you."

His fingers began to slide through slick skin and I moaned. When he pushed one into me, my automatic reaction was to clamp down around it, and a tremor ran through him.

"You're so tight," he whispered with a tortured moan.

I began to move so my clit rubbed against his knuckles. Everything felt so incredible. I moaned and found his mouth again, kissing him hard.

When he tried to pull his hand away, I held it in place.

He broke away from our kiss. "Indy . . . I want you to think about this."

"I have and I know what I want." I sighed and released his hand, giving up. "Do you do this with all the girls you make love to? Try to talk them out of it?"

"This is different," he said.

"Why?"

"Because *you're* different," he said. When I frowned, he sighed. "I didn't love them. But I'm in love with you."

My heart sang. "You love me?"

He smiled and those two beautiful dimples appeared either side of his mouth. "Insanely so."

His fingers found me again and I began to move against him. But this time I reached for his zipper, and this time he didn't stop me. When I touched him, he shivered and began grinding against my palm. Our breathing became heavy. The tension in our bodies coiled and tightened, making us restless, making us move impatiently against one another as we both raced toward our orgasms. We were past the point of no return, and I gave into the sensations crashing through me. Our eyes met as we brought each other to a climax. I clenched around his finger and moaned softly as a bliss so warm and sweet descended on me. I felt him tense up, felt his abs go hard and his breathing ragged, heard him moan into my neck as he spilled his warmth onto my hand. I trembled against him, my heart pounding in my chest as the throb and ache between my thighs slowly eddied away.

Cade kissed me hard. "That was insane," he panted, his chest rising and falling.

"Now will you make love to me?" I asked.

He looked down at me, his eyes filled with immense tenderness.

"After graduation," he said. "Because I don't care what you say, baby, we gotta make it right for your first time."

CHAPTER 50

INDY
Now

I woke up in the clubhouse with Abby sound asleep next to me. We were in Griffin Calley's room. He very rarely stayed at the clubhouse, so Abby crashed there whenever there was a party. Feeling foggy from too much wine, I went in search of coffee. My head was pounding and my mouth felt like cotton, and if I didn't get some caffeine into me soon, there was a good chance I would start swinging.

Red was busy in the kitchen preparing breakfast, and when he saw me he smiled.

"Coffee?" he asked, handing me a cup.

"Please." I accepted it gratefully and took a seat at the bar. Red made good coffee. It was strong. The perfect elixir to my hangover. With my head in my hands, I stared into the rich, dark liquid as I tried to collect my thoughts.

Today was my last day in Destiny. Tomorrow I would fly home to Seattle. Back to my old life. Back to everything that was safe and familiar.

It was the sensible thing to do.

A petite girl in too-tight jeans and a barely there midriff top came over to me. "Can I get you some breakfast, Indy?"

She was attractive. Young. Eager. I felt that familiar pang in the pit of my stomach. There was no shortage of that around here. No shortage of temptation for the guys, married or not.

"No, thank you."

"Are you sure? It's really no problem."

"I'm good."

But for some reason, she wouldn't let it go.

"I'm happy to fix you a plate."

And it rubbed me the wrong way.

"I'm not hungry," I replied sharply.

Abby appeared beside me. She gestured for the girl to leave with a nod of her chin and the girl scooted away.

"You sure you ain't hungry? 'Cos you've got an attack of the hangries, if ever I've seen them," she said, sliding into the chair next to me.

"Hangries?"

"You're angry because you're hungry. *Hangry*."

I stared into my coffee. "If I want something to eat, I can get it myself."

"Sure." She crossed her arms and leaned them on the table. "But whether you like it or not, Indy, you're MC royalty around here. You're the granddaughter of an original, and the love interest of fucking Cade Calley. You're the original wild child whose ghost has lingered in this clubhouse for the past twelve years. You're legendary around here."

I glanced at her. "You sound like my personal cheer squad." She gave me a pointed look and I sighed. "It just gets to me, okay."

"What?"

"All the girls." I took a sip of my coffee. "All the temptation for the guys."

She scoffed. "You talk like this is your first rodeo. This is club life, Indy."

"Doesn't mean I have to like it."

"No. But you don't have to hate on it so much. These girls, they're not the enemy. We women stick together."

She was right. Apart from a few undesirables, *a la Genevieve*, there had always been a strong sisterhood in the club.

I felt bad for snapping at the girl. I would make sure I apologized to her on the way out.

I shrugged. "Anyway, you're wrong. I'm not Cade's love interest. I'm not Cade's anything. Tomorrow I fly home." Even as I said it, my heart skipped. Tomorrow this would all be over and I could resume my old life back in Seattle.

But even as I thought it, my chest felt tight. Because no matter how I decided to spin it, leaving was going to be hard.

CHAPTER 51

INDY
Now

It was my last night in Destiny and the Kings of Mayhem MC decided I needed to be sent off in style.

In big, bad, biker style.

They were going to host a party fit for a princess.

An MC princess.

With a live band and a barbecue. And sexy pole dancing triplets grinding their stuff to Kid Rock's "*Cowboy.*"

And you know what, I kinda loved it.

Two weeks earlier I would've hated it. But now that the pole had been successfully extracted from my ass, I could breathe and be myself again.

I saw Cade as soon as I got to the clubhouse. We were both walking in at the same time and stopped when we saw each other. We hadn't spoken since the night before when we'd danced together and he'd held me tightly in his arms and told me he wanted to kiss me.

After finding him with Cora down by the beach I had left the wedding. I had taken a half-full bottle of wine from one of the reception tables and sat on the rooftop of the clubhouse looking up at the stars, trying to get my thoughts straight.

Now things were weird between us. He didn't know that I'd seen him with Cora. He didn't know that I'd seen the way she had slid her legs on either side of his hips and grinded against him as she kissed him passionately. He didn't know that I'd heard the things he had said to her.

"Hey," I said cautiously. Things were tense.

"Hey," Cade replied.

He looked preoccupied. Distant. His brow furrowed.

"I'm sorry I skipped out early last night," I said. "I just needed some time out, you know? Some breathing space. I think too much wine might have had something to do with it."

I tried to lighten the moment. But Cade was beyond that.

"It's okay," he said, his eyes dark. "I shouldn't have said what I said."

He towered over me and I could feel the power of him radiating around me. I could also feel his sadness.

"I saw you," I said calmly. "With Cora."

His eyes darted to me. "Nothing happened."

"I know." I smiled, hoping he would smile back, but he didn't. "You were very sweet to her."

When I'd discovered Cade and Cora kissing at the river's edge it had taken me a moment to realize what was happening. In a glance, it looked like two people making out. But as I watched, I realized it was Cora doing all the kissing and Cade trying to fend her off. He'd peeled her off him and held her at arm's length as he let her down gently. When she started to cry and question if she was pretty enough, he had tenderly lifted her chin.

"You're beautiful. And I'm a lucky man to have a stunning woman want to be with me. Any man would be, Cora. But I'm in love with someone else. Whole-heartedly."

Cade folded his arms across his chest. "What did you see?"

"You were a gentleman," I said. "You let her down gently."

He shrugged. "She was drunk. She would've regretted it in the morning."

"You're just being modest. Cora has a crush on you."

"Yeah, well." He rubbed the back of his neck. "She's not the one for me."

Awkwardness hung between us.

"Cade—"

"Listen, Indy," he cut me off gently. "You've made it real clear we're done. I want you to be happy. And if Anson makes you happy, then I can't ask for anything more."

I didn't know what to say. It felt like something broke inside of me.

"You have a fiancé," he said. "And just because I hate everything about what that means, it doesn't mean I won't respect it. Just . . . I don't need to see it anymore."

He walked away, and another part of me collapsed in on itself.

I didn't want Cade to walk away from me.

But what did I expect? I'd said goodbye to him by fucking him. Then I'd kept him at arm's length by lying to him about a fiancé.

I had gotten what I'd asked for.

He was done.

I fought back tears as I watched him disappear inside the clubhouse.

Isaac came up to me and put his arms around my neck. "I'm going to miss you when you leave, woman."

I had to blink to keep my tears away. I was going to miss him, too.

"It won't be like before, I promise. I'll be back more often." My throat tightened with emotion because I knew coming back would be hard. Leaving tomorrow would mean giving up Cade for good.

"Hey, who is that?" I asked, nodding to a young man arriving on a mint green Vespa. I was trying to change the subject so I didn't ugly cry in the middle of the MC compound.

Isaac released me to light a cigarette.

"That cool cat is Reuben. He's not a club member in the traditional sense. He is more of an . . . *adoption*." He drew on his cigarette and released a breath of smoke.

"An adoption?"

"Reuben doesn't play well with others," he explained. "I'm not sure he's wired right. He just likes to hang out, and we like his company. So, we've welcomed him to the family."

Reuben looked like Finch from *American Pie* and, according to Isaac, they had a similar personality and style. While his friends drank beer from red plastic cups, Reuben drank whiskey from a tumbler. When his friends drove American heavy metal classics like Dodge, Ford, and Chevy, Reuben got around in his mint green Vespa. While his friends preferred the more casual look of jeans, tees, and a cut, he chose dress pants, button-up shirts, and a bowtie. He walked to the beat of his own drum and didn't care what anyone thought about it.

According to Isaac, Reuben was his own story. He was particular. Precise. He liked things a certain way and would make no apologies for changing things until they were exactly how he liked them.

He was also lethal.

Or, so it was rumored.

"Once, we were driving past the skate park and Reuben spotted some guy mistreating his dog. We pulled into the parking lot and confronted him. Poor dog, it was terrified of this loser. I told the guy I was going to take that dog off him, but the sonofabitch pulled a gun on me, pressed it against my forehead, and told me he was walking away with it.

Two days later, that motherfucker washed up on the riverbank with a gunshot wound under his chin. That's Reuben's signature. He says he likes to look them in the eye as they are leaving. Psycho sonofabitch."

"I don't know what to say about that," I said. And I truly didn't. I couldn't stand animal cruelty, and I believed that the devil kept a special part of hell free for animal abusers, but I also couldn't condone what Reuben had done, even if it was oddly calming to know that someone so psychopathic could actually be on the side of the good guys.

"Not long after, I visited Reuben at his house and he introduced me to his new dog. It was the same dog from the park. I didn't ask questions and he didn't offer an explanation. But I'll tell you what, that dog fucking loves him."

Isaac was a good storyteller but was prone to embellishing his tales. I had to take what he was saying with a grain of salt. There probably was a dog. I knew how much of an animal lover he was. But as for a dead body, who knew?

I looked across at Reuben who had taken a seat at one of the barbecue tables with a plate of food. I watched as he unfolded his napkin and placed it across his grey-suited lap, and then straightened his bowtie in the shine of a steak knife.

Yeah, okay. There probably was a body.

I looked at Isaac, who winked back at me.

Ok, maybe there wasn't.

Isaac left to grab another beer, leaving me alone to take in my surroundings. I watched him walk away, a serene smile on my face as I took it all in. Here, I could be content. With him. With these people. This life. I would be lying if I said this didn't feel right. That here, amongst the leather and the smoke, and the rumble of Harleys, I felt just as much at home as I did in the gleaming, sterile halls of the hospital. If not more. And because of it, leaving weighed heavily on my chest.

I exhaled deeply in an attempt to steady my feelings.

When the band started to play Lynyrd Skynrd's *"Southern Ways,"* the crowd cheered.

I glanced around at my friends, *my family*, and couldn't help but smile.

Everyone was dancing, laughing, and having a good time. Across the makeshift dance floor, Isaac and Cherry joined Caleb and Brandi in dancing to the band, even Grandma Sybil and her boyfriend were breaking out the moves on the dance floor. To the left of the stage, Joker twirled and dipped Abby.

My heart felt light and my smile grew even bigger when I saw little Brax and Vader's little girl, Shelby, dancing to the music.

Suddenly, tomorrow's flight seemed too close.

I stood up.

I didn't want it to end this way.

I scanned the crowd for Cade and found him standing at the bar looking every bit as fuckable as ever as he ordered a drink from Randy. My heart took up a gallop as I approached him.

"Give me one last dance?" I asked.

I offered him my hand.

In that moment, my heart wanted to be free. It wanted to enjoy what it wanted to enjoy.

It wanted him.

One last time.

He looked at my hand and accepted it. "I thought you'd never ask."

He smiled, but it didn't quite reach his eyes. And when he slid his arms around my waist and pulled me close, I could feel the rapid thunder of his heart. Being this close was heaven. But being this close and not being able to love him was torture.

I held him tight and relaxed into his body, and felt engulfed by everything that was him. His smell. His heat. His strength. His protection.

My walls crumbled away.

"Anson isn't my fiancé," I whispered against the warmth of his throat. "In fact, we're not even together."

Cade pulled back so fast I almost lost my balance. "What did you say?"

I looked up at him and his beautiful blue eyes roamed my face.

"Anson and me. We're not engaged. We broke up about eight or nine weeks ago." I sighed. "Truth be told, we'd broken up a lot earlier than that, we just hadn't realized it."

Cade's smile finally reached his eyes.

"That doesn't change anything," I warned him.

But Cade didn't listen. He simply cupped my face in his big hands and whispered, "You're wrong, Indy. That changes everything." And then he kissed me, right there on the dance floor, for the entire club to see.

I broke away to look up at him. "One last time."

Heat filled his eyes. "For now."

And then he kissed me again.

CHAPTER 52

CADE—Aged 18
Then

The only light in the room came from the small candle on her desk. The window was open, and I could see the moon shining through the branches of the sycamore tree. Indy stood across from me, her big eyes shining like large orbs in the dim light and I could see the nervousness on her face. I reached for her, tenderly brushing my fingertips along her jaw.

"You're so beautiful," I whispered, stepping closer so our bodies were a breath away from one another. "You're the most beautiful thing I have ever seen."

She smiled, but I felt her shiver with nerves as my fingertips gently caressed the plane of her throat and across her chest, dropping to skim the polished swell of her breast. I felt her breath hitch when I found the sweet bud of her nipple, and her breath left her when I pulled her to me and planted my mouth to hers.

This is heaven.

I pulled away and looked down into her beautiful face. There was no need for words. I was in love with her and she was in love with me. The time was right. We were both eighteen. We were ready.

She smiled and kissed me again, soft and gentle at first, but it grew stronger and more demanding as our bodies began to respond. I was hard as fuck, but in the base of my belly a desire I had never known before began to spread through me, and I wanted to take this slow. I wanted to savor this moment. Savor her.

"Have you got them?" Indy asked shyly.

She was talking about condoms. I nodded.

"Can I see them?"

The foil pouch was on my nightstand. I passed it to her. Inspecting it in her hand, she looked so unsure, so nervous. But then she looked up at me and smiled.

"Can I put it on you?"

The question sent pleasure tingling through me and I wondered if it was such a good idea. I had wanted her for so long I wasn't sure I could stand it. But I nodded and watched, speechless, as she tore open the wrapper with glittered nails, and removed the latex sheath. Her eyes dropped to my erection and she bit her lip.

"Are you ready?" she asked.

I swallowed deeply, my throat dry, and managed to croak out a yes.

When she touched me, I trembled, and my breath left me in a deep exhale. Sensations crashed through me as her fingers curled around me and slowly rolled the latex down my hard shaft. I sucked in a deep breath. When she was finished, she stepped back.

I drank her in. Standing there naked, looking across at me shyly, her long, blonde hair tumbling over her shoulders. I kissed her, then, walking her backwards toward the bed, and laying her down amongst the sheets. I crawled over her, my body instantly responding to the feel of her beneath me because I had dreamed of this for so long. Her legs parted and I rested my hips between them as I continued to kiss her, letting our bodies find their own way together.

I pulled back to look at her. Somewhere in the back of my mind I thought about asking her, once again, if she was sure. But it seemed pointless, because she had assured me she was ready and wanted me to be her first. So, there was nothing but silence and the locking of our eyes as I slowly pushed into her body and took her virginity from her.

Her brows pulled in and her eyes closed momentarily as I filled her. Pain and pleasure flickered across her face, and I pulled back to give her body a moment to adjust before slowly easing back into her, all the way to the hilt. Indy's lips parted with a moan that was both a mix of desire and discomfort. But she smiled, and when I pulled back again, she raised her hips toward me, seeking me, wanting me.

She rose up on her elbows to watch me sliding into her. She parted her thighs farther so she could see it all, fascinated by the act.

I wanted to take my time with her. But the plain and simple fact was I had fantasized about making love to her for so long, wild horses couldn't hold back the climax. I kissed her hard and strong, and when she whimpered, I gave in to it and came in the most mind-blowing orgasm of my life.

Afterwards, I fell onto my back and pulled her into my arms. My heart thundered in my chest.

"I love you," I said, planting a kiss on top of her head.

She wrapped her arms around me. "I love you, too."

We lay in silence, our breathing in song with one another.

"You know I'm going to marry you, right?" I said, feeling invincible while my girl was next to me.

She wrapped her arms around me and held me to her satiny skin.

"You had better," she whispered. "Because my heart is yours and only yours."

CHAPTER 53

CADE
Now

It was a magical night. The music. The people. The atmosphere. The fact that I had my girl by my side and I could hold her hand and slip my arm around her waist as much as I wanted. She wasn't engaged. She was still mine.

It was like a weight had been removed, a cloud dispersed, the fog lifted, and I could see hope for the first time in a very long time. The years peeled away. All the hurt and heart break. All the sadness and grief, and the deep, dull ache of missing her, was gone. She was my girl again.

We laughed. We danced. We kissed. Then we kissed some more. And it was easy to momentarily forget that tomorrow she would be gone. I couldn't let myself think about it. I wanted to enjoy the night while we had it. I wanted to show her that this is where she belonged. Here with the Kings of Mayhem. With her family.

With me.

I wrapped my arms around her and held her against me. I pushed my hands through her hair as I kissed her hard, drinking in the sweetness of her and falling in love with her over and over again, with every stroke of my tongue.

We drank and partied with our friends, *our family*. And when the band played their last song just after midnight, I took Indy by the hand and led her back to my room in the clubhouse.

"Remember, this doesn't change a thing," she whispered as I peeled her clothes from her body.

She was wrong. This was changing everything. She just didn't know it yet.

"Tonight, you're all mine," I said, lifting my shirt over my head and pulling her to me. "And I'm going to show you exactly what that means."

And I did. All night long, right through to dawn. I loved her body with my body. I kissed her deeply and rhythmically rolled my hips into her hips, savoring the sensations and feelings of love and bliss that consumed the both of us. And when I made her come, I made her come time and time again, kissing her, loving her, making each orgasm last longer, making her moan and whimper my name as she pulsed and clenched around me.

We both clung onto the night, making each other cry out, making each other wish that things could be different and that we could have this for the rest of our lives. And when the first light of the day broke through the darkness, we both fell asleep entangled in one another's arms, our wild hearts slowing to beat as one.

CHAPTER 54

CADE—Aged 18
Then

My head throbbed, but it was nothing compared to what my cock was doing. Indy was waking me up in the best possible way. Her delicious plump lips were sliding up the length of me and I groaned, throwing my arm across my face to drown out the bright morning light fighting its way through my closed lids. I couldn't remember coming home or slipping into bed next to my girl. My daddy had been pouring drinks into me all night, and I couldn't remember much of anything.

The flick of Indy's tongue sent pleasure tearing through me and I groaned. Despite my hangover, my body started to wake up real good. I licked my lips and tangled my fingers in her hair.

"That feels real good, baby . . ." I rasped.

She slid up my body and sank down on my cock, gasping as I filled her. I kept my eyes closed as she rode me, fighting off the hangover and the pain of daylight, hoping the hazy pleasure of an orgasm was going to ward off the headache.

Indy moved slowly against me, riding me at a perfect pace, lazy and slow, expertly coaxing the pleasure from the base of my belly. Just before I was about to come, she gasped and the sound pierced the haziness in my brain, sending my eyes wide open.

The girl riding my cock wasn't my girlfriend.

I was fucking someone else.

I gasped. Unfortunately, the realization I wasn't fucking Indy coincided with my orgasm, and I shot into the stranger on top of me.

"No!" I cried, shoving the girl off me while my cock continued to pulse with my climax.

She tumbled onto the bed. "Hey!"

"What the fuck are you doing?" I yelled at her.

Before I could answer, a voice came from the doorway.

"Funny . . . that was my question."

Horrified, I turned to see Indy standing in the doorway. She looked both shocked and heartbroken. My heart exploded in my chest.

"Indy!"

"How could you?" she screamed at me. The water bottle in her hand hurtled across the room and hit the wall behind me. "How could you fucking do this to me?"

She didn't wait for me to answer. With a heartbroken sob, she took off.

My stomach recoiled in panic. What had I done? In two hours we were due to leave for college to start our new life together—away from the club. We would be college kids, and in a couple of years I was going to make her my wife, and eventually we would have kids.

But one look on Indy's face and I knew that world had just been ripped away from me.

I ran after her, tearing down the hall of the clubhouse, completely fucking naked. My dad was still in the bar, smoking cigarettes and laughing with Tex and Griffin, and one look at him and I knew this was his doing.

Outside, Indy's beat-up Honda screeched out of the club parking lot, leaving a plume of dust and smoke behind her. I hightailed it back to my room, shoved on a pair of jeans, pulled on a plain white tee and flannel shirt, and got into my boots in record time.

"Why?" I yelled at the girl still on the bed. "Everyone knows I'm with Indy."

The redhead looked like the cat that ate the cream. "It seemed to me you had forgotten all about your girlfriend when you fucked me last night. You enjoyed it. Kept telling me how much you loved my tight pussy." She opened her legs so I could see all of her. My cum glistened on her skin, and I felt sick. I ran to the bathroom and vomited.

"Get out!" I screamed at her when I walked back into the room and saw her on the bed. "Get the fuck out."

Without a word, she left. Butt naked and proud of it.

When I raced back through the clubhouse, my father was looking pleased with himself. I was furious, but I wasn't even going to bother with him.

Until he opened his mouth.

"Guess the trip to college is off the cards now—"

I paused at the door but didn't turn around.

"—college boy."

My breath left me, heavy and heartbroken. I didn't give him the satisfaction of seeing my face. Without further hesitation, I ripped the door open and left the clubhouse.

Within seconds, my Harley rumbled with life and I took off after my girl.

CHAPTER 55

CADE
Now

I awoke with a start to find the bed beside me empty. I checked my phone, and when I saw nothing from Indy, I dressed quickly and went out into the clubhouse to see if she was in the kitchen making coffee.

She wasn't.

I checked the bathroom. Nothing.

She was gone.

Feeling the fantasy of the night before slip further and further away, I rang her but she didn't pick up. I went for the door but stopped. She had given me one last night. Made me promise I wouldn't try for more because we both knew it wasn't possible. She had a life back in Seattle. One that didn't involve me.

She had left without even a goodbye.

Last night was her goodbye, asshole.

Worked up, I took a shower to calm down because my body was tight and prickly with frustration. My girl was on a plane back to Seattle and I couldn't do a fucking thing about it. I slapped my palms to the tiled wall and let the water roll over me. I promised her . . . one night and then . . .

Fuck it.

Promise or no promise. She belonged with me.

I flicked off the shower and wrapped the towel around my hips. A quick phone call to Lady and I knew Indy was on her way to the airport.

In ten minutes, I was sitting in traffic.

If Indy thought she could just walk away from me without talking this through, then she had another thing coming. If there wasn't anything left to fight for, then fine, she should leave. Just walk away and get on with her life. But there was something left to fight for. She'd let me know that the moment she had made love to me.

Lady said her flight was in just under an hour. But even if I missed her at the airport, I knew I would keep on riding—all the way to Seattle if I had to. Indy was my girl and I was going to ride to the ends of the Earth if it meant bringing her back to me.

She was lining up to board her plane when I found her. I slowed down as I approached, not wanting to startle her. But she must've felt me because her head lifted and she turned as if she was suddenly aware of me being there.

Her face fell.

"Don't," she whispered.

"Don't what? Stop you from making the biggest mistake of your life. Stop you from walking away when I know you don't really want to?"

She glanced around us. "I thought we agreed."

"No, we didn't agree on anything. I don't want this. You can't fucking leave."

When the lady behind us gasped and covered her kid's ears, I gave her an apologetic look and pulled Indy out of the line. To my surprise, she let me.

I took her hand and looked into her big brown eyes. "I love you more than I know how to handle. I can't let you walk away from us."

"I have a life back in Seattle, Cade."

"I know. But I'm asking you to have a life *here*... with me. With your family and friends. Let me be the man you deserve." My heart pounded in my chest. "I don't want this to be the end."

"It has to be." She looked away. "You'll find someone else."

I grabbed her by the arms as if it would somehow make her come to her senses. "I want you! It doesn't matter if I find someone else—they're not you. So, I'm fucking doomed, do you understand me? Because I don't want anyone else. And believe me, I've tried. But it seems that choice left me when I was five and my heart decided it belonged to you."

She started to cry. "I can't do this again."

"You still love me. Somewhere behind that wall you've built, you still love me."

"And what makes you so sure?"

"Because I still love you, just like I did when I was eighteen. It never ended for me. Do you understand that?" I knew I sounded desperate. But I needed her to understand. For me, there was only her. "It simply got stronger, day after day, year after year, and you know what that tells me? It tells me that what we had was real. That it was something special. Something strong. Something magical. That doesn't just fade away."

She took a step closer to me. "No, it doesn't. But I can't—it took so long to get over you. I can't do that again. The pain..." Her eyes filled with tears and she squeezed them shut. "It would end me."

Her words slayed me. I knew what I had put her through, and I was so damn sorry.

"Don't go," I whispered.

She shook her head again.

"Goodbye, Cade."
And just like that, she was gone.

CHAPTER 56

INDY—Aged 18
Then

Rain battered the window. I hugged the cushion tighter to my chest and stared out at the gray day. Outside, a cold wind moved through the trees, sending leaves falling to the ground.

It was my fifth day in Seattle, my third day of college, and six days since I had walked in on Cade having sex with the girl from the clubhouse.

Six days of a broken heart.

Six days of hibernating in my room, and only venturing outside to go to class.

My chest was heavy with heartache and longing. How was it possible to hate and ache for one person at the same time?

"Okay, enough is enough," my roomie said, flopping down on her bed across from mine. Trinity was a New Yorker with a big smile and a halo of auburn curls. "This is your sixth day here, and apart from a couple of classes, you haven't left this room." She sat up. "Get your coat. We're going out for coffee."

"I don't want to go out," I murmured, still staring out the window.

I had no desire to be sociable.

"You know, people don't believe me when I say I have a roommate. They think you're a ghost."

I knew I should be embracing college life. I had wanted it for so long. *But not like this. Not without Cade.* Another wave of grief crashed through me and I squeezed the cushion tighter to my chest. It was a hard enough putting one foot in front of the other, let alone making an effort. *I missed him.*

Trinity threw my coat at me. "One coffee. And then I will personally escort you back to our room and you can resume the recovery position."

If there was one thing I had learned about Trinity in the six days I had known her—she was determined. She wasn't going to let this go until I gave in, and right now I didn't have the energy to fight her.

I glanced at her. "Just one?"

She grinned. "I promise."

Outside, it was as cold as it was bleak. The rain had stopped but the sky was dark with rain clouds. Leaves skipped across the footpath as we made our way through the deserted park toward the campus café. I ducked my head down and pulled my coat tighter around me.

"Um, Indy, this is just a guess, but I'm pretty sure that's your Mr. Wrong waiting for you up ahead," Trinity said.

I looked up and she was right. Cade was waiting for me farther along the footpath. Wearing a Kings of Mayhem hoodie with his hands shoved in his jeans, he looked like he hadn't slept in days. He looked like hell.

Trinity turned to look at me. "Do you want me to tell him to go away?"

Kings of Mayhem

I had never seen Cade look so desperate. He was usually so confident, so self-assured. But not today. He was pale with dark circles under his eyes, and while he was still big and broad, he looked like he had lost weight.

I shook my head and walked toward him, while Trinity took a seat on a park bench a few feet away.

"What are you doing here?" I asked, unable to keep the sharpness out of my voice. A deep, searing pain made me tremble. Seeing him was hard. "You shouldn't be here."

Cade shifted with uncertainty. "I had to see you."

"Why? We're done."

"Please don't say that," he begged. His Adam's apple bobbed. His lips were red from the cold. He was desperate. "I can't breathe without you."

"Then you should've thought about that before . . . you know what, I'm not doing this." I put my hand up. "I'm not rehashing this. Like I said, we're done."

I went to walk past him but he grabbed me and pulled me to his chest, desperately squeezing me to him. His smell and the familiarity of his warmth broke my heart all over again and I longed to melt into his embrace. "I need you. I can't live without out. Please, Indy, you have to give me another chance." His arms tightened around me. "Tell me you want me again."

His words cut through me and I couldn't stand it, so I pushed him away. "I told you we were done."

"Please," he begged. "I made a mistake."

"You had sex with someone else!"

Images of him and her haunted me every day.

"I didn't know . . . I thought she was —" He stopped when my eyes widened.

"You thought that skank was me?" I cried. Despite the cold and the rain, my blood boiled and I shoved him in the chest. Out of the corner of my eye, I saw Trinity stand up. "You couldn't tell the difference between the girl you supposedly love and some club whore?"

Later, I would be pleased that there was no one in the park to witness the meltdown that followed.

"I heard you moaning. I heard how much you were enjoying her riding you. At first, I thought someone else was in your room. I mean, there was no way, right? You wouldn't be in there with another woman. But there you were, mid-orgasm with some MC groupie on top of your . . ." My chin quivered and I had to look away for a moment. "For as long as I live I will never be able to forget or forgive what you have done." I bit my lip to stop it from trembling. "Go home, Cade. You don't belong here."

He grabbed me by the shoulders. "I fucked up. I own it. But it's killing me, Indy."

I knocked his hands off me. "It's killing you? What do you think it's done to me?"

He looked desperate.

"Indy, please—"

My heartache bubbled up and burst from me.

"How could you be so reckless with my heart!" I yelled. I was in so much pain I was almost doubled over with it. "I gave it to you and you *broke* it!"

He reached for me but I stepped away from him.

"I know and I'm so sorry—" He breathed brokenheartedly, barely able to contain his tears.

"Sorry doesn't even begin to make this better!" I rasped. I pushed him away and stood in front of him, my pain wide open for him to see. "You've taken everything from me. You broke us and there just aren't enough pieces left to put us back together again. Go away, Cade."

"But I love you," he breathed desperately.

Standing in front of him with my grief so exposed, I felt vulnerable. So I grabbed onto my anger to protect myself.

"Well, I don't love you," I cried, knowing my words would slay him. "Not anymore."

He looked at me as if I'd just pulled his heart from his body.

In that moment, he realized we were done, and a hundred different emotions crossed his face before he finally shook his head. A look of absolute grief crossed his face. And in that last moment we just stared at each other as our future dissipated like mist in the dreary afternoon light. Finally, he walked away and I burst into tears.

That night I wrote him a letter telling him to stay away . . . and he did.

For twelve years.

CHAPTER 57

INDY
Now

It was raining. *Of course, it was.* Because this was fucking Seattle and not Destiny, Mississippi.

Still feeling grim from the scene with Cade at the airport, I pushed back my heartache as I paid the taxi driver, and reluctantly trudged up the stairs to my apartment.

I closed the front door behind me and leaned against it, feeling my heart break all over again. I could move to another country—another planet—and I was never going to be able to outrun my feelings for Cade.

During my seven-hour flight and the fifty-seven-minute layover in Houston, I had tortured myself with a tangle of confused thoughts. But they all came back to the one conclusion. That I had made a huge mistake walking away from him.

Now I was simply exhausted. I had used the last of my resolve to walk away.

I banged the back of my head against the door and closed my eyes.

"Damn," I whispered to myself, suddenly feeling very lonely.

Kicking off the door, I threw my keys in the ashtray on the kitchen counter and dumped my overnight bag on the couch. I lit a fire to push away the dreary Seattle chill and put on some coffee. Feeling alone and just plain weird about things, I crossed the room to the huge bay window overlooking the park. I leaned against the windowsill and stared out into the bleak night feeling an overwhelming urge to cry. Outside, glittering ribbons of rain fell from the eves in front of the window, and in the light of the streetlamp they glittered like diamonds.

When I felt the tears prick my eyes I got mad. "Don't you dare fucking cry. You chose this. You chose Seattle over him. You—"

My phone buzzed in my hand, making me jump.

To my surprise, it was Cade, and seeing his name on the screen filled me with so much warmth I wanted to run out of that apartment and hightail it back to Destiny.

After the scene at the airport, he was the last person I expected to hear from.

Smiling through my sadness I answered it, trying to conceal the emotion in my voice and the tears that had started to fall down my cheeks.

"Stop crying," he said softly.

God, it was good to hear his voice. "I'm not crying."

"Yes, you are."

I smiled. Thinking how typical it was of him to think he knew me so well. "Is that right?"

There was silence for a moment before he spoke again, "Indy?"

"Yeah?"

"Will you answer me one thing?"

Not sure if I should agree or not, I answered quietly, "Sure."

There was more silence, and then Cade's voice was husky as he asked, "Are you crying because you're still in love with me?"

I started to nod and cry harder.

"No," my voice cracked as a new wave of heartache stiffened my face with emotion.

"Don't lie to me," Cade said gently.

"I'm ... not."

"Then why are you nodding?"

"I'm not . . . wait, how—"

My head shot up, and my eyes frantically searched the street outside my window. And there he was, slowly stepping out of the shadows of the chilly Seattle evening and into the streetlight.

Cade.

The love of my life.

The dam broke then and I didn't need to think, I just ran, not even closing my front door behind me. I flew down the steps and out into the rain, not stopping until I reached the comfort of his arms and the sweet, sweet bliss of his lips against mine.

Rain poured over us, but neither of us cared. All we knew was each other. All we knew was the emotion between us.

Cade's palms were strong against my jaw as he held me tight, his mouth moving strong and demanding over mine. A low moan came from deep within him and I could feel his desperation in the way he kissed me.

He pulled away and looked at me desperately.

"Tell me how I let you go without it killing me and I will," he said, his voice rising over the rain. "Tell me how I live without you without it destroying me."

I shook my head, my hair saturated with rain. "I don't want you to let me go."

Cade pulled back, his brow dug in. "But—"

I reclaimed the space between us and smashed my mouth to his, kissing him fiercely. My palms pressed hard against his face, holding me close to him. Because I couldn't get close enough to him.

He pulled back to look at me, searching my face for the answers.

"What are you saying?" he asked, rain bouncing off his lips.

"I'm saying you're right, Cade. You're right." I shook my head a little. "I shouldn't have left you at the airport. We do have something magical, and no matter how hard I try, I can't outrun it. But that's the thing—I don't want to. Not anymore. I don't want to run away from you or the club, or us." My voice continued to rise as my emotions did, and I gave a small, disbelieving laugh. "It's like I've been asleep for the last twelve years, and I've just woken up." Tears mingled with rain on my face. "I don't want this life I have if it's without you."

It was true. And it was a relief to finally admit it.

Oh God. It felt so good to finally say it.

"You don't have to, Indy. Not if you don't want to." He pointed to his broad chest. "I'm all yours. All of me. If you want me. And I promise you, on my life, I will never let anything come between us again."

He kissed me again. Hard and urgent. And I kissed him back

"Tell me you're mine," he begged against my mouth.

I kissed him. "Haven't I always been?"

We barely made it inside my apartment, separating our mouths only long enough to remove our wet clothes. Then Cade lay me down on the plush rug in front of the fireplace and made love to me, exquisitely slow, exquisitely meaningful, every push into my body deliberate and deep. His hands roamed my body and his lips and tongue trailed along my throat, engulfing me in the heat of his kiss, of his lovemaking, of him. And I moved beneath him, slowly, wrapping my legs around his hips and welcoming every deep plunge into my body. Feeling every stroke to my very core, feeling the fierce swell of my orgasm as it moved through me to finally erupt in white light across my brain.

"Cade!" I cried out his name, not once, but over and over as my body and mind were completely and utterly overwhelmed by the potent ecstasy flooding every cell of me.

He drove into me one last time and buried his face into my neck and grasped at the rug beneath us, twisting it in his hands as he came.

Still inside me, he looked down into my face.

"I love you, Indy." Light from the fire flickered across his handsome face. "Stop running from me."

I looked up at him. "Don't give me a reason to run and I won't."

The light from the fire reflected in his blue eyes.

"Never again. You have my word."

And with that, he began to make love to me all over again.

CHAPTER 58

CADE
Now

"So, Indy, are you back for good?" Isaac asked, leaning across the table and digging a handful of peanuts out of the bowl next to a bowl of sugared almonds. My mom was crazy for nuts. Brazil nuts. Peanuts. Chocolate-covered almonds. You name it; there were bowls of the stuff all over the house.

We were sitting at the twelve-seater dining table.

I looked across at Indy who grinned back at my cousin.

"Maybe. Why, you miss me?" She threw a sugared almond at him.

He grinned and nodded at me. "Nah, just sick of his whining is all. I was worried he'd grown a vagina."

She chuckled. "You know that's an impossibility, right?"

"I'm serious… the dude was one step away from crying into his fucking Lucky Charms, every day." He winked at Indy. "If you're back, then I'm fucking happy. It's a good thing."

Indy looked up at me and then turned back to Isaac. "I thought I might hang out for a while… see what happens."

"What about your job at the hospital? Were they pissed?"

"I applied for a transfer to St Gabriel's. They have a vacancy coming up in emergency."

"That's almost like a sign," he said with a wink. "It's good you're back. 'Bout time you two got your shit together. Don't think there's been a finer match made in hell."

He stood up and stretched, yawning, and then grabbing his cigarettes off the table, put one in his mouth. "I gotta shoot. You bitches play nice."

When he was gone, I looked at my girl sitting across the table from me.

"You know, we've got the house to ourselves for a couple of hours," I said.

Since returning from Seattle, we alternated living between all three homes: my mom's, Indy's mom's, and the clubhouse.

Indy grinned with a mischievous sparkle in her eye. "Best we make the most of it then."

In my room, I took my time removing her clothes and making love to her. I wanted to make her pregnant. I wanted to fill her with my babies and make her my wife. I wanted to make it so nothing would ever come between us and keep us separated again.

I knew it was crazy wanting all those things so quickly. But I had grown up wanting them with her, so it was only natural for them to resurface with her return to Destiny.

Looking down at her, I looked into her eyes. I had won the lottery. I had everything I wanted. I just hoped she felt the same way.

"I love you," I said. And I had never meant anything more in that one moment. "Tell me what I need to do to keep you with me."

"I need to take things one step at a time," she replied soberly.

"We can work things out together." I wiped a strand of hair from her cheek. Still inside her, I felt her clench around me. "Promise me that we can. That you won't run away again."

She nodded and slid her hand behind my neck, pulling me down to kiss me. "I'm not going anywhere," she whispered against my lips.

I rose up on my forearms again. Sliding my turquoise and silver ring from my finger, I reached for her left hand and slipped it over her ring finger. "You're my girl."

"What are you doing?"

"Making you mine for good."

Surprise turned into a big smile. "Are you asking me to marry you?"

"I don't want any other girl, Indy. From the moment I met you, we were meant to be together."

"This isn't really taking things one day at a time," she said with a soft chuckle.

I smiled and curled my hand around the ring and her finger. "This is permanent."

She gave me one of her serious looks. "I won't cook for you."

"You can't cook anyway."

She grinned "And I don't iron."

"Baby, do I look like the kind of guy who gives a fuck about ironing?"

I was hard as fuck now, and when I started to move inside her again, an involuntary moan escaped her parted lips.

"In fact, I won't wash, clean, or run after you in any way, shape, or form," she said. She was trying to keep focused on her argument, but the fact that I was slowly fucking her was becoming a distraction.

"And I won't be at your beck and call, like the other old ladies." She tried to sound tough, but she was close to whimpering as my cock moved in and out of her. I pressed in deep and hard against her pelvis with mine.

"Aha," I said, running my tongue along her neck.

"And don't expect me to wait at home for you to come home. I'm an independent woman."

I pressed harder into her. "Indy…"

"Yes?"

"Are you always going to be such a pain in the ass?"

I felt her grin against my shoulder. "You can count on it, Cade. I ain't one of your club bunnies."

I looked down at her. "Club bunnies?" God, I was in love with her.

"Like Sandy or Candy, or whatever the fuck their names are."

The beginnings of another orgasm began to swell in me.

"I think I got it. You ain't no cooking, cleaning, ironing, wait-at-home, club bunny."

"Exactly."

When she gasped at my sudden thrust, I knew it wasn't going to take me long to make her come, and I was right. After moving deep and slow into her, she came beneath me in tiny shudders, pressing her fingers deep into my shoulders and squeezing her thighs tight around my hips. It was enough to set me off. My second orgasm was long and drawn out, sinking into my brain and dragging me away on a hazy wave of bliss.

That's when I made a silent vow to myself. I would only ever do right by this amazing woman. No matter what it took.

CHAPTER 59

CADE—Aged 23
Then

The room smelled like old timber and aged leather. I glanced around me, taking in the rows and rows of old books in the wall-to-ceiling bookcase, and the old desk in front of me that seemed too big for the room. Outside, rain fell like nails from a grey sky.

"This is very generous of you, Mr. Calley," said the man behind the desk. He was a good-looking man in a suit. African American and big, he smiled at me as he joined his hands together.

"She deserves it," I said.

"Yes. It is a shame her scholarship fell through. But your generosity will ensure she gets to complete her education and earn her doctorate."

I nodded. When Lady told me about Indy's scholarship falling through, I knew I had to do something. Bolt's illness had drained money from Indy's college fund and more. Hefty loans meant Lady and Jackie didn't have the money to spare. And unless they could find the money for her to finish med school, Indy would have to drop out. The club would help out. There was a lot of money in the club because of their lucrative businesses. They would pay for her to finish, Bull had assured them. But I stopped the club from stepping in because I wanted to pay for it.

I owed her at least that much.

In five years, I had managed to save a lot of cash. Enough to ensure Indy would see her dream through to the end.

"Would you like to see her?" The gentleman behind the desk asked. "I had my secretary find out where she'd be this morning in case you wanted to—"

"That won't be necessary. And if we could keep this between us, I'd be grateful."

I stood and so did he.

"You don't want Miss Parrish knowing the donation is from you?"

I shook my head.

"Not from me," I said. "Let her know it was from someone who believes she is going to do great things."

We shook hands and I left his office. Outside, the rain had stopped but it was cold and wet, and I shoved my hands in my jeans. Despite the weather, the campus was crowded with students making their way to and from class. I wasn't wearing my cut and was able to blend in easily as I made my way toward the parking lot. In another life, one where I hadn't fucked up, I would have walked these grounds as a student. But in this life, I walked it as a stranger who had no business being there, other than to ensure someone very special got to follow her dream.

If I hadn't glanced to my right I would have missed her. But I did and the sight of her stopped me in my tracks and sent a ferocious pain spiraling through me. She was walking with a group of people, her beautiful blonde hair almost hidden by the beanie she wore, her face pink with cold. She was clutching a Styrofoam cup of coffee between her gloved hands as she chatted happily to the guy walking beside her. Suddenly, her beautiful, pink lips broke into a devastating smile as she laughed at something he said and my heart squeezed painfully in my chest. She didn't see me and I was glad. Five years had passed since I'd spoken to her, and the agony in my heart was as real as the last time I'd seen her. Her seeing me and walking away would end me.

I turned my back and began to walk away.

It would be years before I would see her again.

And by then she would be with another man.

CHAPTER 60

INDY
Now

It was Wednesday. And every Wednesday night, apparently, there was a fight for money at the clubhouse. Tonight, it was Cade and Hawke.

Typically, it was a club member thing only. But Cade seemed determined to keep me close and brought me along.

Isaac sat down next to me, and for a moment he didn't speak, he just joined me in watching Cade in the ring, occasionally raising his bottle of beer to his lips to take a sip.

"He's different around you," he said finally.

"He is?"

Isaac smiled and it was the gorgeous, perfect, pearly white smile that made all the girls drop their panties. Of course, it did. He was a Calley, and they all possessed a spell-binding allure about them that they used to mesmerize women to get exactly what they wanted.

"Yeah, he is. But then again, that boy always was a fool for you." He lit a cigarette and it hung off his lip. "Good to see some things don't change."

"He's changed," I said, turning back to the action in the ring.

"Yeah?"

"He's harder. Something's changed in him."

Just as I said it, Cade unleashed a vicious right hook on Hawke's left cheek and split it open, and the crowd of bikers cheered.

"Yeah, well, a lot of water has rushed under that bridge," Isaac said. "We all have to grow up sometimes, I guess."

"It's not that. There's something else. Something I can't quite put my finger on. But it's made him harder than I remember. Darker."

Isaac put down his beer bottle and drew on his cigarette. "Travis Hawthorne."

My eyes darted to his. I recognized the name immediately. Once upon a time, Travis Hawthorne had held us all in a state of terror for more than an hour as he roamed the school hallways with a loaded shotgun, a Glock, and enough ammunition to arm an entire infantry.

"What about him?" I asked.

Isaac drew on his smoke and then forced it out both nostrils.

"He got out. Some years back."

I gasped. "How can that be? He was a psychopath!"

"Not according to his doctors." He shook his head. "They let him out about four years ago."

"That's crazy," I whispered.

"That's not the half of it," Isaac said. "Two months after he got out, Travis killed a young woman and her elderly parents."

My hand went to my mouth. "Why?"

"Because he is a psychopathic asshole."

Jesus.

"What happened?"

"He came across them at the supermarket, followed them to their farmhouse, and then did what he did. Why, because that kid was crazier than a cut snake. Did all kinds of terrible things to the woman, before and after he killed her." Isaac shook his head. "Cops caught up with him in Tennessee. He was driving her car, and apparently the taillight was out. I guess he figured he was busted, so he decided to go out in a hail of bullets."

"Goddamn."

Isaac relit his cigarette because it had gone out. "Cade blames himself. Believes if he had killed Travis all those years ago instead of wounding him, the woman and her parents would still be alive."

"But it's not his fault."

"I know that, and you know that. But Cade? He thinks he's responsible for three lives when he could've taken just the one." He looked regretful. "He had a real hard time after that, Indy. He took it hard. At the time, he was dating a girl named Krista and we all thought he would end up marrying her. Then all of a sudden, he broke up with her and withdrew into himself. It took him a while to get his head right again." He sighed. "Not that I'm sure he ever did."

My stomach heated with jealousy at the mention of an ex-girlfriend. The thought of him with someone else made me feel vulnerable because it was a reminder of how close I had come to losing Cade for good.

I leaned over and took Isaac's cigarette from him, inhaling deeply. I hated asking, but I couldn't help myself. "Do you think he would have married her?"

Isaac thought for a moment, squinting at me through a furrowed brow. "At the time, I did. But looking back..."

"What?"

He shrugged. "She wasn't you."

We both looked up in time to see Cade drop Hawke to the floor with a powerful right hook. Bull signaled he was the winner by raising one arm above his head and the crowd cheered, except for the bikers who had put money on Hawke.

I handed Isaac his cigarette back. "Am I making a mistake, Isaac?"

"Only if you don't mean to stick around. That kid has always had his head bent out of shape over you. He's come close to losing his shit before, and I would fucking hate to see it happen again."

I found Cade in his bathroom.

"You broke Hawke's nose," I said, leaning against the doorway.

He cocked an eyebrow at me. "You checked on Hawke?"

"He was the one lying semi-conscious on the ground," I said, cocking an eyebrow right back. "Besides, I figured taking care of you might take a little longer."

My innuendo wasn't lost on him. He grabbed my wrist and pulled me to him. "I know exactly how you can take care of me."

He kissed me hard, but I broke it off.

"Let me tend to those cuts and bruises," I whispered, kissing his jaw. "And then I'll let you do whatever you want to me."

I couldn't lie. Seeing Cade take down Hawke had turned me on. Fist to face. It had been so primal. So, after I dressed his knuckles and sutured a split through his eyebrow, we got naked and I let him do whatever the hell he wanted to me. Which involved a lot of licking, rubbing, touching, and thrusting, and me getting two toe-curling orgasms.

Afterwards, we lay breathless on his bed.

"Isaac told me about Travis Hawthorne," I murmured against his chest.

Cade didn't move, but I felt his breathing pause for a moment. "What about him?"

I sat up and pulled my hair over my shoulders.

"That he got out." I bit my lower lip, not sure how Cade was going to react. "And that he killed a woman and her parents not long after."

Sitting up against the pillows, Cade reached for a cigarette from the nightstand and busied himself lighting it. He took a deep drag and let it out with a heavy sigh. In the dim light, his broad chest looked massive.

"He said you blame yourself. That if you had killed him all those years ago, then those people would still be alive."

He didn't deny it. "What else did Isaac tell you?"

"That you broke up with Krista not long after." My eyes met his. "That everyone thought you and she would get married. But then all of a sudden, you broke up with her."

Again, my stomach knotted at the idea of him with her.

"And?"

"That's it. That's all he said." I couldn't help but want him to tell me why he broke up with her.

"You want to know the real reason I broke up with Krista?"

"Yes."

He drew heavily on his cigarette, his blue eyes sparkling across at me. "She wasn't you."

"Cade—"

"That's not a line, Indy. It's the truth." He stubbed out his cigarette. "There are only two things I regret in my life. One of them was taken care of by seven police bullets on the side of the road just outside of Hazard, Tennessee. The other just walked back into my life." He reached over and tucked my hair behind my ear, and he studied my face as he ran the back of his fingers across my cheek. "Losing you was my biggest regret. And after Travis got out and did what he did, it made me realize that I had to make right the one other thing I could change. So, I broke up with Krista and climbed on my bike."

A strange tingling sensation took up in my stomach.

"I rode all the way to Seattle to find you."

"You came to Seattle?"

I didn't know. He had never come to see me. Or contacted me to let me know he was in town. But, why would he? The last time we had spoken I'd told him to stay away from me.

"I rode to your hospital. Waited for you to finish your shift."

I couldn't believe what I was hearing.

"But when I saw you, you were leaving with someone. He had his arms around you, and just as you stepped outside, he paused to kiss you. You were smiling, Indy. You looked so happy. And I knew then, in that moment, that I had no right to be there. I'd had my chance with you and I had blown it. But even then, I couldn't walk away. I made myself watch you walk off with him, even though my body ached and my mind screamed at me to run after you. How could I? He said something and you laughed, and I could see he made you truly happy. So, I accepted that you were gone and I had to get over it and move on."

The man he was talking about was a guy called Peter. He was a plastic surgeon at SeaTac Medical where I worked. He was also a huge dating disaster. We had dated for a month and he was charming and interesting. But it ended when I walked in on him eating his receptionist's pussy during his lunch hour.

I let out a deep breath. I didn't know what to say.

"He meant nothing," I finally said. "We dated for a few weeks. But it was nothing."

"What about Anson?"

His question surprised me.

"What about him?" I asked.

"Did you love *him*?"

"That's a random question," I said.

It wasn't really. But it caught me off guard.

"Did you?" he asked again, an edge to his voice.

I thought about it and then nodded. "I loved him, yes. But I wasn't *in love* with him."

I felt Cade's body weaken against me, and when I looked up I saw his jaw was fixed as he stared up at the ceiling.

"That makes me feel insane," he said finally, his voice hoarse and dark. The silver rings on his fingers glinted in the dim light as he ran his hand through his hair. And he exhaled deeply to calm whatever storm was taking place inside of him.

"I'm pretty sure you weren't celibate during the past twelve years," I reminded him.

"No. I wasn't. But I was never in love with anyone."

"What about Krista? You didn't love her?"

"No."

"Isaac said everyone thought you would marry her."

"Clearly, they were wrong."

"But you would marry me?" I held up my left hand where Cade's pinky ring was still on my finger.

"In a heartbeat." He gave me a sexy, close-lipped smile that pressed his dimples deeper into his cheeks.

I smiled and settled back into his chest.

And then, for reasons only God would know, that was when the realization hit me.

Out of nowhere.

I lifted my head, and my brows pulled in.

"It was you, wasn't it?" I said with the breathiness of disbelief.

It wasn't a question. I already knew the answer. And it seemed crazy to me that I had never put two and two together before now.

Cade frowned. "I'm not following."

I sat up. "When I was in med school my scholarship fell through. The school received a payment from an anonymous benefactor. I figured it must have been the club. My mom said she didn't know who it was. For years I wondered." I looked him in the eye. "It was you, wasn't it?"

He half sat up, his hard stomach rippling with the deep curves and dips of his abdominal muscles. Heat radiated off his strong body as he fixed me with his blue gaze.

"Does it matter?" he asked.

A love so powerful, and so overwhelming washed over me. This man, this towering beast of a man with all his tattoos and muscles—he was the most beautiful soul I had ever met. A fierce love soared through me. My heart swelled, completely seduced by his love for me and the lengths he would go to make me happy.

"I love you so much," I said, tears welling in my eyes. I rose up onto my knees and felt his strong abs flex and clench as I slid onto him and took his face in my hands. Leaning down, I kissed him tenderly. "Thank you for loving me so much."

His hands slid up my thighs to my back, his strong fingers trailing up and down my spine. Here, with him, I felt so cared for, so loved, so honored. I sealed my mouth to his and pushed my fingers through his hair as our kiss deepened and I lost myself in the beauty of the only man I could ever love this fiercely.

CHAPTER 61

INDY
Now

The next afternoon, when I finished work, Cade was waiting for me.

"Where are we going?" I asked, taking the helmet from him and climbing onto the back of his bike.

"It's a surprise."

"I hate surprises."

"I know," he said with a grin.

With a flick of his wrist, we roared off into the late afternoon light and I relaxed behind him, enjoying the warmth of his big body in my arms and the hot summer breeze whipping at my skin. Ten minutes later we pulled up outside of a two-story, brick home and Cade killed the engine.

"Where are we?" I asked, undoing my helmet and placing it on the bike.

Cade winked and grabbed my hand, leading me along the little pathway to the front porch. Three steps and we were at the big oak front door with huge silver handles. He dug into his cut pocket for the key, and opened the door.

Still wondering what we were doing here, I followed him inside and looked around me. Inside, the house was stunning. Polished timber floors. Pale yellow walls with bright white trim. Plush carpet on a sweeping staircase leading up to the second landing.

"What is this?" I asked, trying to take it all in. The tall, arched windows. The French doors leading out to a patio.

"Our new home," he said. "If you want to live here."

I raised an eyebrow. "This is ours?"

"I bought it a couple of years ago and have been leasing it ever since. Up until last week, a British couple rented it but they had to return to England, so now it's vacant. I considered selling it. But it's only ten minutes to the hospital and it's close to everything."

I had another look around me.

"What do you think?" he asked.

My gaze came back to him, a rising excitement curling its way through me. "I think it's our new home."

He grinned, his dimples deepening in his cheeks. "You want to live here?"

"Are you kidding me? Of course, I do!" I twirled around and started to laugh. "Cade, it's perfect."

I walked through the beautiful home. Through the large lounge room and into the formal dining room where a massive mahogany table gleamed in golden light. Through the bathrooms with the Italian tile and gleaming marble vanities, and into the guest bedrooms where my feet sank into the plushest carpet I'd ever felt.

When I walked into the kitchen, I stopped. It was incredible. Breathtaking, almost. All glossy and white with stainless steel appliances. I ran my hand along the smooth, marble countertops. "It's so beautiful."

Cade came up behind me and put his arms around my waist.

"Welcome home, baby," he murmured against my throat.

I twisted around in his arms and he kissed me. His mouth moved erotically over mine, his lips taking command, his tongue filling my mouth and tangling in a sensual dance with my tongue. It was a passionate kiss. Luscious. Delicious. Addictive. And I curled my fist into the front of his shirt to hold him close to me as I drank him in.

Home. We were finally home.

Cade groaned hungrily, cupping my face in his strong hands.

Breathless, I pulled back and laughed. "Here?"

"As good a place as any," he said, kissing me again. He scooped me up into his big arms and carried me through the kitchen and up the stairs to our new bedroom. He laid me down on the freshly made bed. "Just so you know, no one has slept on this bed," he said as he crawled over me. "I brought it to help the place sell if you didn't want to live here."

"Then best we christen it," I said with a seductive raise of an eyebrow.

He kissed me slowly, and then pulled away to slide down the length of me, removing my clothes as he went, and I was grateful for the shower I'd taken before leaving work because I'd been projectile vomited on by a nine-year-old.

When I was in nothing but my panties, he buried his face against the satin and my body ignited. Slowly, he slid them down my legs and buried his face between my thighs.

I pushed my head back into the pillow while he pushed his tongue in deeper. If it was one thing Cade Calley had mastered, it was his tongue and what he could do with it. I moaned and tangled my fingers through his hair as my orgasm began to swell. *Holy hell.* Less than a minute down there, and he already had me ready to come. My toes curled into the mattress.

"Cade..." I breathed.

One more flick of his tongue and I came undone. I grabbed the bed sheets and cried out as my clit throbbed against his mouth, and raw pleasure streamed through me. I unleashed a cry, my mind utterly unraveled with ecstasy. With a growl, he pulled away and rose to his feet, his face dark with an urgent need he could no longer contain. His cock was in his hand and he stroked it, his eyes full of heat as he looked down on me sprawled on the bed.

When he reached for a condom in his wallet, I stopped him. Since returning from Seattle we'd both been to the doctor. And because I was on the pill, there was no need for further protection.

"Are you sure?" he panted.

My clit throbbed with excitement. I wanted his naked cock inside of me.

I nodded and he dropped his wallet, giving me a look that was nothing but raw desire.

He crawled over me, his naked body engulfing me in his warmth as he rubbed himself through the slippery skin he had just tortured with his tongue. With one hard thrust, he was inside of me but he stopped, completely overwhelmed by the sensation.

"Oh, baby..." His face shimmered and his brows drew in.

When I began to move beneath him, he hissed in a deep breath.

"This feels too good," he moaned.

He wasn't lying. It felt more than good. It felt out of this world. And I was wet with longing at the idea of him coming inside of me. When my pussy clenched and pulsed at the thought, Cade groaned.

"It's not going to take me long, baby. Your tight little pussy is too much."

It was a hot Mississippi summer and our skin was slick as we rolled around on our new bed. Sweat beaded on Cade's brow and his naked chest gleamed in the late afternoon light. It was hard and fast. With lots of dirty words being moaned and mumbled as the pleasure swelled.

When his phone rang, Cade ripped it of the bedside table with a growl and threw it across the bed to stop it from ringing just as his orgasm tore through him. He gripped my hips and thrust harder, his eyes closed and his lips parted as he pumped and pumped his climax into me.

When he came back down to Earth, he started to laugh and collapsed against me. He covered me with his slick body and buried his face into the crook of my shoulder. Skin to skin, I could feel the wild thud of his heart against my chest.

"That was fucking amazing," he murmured into my throat.

"You know, we are going to have to stop having sex long enough to do other things," I said.

He lifted his head. "If it's going to feel like that every time we have sex then I'm not leaving this room. Ever."

Since returning from Seattle, we'd spent a lot of time in the bedroom. Talking. Fucking. Sleeping. Fucking. Losing ourselves in the little bubble we had wrapped around us. *Fucking.* For the first two weeks, we barely put on clothes.

But now I was working at St Gabriel's as an emergency physician and the hours were crushing. Eighteen-hour shifts that usually turned into twenty-four. So, when I got a couple of days off, we were lucky if we emerged from the bedroom at all.

"I'm surprised your mom hasn't sent out a search party for you," I said. "I really haven't seen her that much since we got back."

"Oh, damn," Cade replied, rolling off me and pushing his palms into his eyes. "I forgot."

I rose up on one eyebrow. "Forgot what?"

"Mom invited us to dinner."

"When?"

He looked at his watch. "We're supposed to be there in ten minutes."

"You mean I have to face a hundred-and-one questions about us with sex hair? I need to go home and shower." I went to get up but he pulled me back and held me against his rock-hard chest.

"Or we could call in a rain check and stay in our new home," he whispered against my neck.

"We have to go," I said soberly, sitting up and sliding my legs over the side of the bed. Apart from one afternoon at his mom's house, we hadn't seen much of his family. I walked toward the bathroom, fully aware of Cade's eyes roaming over every inch of me. I could feel them, like the sweet caress of fingers along my skin. I looked at him over my shoulder. "Or they may actually send out a search party."

My eyes dropped to his cock. It was still hard.

I raised an eyebrow. "That's not going to get us to your mama's on time."

He began to stroke it. "This?"

A pulse took up between my thighs. Seeing my tattooed god fisting his cock on the bed was too irresistible. The shower would have to wait. I would have to go to dinner smelling of Cade and the things he did to me. I walked back to the bed and crawled over him, sliding my thighs on either side of his hips.

"Fine, but just so you know, you're explaining to your mama why we're late."

CHAPTER 62

CADE
Now

We arrived at my mom's almost an hour late. But it was hard to feel apologetic while my body still throbbed with the echo of two mind-blowing orgasms.

Everyone was there. Mom and Ari. Griffin. Sybil and Jury. Lady and Abby. Isaac and Cherry with little Brax. Caleb without his annoying girlfriend, Brandi.

And they were already seated at the table when we walked in, which was good because I'd spent the last few hours working up one hell of an appetite.

"So, Cade, I hear you chased down our girl all the way to Seattle," Ari said.

Ari was the manager of *Sinister Ink*, the Kings of Mayhem tattoo shop. He was also my mom's boyfriend. At six-foot-seven, he was mammoth. He also didn't say a hell of a lot, but when he did, you listened.

"I was lucky there was another flight leaving not long after hers," I explained, heaping mashed potatoes on my plate. "I figured it was going to get me there a lot faster than the Harley."

"That's my boy," my mom said with a wink.

"Pussy," Isaac muttered with a grin.

Cherry elbowed him. "I would expect nothing less from you, Isaac Calley," she said.

"And you would get nothing less, baby doll," he replied, kissing her on the cheek.

Brax screwed up his nose and rolled his eyes dramatically at his parents.

I laughed. Suddenly consumed with a want to have my own son. I looked across the table at Indy, and our eyes locked as she buttered her corn. I wanted to start a family straight away. Get married. Make babies. I had always wanted a family with her. But this was the first time in a long time that it was possible. She smiled and it took my breath away. This woman. She was everything.

Tomorrow I would ask her to marry me.

Properly.

On my knee with a fucking ring.

Not one I'd ripped off my finger and put on hers while I was still inside of her.

"Well, now that we're all here, I've got an announcement to make," Cherry said, standing up with a huge grin on her face. Everyone at the table went quiet. "Well, there really isn't any other way to say this than—we're having another baby."

To say the table erupted with excitement would be an understatement. Family was everything in the MC. Kids were adored and raised with a hundred uncles and aunts. It was a massive family. So, when one of our own was expecting a baby, it was a big fucking deal.

"Congratulations, brother," I slapped Isaac on the back.

He smiled but there was something odd about him tonight. Something I couldn't put my finger on. He was genuinely excited about Cherry, but something was off. Like he had something on his mind. Something big.

"I really need to talk to you," he said when the table was being cleared and everyone was preoccupied.

By his tone, I knew he wasn't going to tell me anything good.

We went outside for a cigarette so we were away from everyone.

"Look, I've set up this deal," he said, lighting up a cigarette. "A really fucking good deal."

"What sort of deal?" Club members didn't set up anything without it going to the table for a vote.

"Just hear me out, okay." He drew heavily on his cigarette and looked up at me through his brow. Isaac had this James Dean in *Rebel Without a Cause* thing going on. It drove the girls crazy—like panty-dropping crazy. His eyes would squint to almost closing, and his brow would furrow up like he had the world resting on his shoulders.

But I wasn't a horny girl, and his furrowed-brow, tortured-biker routine didn't work jack on me.

"What sort of deal. Isaac?"

He flicked the ash from his cigarette.

"I was down in Tuscaloosa, met up with some guys. They offered me a good deal."

"What guys? And what kind of deal?" I asked, my eyes narrowing. This was beginning to sound like a rogue deal, and I prayed he hadn't made any promises on behalf of the club.

"Just a little heroin."

"You mean to tell me you went rogue? You went behind the club's back and made a deal you're not authorized to make?" I gritted my teeth and sucked in a deep breath in a poor attempt to keep my temper in check. "Damn it, Isaac. Do you know what you've done?"

The Knights of Hell and the Kings had an understanding. We didn't touch their profitable heroin and gun-running trade, and they stayed a certain distance from our interests. It was a gentleman's agreement.

But, let's face it. None of us were gentlemen.

Who knew what kind of retaliation The Knights would unleash on The Kings.

It was just the type of shit the club didn't need right now.

As clubs went, The Kings were bigger, better, and a hell of a lot smarter. But, The Knights were like an over enthusiastic kid brother—full of bravado and bite. They were just itching to pull their dicks out over some feud. The tension between the two clubs had been building for years, and Isaac had just given them a reason to release some of that tension.

"It was an opportunity for The Kings to explore another lucrative market."

"It was an opportunity for The Knights to start a fucking turf war!" I seethed. Isaac had no place making this kind of deal.

There were so many things wrong with this scenario, I didn't know where to start. The last eighteen months had seen a lot of deals fall through for the club. In fact, we'd had a long run of bad luck lately. We didn't need any more trouble.

"The Kings don't run drugs. And we sure as shit don't make rogue deals behind our brothers' backs," I growled.

"There's money to be made here, brother," Isaac demanded. "Good money."

"Not for our club, Isaac."

"It's a missed opportunity for every single one of us if you don't explore this."

"We're not pieces-of-shit drug dealers!" I seethed. "We're more honorable than that gutter-feeding bullshit."

"Because porn and prostitution are such noble industries," Isaac said.

"At least they don't kill people. What's a guy gonna do? Fuck himself to death?"

Isaac ignored me, and his face remained serious. "It's an untapped supply of coin, Cade. Lots of coin. We've got to take this to the table. Give our brothers an opportunity to vote on it. We can make some serious money. We need this. *I* need this. I've got a wife, a son, and another kid on the way."

"Bull will never go for it. None of our brothers will go for it. It's not what we do." I turned my back on him. He wasn't listening. While I had anything to say about it, The Kings were never going to be drug-dealing pieces of shit.

"Just because that's the way it's always been, doesn't make it right," Isaac continued. "It's time to move into this century, brother."

My patience gone, I swung back to him. "The Kings don't run drugs. It's club code!"

"It's soft!" he yelled.

I leaned in close and said, "It's not soft. It's right!"

While his body remained ready to fight, I could see all the fight drain from his eyes. He knew he wasn't going to convince me otherwise. No matter how many dollar signs he tried to dangle in front of me, I wasn't going to see this deal as anything other than a really bad fucking idea!

I ran a frustrated hand through my hair. "Who else knows?"

"No one." His eyes found and held mine. "But I want to bring it to the table."

"Have you completely lost your mind? Our granddaddy would turn in his fucking grave if you bring that shit to the table."

"Our granddaddy is dead, Cade. It's time to move forward. Bring the club into the twenty-first century and not keep living by the hippy, free-love bullshit of a dead man."

Taking him by surprise, I grabbed him by the collar and put him up against the wall.

"You disrespect Granddaddy again and I am going to put you through this wall. You got me?"

Nobody was going to speak smack about my granddaddy.

Nobody!

Isaac nodded. I had been close to Hutch Calley right up until his death when I was thirteen years old. He was a man of honor.

"The Kings will not touch any heroin deals. Not while I'm breathing. Understand?" He nodded again and I let him go. "Put it to bed."

He nodded and straightened himself. "Yeah, brother. Consider it done."

CHAPTER 63

CADE
Now

That night, someone set fire to Head Quarters. The phone call woke me just after 2 am. It was Sheriff Buckman telling me that the club's film studio was well alight and couldn't be saved. I rang Isaac who said he would meet me outside the clubhouse in ten minutes.

When I slipped my cut over my sweatshirt and grabbed my keys from the bowl on the table by the door, Indy appeared in the doorway. She was fully dressed and pulling her hair into a ponytail.

"What do you think you're doing?" I asked, shoving my billfold into the back pocket of my jeans.

"I'm coming with you."

"Ahhh, no, you're not."

"Ahhh, yes, I am." She smiled up at me and kissed me quickly on the chin. "I feel like a ride."

"It's 2 am."

"Good. Then there'll be less traffic on the roads."

There was no point arguing. I would get out of there quicker if I just took her with me.

By the time Isaac pulled up out front, we were waiting for him. He took one look at Indy on the back of my bike and raised his eyebrows to me. But he said nothing. He didn't have to. The amused grin on his face said it all.

We took the back highway toward Humphrey where our studios were, and as we neared, you could smell the smoke and see the glow of the flames in the distant darkness.

Sheriff Buckman met us as we pulled up. "You know who did this?"

"You think it's arson?" I asked, as Indy slid off the back of my bike.

"Like the stars are out and the moon is bright." He nodded in the direction of the firefighters putting the last of the flames out. "This fire reeks of arson."

I climbed off my bike. "You're telling me someone torched this place?"

Buckman looked uncomfortable, glanced around and then leaned in. "You guys got something you need to fill me in on? Something I should see coming before it shits on my doorstep?"

"Relax, Bucky. This wasn't us," I said. He didn't look convinced. "I swear to God. We've got no cause to torch our studios."

"Great." He shook his head. "I don't know what's worse. A half-cocked insurance job I didn't know about, or —"

"Or what?" Isaac asked.

"The person trying to get your attention."

It took them more than an hour to put the fire out, and what was left was a smoldering pile of rubble. More than six-million-dollars' worth of pussy and ass, gone.

Isaac, Indy and I did a walk around. If a rival club were responsible, then it would be easy for us to spot. To make sure we got the message loud and clear they'd leave something behind... but we found nothing. I called Nitro, because if anyone knew about fire, it was our friendly pyromaniac club member. He arrived twenty minutes later with Hawke and they did a subtle circle of the scene.

When a falling portion of the roof injured one of the firefighters, Indy left us to tend to him until the ambulance arrived, while Nitro and Hawke met us by the smoldering rubble of what had been the entrance into the studio.

"You find anything?" I asked Nitro.

"It's definitely someone's handiwork." His eyes skimmed the still glowing and smoky ruins of collapsed timber and steel behind us. "Probably broke in through the rear, found the film reel room and doused it with some accelerant. Gasoline."

"How do you know that?" Isaac asked.

"Because it's exactly what I'd do." Nitro's eyes glittered with some weird respect at the thought. "Whoever lit this wanted to cause as much damage as possible."

Isaac looked at me. "What do you think? Is it someone we know?"

I glanced around feeling a rush of unease. "I don't know."

"You think it's The Knights?"

I kicked a charred piece of rubble with my boot. Was it The Knights? Had they heard about Isaac's rogue heroin deal and decided to send us a message?

"Did you speak to your contact and sort out the heroin situation?" I asked.

Before he could answer, Buckman walked up to us.

"You boys might as well leave it for the forensics team," Buckman suggested. "Go home and get some shut eye. We'll let you know if we find anything."

I took out my phone and snapped a picture of the smoldering skeleton that had once been our studio and sent it to Bull who was in Jacksonville on business.

Shoving my phone back into my cut, I nodded at Buckman. "As soon as you know something, *I* want to know something."

I didn't need to tell him. He would call me the moment forensics turned up something—a fat, monthly retainer ensured it.

Indy approached us, her face dusted in soot.

"How is he?" Buckman asked her.

"He'll be fine. He's on his way to St Gabriel's now." She turned to me. "Any idea on what happened here."

I shook my head. "No. Not yet. But one way or another, we're going to find out."

Nitro and Hawke walked up to us.

"We're heading home. Unless you need us," Nitro said.

I shook my head. "Go home. We'll catch up at the clubhouse tomorrow." We did the typical MC brother hug goodbye, and then they were gone.

"You ready to go home?" I asked, guiding Indy onto the back of my bike.

It felt good to feel her body in close proximity to mine.

"Yeah, take me to coffee."

I grinned and nodded at Isaac. "Ready?"

He agreed. "Yeah, let's get out of here."

We took the back road through Humphrey, a windy, long stretch of smooth highway flanked by misty forests on either side. Dawn was breaking over the tall pines as we pulled up at the set of lights just before the train crossing that would lead us back into Destiny.

I glanced over at Isaac. He was checking a message on his phone. "It's Cherry. She wants a slice of Mavis's pecan pie. And if there is one thing I've learned, it's that you don't fuck with your pregnant wife's cravings."

He was putting his phone back into his pocket when he was suddenly thrust backwards. It happened so fast that it was already over by the time I understood what had gone down. Isaac fell from his bike, disappearing underneath it as it fell on top of him.

"Isaac!" I jumped off my bike and ripped his off him. He was lying flat on his back with a red stain spreading across his chest. Eyes wide with terror, he was coughing up blood as he struggled to breathe. I dropped to my knees. He'd been shot. Isaac had been fucking shot.

"No, no, no!" I yelled, putting my hand over the wound to his chest to stop the flow of blood. God, there was so much blood. So much. "Indy, he's been shot."

Indy was already there, kneeling beside us, but I could tell by the look on her face that this wasn't going to end well. She felt for the wound and blood bubbled up through her fingers.

"Okay, baby, you need to call an ambulance," she said calmly, her experience in a trauma ward taking over. She looked at me, the sharpness in her eyes telling me to hurry. When she looked back down to Isaac, her voice was reassuring. "Okay, buddy. You're doing all right. You've been shot, but I'm going to help you, okay?"

With my hands covered in blood, I rang for help, and while I yelled into the phone for an ambulance, I watched my cousin fight for his life at my feet. He stared up at me with terrified, wide eyes. He was gurgling and trying to move, his arms flaying at his side.

"I need you to try and stay still," Indy said. "You have a wound to your chest, Isaac, so I need you to try and stay calm. Cade is calling for help and they're going to be here real quick. I promise you, okay."

But then Isaac started shaking and shuddering, and coughing up big mouthfuls of dark red blood. His shaking got more violent, and then all of a sudden, he stopped moving.

The second bullet got him right between his eyes, killing him instantly. Blood splattered across Indy's face as the impact of the second bullet hit him with high-powered velocity.

I dropped the phone and reached for Indy. I couldn't see the gunman, but I knew the direction he was firing from and I had to protect her. I pulled her into my arms and turned my back toward it, sheltering her with my body.

All the air in my lungs vanished in an instant, and I was only vaguely aware of headlights and the sound of a vehicle disappearing into the shadows of the dawn.

For a long moment, the world was still. Then slowly, it all started up again as my brain processed what had happened.

Isaac was dead.

Someone had just murdered my cousin.

TO BE CONTINUED
in
Brothers in Arms: Kings of Mayhem MC Series Book 2
Due for release 26 February 2019

Penny Dee

BROTHERS IN ARMS
Kings of Mayhem Book Two

Chapter One

CADE

Kneeling in your loved one's blood and having them die in your arms changes you.

I know it changed me.

When Isaac died, my heart hardened.

My anger was palpable.

As I watched them remove his lifeless body from the pool of his blood, I vowed revenge. Fury thundered through my veins. Life changed in a heartbeat, and every part of my being could feel it. Rage tore through me, spiraling into every nerve and fiber, every muscle, every tendon, every shard of my shattered heart. Pain ripped at my guts and opened me up. But it was nothing, *nothing*, like my need for retribution.

Bull and Caleb showed up. God knows who called them.

Despite Indy's protests, I sent her home in the safety of a police cruiser while I followed Buckman and the ambulance to the county morgue. I didn't know why, but I needed answers, and for some reason, I felt they were with Isaac's body.

Isaac's body.

My chest caved in under the weight of my grief.

"You can't be here," Buckman said as I bounded the steps of the county morgue.

"Try stopping me."

He pressed a hand into my chest to stop me from going inside. His old brown eyes sought out mine. "Don't make me arrest you, son."

I expelled a deep breath of air. "Isaac is in there…"

"I know." Buckman stepped in front of the doorway. "And you need to let us do our job, Cade. Let Zachariah take care of him."

Zachariah Sumstad was the county medical examiner.

I sucked in a deep breath and looked away. My grief was dizzying. My head spun. I wanted to rip someone's head off to somehow release the growing agony inside of me. I wanted to find out who did this to Isaac and choke the hell out of them and watch the life drain from their eyes.

I inhaled deeply, the muscles in my jaw clenching. "You find out who did this. And you let me know." My voice was low, dangerous, and dripping with a barely controlled rage.

Buckman nodded. "As is protocol."

I leaned in. "No. I want this guy."

"I can't do that, Cade."

"Then I'll just make sure it happens. You won't be able to protect him."

Buckman put a hand on my shoulder. "One step at a time, son."

I turned and stormed down the steps to my bike. Then, gunning the engine, roared off into the morning.

I was going to find out who killed Isaac.

And I was going to make them pay.

CONNECT WITH ME ONLINE

Check these links for more books from Author Penny Dee.

READER GROUP

For more mayhem follow:
Kings of Mayhem MC Facebook page.
http://www.facebook.com/TheKingsofMayhemMC/

GOODREADS

Add my books to your TBR list on my Goodreads profile.
https://www.goodreads.com/author/show/8526535.Penny_Dee

AMAZON

Click to buy my books from my Amazon profile.
https://www.amazon.com/Penny-Dee/e/B00O2OKT5G/ref=dp_byline_cont_ebooks_1

WEBSITE

http://www.pennydeebooks.com/

Kings of Mayhem

INSTAGRAM
@authorpennydee

EMAIL
authorpennydee@hotmail.com

FACEBOOK
http://www.facebook.com/pennydeebooks/

ABOUT THE AUTHOR

Penny Dee writes contemporary romance about rockstars, bikers, hockey players and everyone in-between. She believes true love never runs smoothly, and her characters realize this too, with a boatload of drama and a whole lot of steam.

She found her happily ever after in Australia where she lives with her husband, daughter and a dog named Bindi.

Printed in Great Britain
by Amazon